MISFORTUNE

by

A. J. Zurn

This is a work of fiction. Names, characters, places, and incidents are either the product of the author's imagination or are used fictitiously, and any resemblance to actual persons, living or dead; events; or locales is entirely coincidental.

All Rights Reserved
Copyright © 2024 by A.J. Zurn

No part of this book may be reproduced or transmitted, downloaded, distributed, reverse engineered, or stored in or introduced into any information storage and retrieval system, in any form or by any means, including photocopying and recording, whether electronic or mechanical, now known or hereinafter invented without permission in writing from the publisher.

Dorrance Publishing Co
585 Alpha Drive
Pittsburgh, PA 15238
Visit our website at *www.dorrancebookstore.com*

ISBN: 979-8-89211-232-1
eISBN: 979-8-89211-730-2

MISFORTUNE

Chapter 1

"Open it!" Gen cried. "Mommy, open it, open it!"

Lidia rubbed her tired eyes that were crusted with sleep as she ungracefully shoved the pair of scissors towards the plastic prison that held her four-year-old daughter's small doll—its blond hair and flimsy fabric dress held down by string on top of the faux cage. "Gen, honey, have patience. I'm working on it."

In truth, Lidia was half-assing the job. Ever since Joel quit from their office, Lidia had been forced to work both of their shifts. When Lidia had made complaints her boss, she was explicitly told that it was either fifteen-hour shifts or unemployment, and as a single mother that was barely getting by, she had no choice but to comply. And so, waking up at four, slaving away at her office computer, and getting home at eight for eternity was Lidia's week.

"Mommy! Please!" Gen stretched her little arms and grappled for the still unopened package with her stubby fingers, the same brown hair as her mother's falling back behind her shoulders.

Lidia may have been tired, but she wasn't going to allow her toddler to wield the two sharp blades. Shaking herself awake, she twisted and turned away, angling her body to face the kitchen's stove. "Gen, honey. I said give me a second. If you don't calm down, I'll have to take it for the night, and you'll get it in the morning."

Lidia heard a pout of irritation from behind her, but fingers no longer probed at her waist to reach the wretched toy. Sighing, she actually looked at the item in her hands. Kaylee, Gen's baby-sitter, had given it to the child as a consolation present, as her family was going on vacation to California. Lidia had wished Kaylee had given her a consolation present, because now she was left with a highly demanding job and an energetic kid stuck home alone.

Finally, after almost slicing her thumb, Lidia split the hell-sent plastic open, flinging the doll into the air. It bounced on the counter and landed on the floor, snapping the head off on impact.

Gen did nothing at first, staring at the doll with innocence, until her eyes began to brim with tears and the bawling started. She threw her head into the air and gave a glass shattering screech.

Lidia fought the urge to yell at her daughter to be quiet, but deep down, she knew the attempt would be futile. Without losing her cool despite her heavily building vexation, Lidia bent down and snatched up the toy, which she was beginning to hate very much. The childish sirens continued to blast through her thoughts. Snapping the head on without much effort, Lidia stuck the toy in front of her daughter's face, shaking it to get her attention. "Look, Gen. All fixed."

The fit ceased immediately, but the sniffling remained. Gen scrubbed her eyes with her chubby child hands and reached up tentatively, as if she believed that if she moved too fast, the doll would once again combust and lose a body part. After discovering her mother had done a sufficient job in fixing her doll, a smile burst across the child's face. Gen seized the toy and began to bolt through the small living room and kitchen, weaving through the short hallway to her and Lidia's rooms, before returning and repeating the route.

Leaning back against the stove, Lidia watched her daughter run momentarily, before scrubbing her eyes again and unhinging her jaw to break the record for the most worn-out yawn.

Lidia prayed that someone else would fill in for Joel in the near future even though she wasn't big on religion; her grandma had always pushed Catholicism on the family, attending each and every Mass and Sunday school, sicken and menstrual cramps and weather and plain defiance be damned. She'd used excessive force with the back hand of a tongue and a hand if needed. All which in turn made Lidia reject religion in a whole. The same had gone for claims for the whole family to consistently return to their hometown for terribly awkward Thanksgivings. Though, Lidia knew she claimed her annoying Grandma Eunis for being her reason for not showing up for the holidays. She stopped going after Cousin Eddie made fun of her for getting pregnant with a thirty-two-year-old-man's baby at sixteen. The whole family had laughed when they found out Gen was mixed, as her father was from Mexico. They claimed his heritage was the reason he left Lidia when she announced she was pregnant.

Damning Kyle, Gen's deadbeat dad, and the bullshit story she gave her for leaving—a goddamn ghost story, of all things—once more in her head, Lidia cracked her back with her fingers in between the ridges of her spine and went about making supper, even though it was nine o'clock. Lidia knew four-year-olds most definitely should not be up this late, but neither of them had eaten yet, and Lidia was too tired to care.

She slammed the microwave shut and tapped the few buttons to warm up their shared T.V. dinner. Even though she worked fifteen hours a day, her job still paid shit. It was the only place that would hire a twenty-year-old that lived with a child and without prior qualifications.

Lidia reveled in the quiet. Gen had sprinted to one of the rooms down the hall to play with her doll, leaving Lidia to cool her headache that had been forming from all the noise. Closing her eyes momentarily, Lidia found that the five minutes she had pressed into the machine suddenly fell into what felt like a few seconds.

Blinking herself awake, Lidia pulled open the microwave and grabbed for the hot disposable bowl, effectively burning her fingers.

"Fuck!" she whispered to herself. Lidia twisted around guiltily to check if Gen had heard, but she was still down the hall.

She tentatively reached in once more, this time with a towel as the first defense, Lidia pulled out their meal. She walked backwards from the kitchen, holding the platter with precision, both her and the platter daring the other to do something wrong. She pivoted with the likeness of a slow dance and bent down to set the food on her little table. But she had let go slightly too early, causing the soupy white mix that was supposed to serve as mashed potatoes to spew out molten driblets. She was able to avoid the attack by yanking her hands back with a scowl.

Slapping down the towel and tossing out dishes, Lidia called for her daughter as she sat down and distributed the food among their paper plates and plastic silverware.

Lidia was so drained that she didn't even realize Gen wasn't at the table with her until after her third bite. Lidia sighed with building anger. "Genevieve! I will take that doll right now if you do not come to the table!"

Gen did not appear from the hallway.

"I will count to three, young miss!" Lidia counted to ten before her fuse for the shenanigans finally fizzled to a stub. Lidia shot up from her chair, hard enough that it over corrected and slammed to the floor. The thought that her landlord would be knocking on her door at any moment to stop the noise hit the back of her head, but Lidia was too angry to care about that now.

She stomped down the hallway, eyes fixated on the nearest door to the left, where she heard whispers. "Genevieve Thompson! I have had it with your naughtiness. You are having supper and going to bed. You won't be seeing that damn toy till—"

While Lidia had been rambling to Gen, she had thrown open the door, expecting to find her rapscallion child disobeying her. Instead, Lidia found Gen sitting on the ledge of her windowsill, feet dangling out in the night's cold and beyond Lidia's sight. The screen had been taken out due to another stunt Gen had caused in the past. Usually, Lidia would simply scold her daughter for doing this, but what was different this time was a grown man standing outside the house, an arm latched lightly around the child. He was draped in all black clothing and wore a goat's skull as a mask that held old blood and broken lines under the left eye. From the doorway, Lidia could see maggots traveling along the skull's sinister horns. It was odd, but the streetlamp from outside illuminated his wispy, silky colored skin just right, to where he looked *transparent.*

Lidia stared in shock for a moment, her hand cemented to the now sweaty doorknob, as Gen happily turned around and glanced at her mother. "Mommy! I made a friend! Come meet him." Gen turned around to inspect the skull that held shadowed eyes beneath. "I'm going to call you 'Goaty'!"

After what felt like an eternity, Lidia snapped out of her stupor. "Gen! Get away from him!" she screeched, lightheaded. Lidia propelled herself forward to grab her daughter, but the goat man was faster. His grip on Gen tightened, and he pulled her away from the window, away from the reach of the light from the streetlamp and out of the house. Snatched from the safety of Lidia.

As Lidia stopped momentarily to look dimwittedly out the house, she faintly registered a sound, which identified itself as a scream that consistently rang into the air. Lidia hurdled out the window, as her throat became scratchy. She didn't put the pieces together that she was the one making the noise as she bolted into the night.

Only time knew, but Lidia's frantic chase would turn up fruitless. Lidia would spend the whole night screaming into the woods by her house for Gen, catching limbs on branches and alerting neighbors that Danger was lurking nearby, who watched from the shadows, as the searches for It returned fruitless. As humans reached their stubby fingers to try and grasp the truth to the location for the unended lives and reared no success. As long as Its need went unfulfilled, It wouldn't pay back what It stole.

Chapter 2

Charlette Kezben had the increasing suspicion that everything in her life was going to be late. As the past had so evidently shown, it had turned her father into her late father. Made the day that she was supposed to tour her new college get pushed back a week because the email for it was sent late. Now, it made the moving truck that held all of her and her brother Martin's belongings backed up by a week.

"You've got to be kidding me!" Charlie fought to keep her voice down as she stood in the living room of her new and desolate house. She pinched the bridge of her nose and reminded herself that the front desk wasn't responsible for the error.

"I'm sorry, ma'am," said the man on the line, his accent so thick Charlie couldn't even begin to place it. "The truck that holds your belongings has always had difficulties with the wheels."

Charlie let her mouth fall, and glanced at her little brother, who sat on the old carpet to her left. Martin met his sister's stare, his face built with bricks of boredom at the moment. "Our stuff was delivered to the wrong address. What do the wheels have to do with anything?" Her voice was involuntarily high.

The front desk man went quiet momentarily. "Thank you for calling," he said quickly. "Your belongings will probably arrive by Tuesday."

Charlie opened her mouth to try and ask her question again, but was met with an empty dialing tone. She glanced at the screen, and behold, found the man had hung up on her. She huffed and shoved her phone in her pocket, quickly returning her hand to her face, this time to rub her forehead stressfully.

"What'd they say?" Martin sat with his lanky knees pressed against his chest while he picked at a stain on the ground that had been covered up by furniture when Charlie had toured the house.

Charlie sighed hardest to make the hair that bordered her face rustle. "Tuesday."

"God, this neighborhood is smaller than you. How the hell did they mess it up?" Martin stuck his hands out in front of himself to emphasis the point.

Charlie twisted around, hands on her hips. Martin loved to talk about her height, or lack thereof, since he passed her completely average and perfectly normal 5'6" in sixth grade. "Ha-ha. Very funny. Haven't heard that one before. Did you come up with that yourself?"

Martin smiled sweetly. "I did, thank you for asking. Like how I also came up with the idea that you should get stilts. That way, you might be able to see yourself in the bathroom mirror."

Charlie's smile was just as sweet, just as innocent, and just as malevolent. "Aw, how caring. I'm sure Aunt Mary would love to hear those jokes again. I bet she would be thrilled if you wanted to go back to living with her."

That got through to Martin. He dropped the smile. "God, no." He leaned back against the wall dramatically. "I'm sorry for hurting your feelings, but I'm not sorry for being tall. At least one of us can make use of the top shelves in this house."

Charlie pivoted away from her brother to hide her smirk. Martin was a shy creature to the world, but he never had any problems talking to his sister. Especially after their father died. The death was three years old, but it always felt fresh. Like celebrating the birthday of an infant that died at birth.

They'd lived like any other nuclear family in an average neighborhood with their average jobs and average lives. Father a businessman. Mother a store clerk. Children attending their local high school and returning home with mediocre yet sufficient grades.

They were perfectly happy in their perfectly normal lives.

That was until Brandon Fredricks, a man they'd never met in their lives, stomped off to the bar after finding his wife cheating on him, which left him feeling betrayed and spitting fire over it, something that he decided many drinks of alcohol would solve. Bartenders reported that Brandon ordered glass after glass to drown his sorrow and feed his fury. After deciding to drive himself home, Brandon tore down the highway at thirty miles over the speed limit.

On the same road that night was their father, who was out late after picking up a birthday present for his wife.

Brandon, in his haze of alcohol and rage, lost control of his car and drove into the opposite lane. The lane their father had been in.

The funeral had been abrupt and traumatic. One day, the Kezben family had a loving father and husband. And the next day, they didn't.

Charlie and Martin had both responded to the death by looking towards family for comfort. Even though they were at the ages of nineteen and fourteen, neither child had experienced a death in the family before. For the first few months, they depended on each other more than ever.

It was their mother that sent everyone spiraling.

Their father had a moderately nice paying job, and they would've stayed afloat with the death benefits if their mother had continued to show up to work. The store she worked at was only filled with so much sympathy before they got sick of her flaking out on her shifts. Widow or not.

The house and groceries and bills no longer paid for themselves after their mother shut herself off from the world and her kids. Charlie did her best to coax her mother out of the depression and take care of her brother during this time, but when Martin let it slip to their school councilor that they couldn't afford to pay the water bill because their mother stopped working, Charlie couldn't stop CPS from arriving on their doorstep.

They were forced to move in with Aunt Mary, leaving behind their childhood home and friends. Technically, only Martin had to go, but Charlie would never let her brother move away from her just because of CPS. Their mother had then followed along with them like a dejected dog after she lost the house.

The most CPS did for them was dump them in a house of a relative they hadn't seen in years that didn't want them. Aunt Mary was their mother's aunt, but she would deny them attention if they called her Great Aunt Mary. She claimed the title made her feel old. Aunt Mary most likely meant well, but there was a reason the woman never had children.

Due to their mother no longer being a functioning adult, it fell onto Aunt Mary to be her full-time servant, bringing her clothes and taking away dishes. All while leaving the children that were supposed to be in her care to govern themselves.

And after Charlie saved enough money from her multiple jobs, took out a loan, and begged and pleaded for extra money from Aunt Mary, she was out of that hellhole house and off to college a state away, little brother in tow.

For the past three years, her life felt like it was spiraling out of control—that no matter how hard she gripped at it, it still melted through her fingers. And even now, in a different state and house, she still felt like nothing changed.

"Where are we going to sleep?"

Charlie continued forward after turning around. She shrugged heavily for an answer as she walked out of the living room and into the kitchen that was deeper in the house. "How about you go unpack the car and I'll run to the store?" she called back mindlessly, busy surveying the cabinets and oven for wear and tear that the landlord might have left out in the house description. Save a scratch on the fridge at eye level, nothing looked like it would explode if she used it.

A groan rumbled from the living room. "Like I'm going to find my stuff through your pile of junk." Despite that, the doorknob opened and the screen door squealed anyway. Charlie was not too old to roll her eyes at her brother's dramatics.

A quick check around the house proved that their landlord had been mostly telling the truth, save a faucet in the upstairs that failed to work half the time. Otherwise, both bedrooms next to it and both the kitchen and living room downstairs were in the condition to be expected from a leased home. Even their one-car garage that sat off the side of the house like an unwanted child was in acceptable condition.

Joining Martin outside by the car's trunk, it was obvious that even though he was nearly eighteen and tremendously tall, he really *didn't* have the muscle strength to haul Charlie's boxes out of the way.

"Jesus, just put them down, you're going to snap in half!" Charlie rushed over like a concerned mother as Martin set the box down hard. A rattling that sounded dangerously close to glass shattering came from within. Charlie cringed. "Honestly, Martin! What are you doing?"

His face was red with exertion. There were three other dry brown boxes next to him, not including the one that likely held something of hers, now broken. "I wasn't kidding when I said you put too much stuff in the car. Especially from the back."

She frowned at him. "Then why didn't you just grab it from the backseat?" She gestured at the backseat door for effect. Even going as far as to open the door and pull down the seat. Sitting there, in all its cubey glory, was Martin's single box that he packed in the car.

He huffed for a second more, shoulders slouched. "Oh," is all he said. Filling his arms with the cardboard, Martin waddled in through the front door. Embarrassment wafted off him for miles.

Charlie shifted her hair out of her face with hands a shade darker than it, the light brown curtain always obstructing her view every time she looked down. It only fueled her irritation as she stared down at the boxes left discarded by her car. Martin was a smart kid, always doing his best in school, even under their not-so-great circumstances, but he wasn't the brightest bulb in the bunch.

"I was wondering how long he was going to try and lift that box for."

Charlie flicked her head to the voice. Standing on the porch connected to the house to the right of theirs was a man with deeply sun-kissed skin, and a fatherly smile—one that was surrounded by wrinkles that only appeared after living half a lifetime. There were multiple cars out front, and his garage, which was marginally larger than hers, showed there were more vehicles within. The models were older looking, giving the impression their next-door neighbor either collected vintage cars, or was a stage ten hoarder.

She mimicked his look politely, turning to face him fully. "Martin means well. Sometimes he just needs a little bit of help to find his way." Charlie almost felt guilty for teasing her brother behind his back. Almost.

"I'm sure he was just trying to be helpful. Not many kids are these days." The man kept his face soft as he descended the few stairs to his driveway and crossed the minuscule amount of grass that separated their driveways. He stood before her with a gnarled, knuckled hand extended. "Bill Forester. You must be the new neighbor."

Charlie obliged the handshake. "Charlie Kezben. Martin's my brother. We moved here from Iowa."

Bill shook her hand firmly before letting go. "It's a pleasure to meet you and your brother. Can't say I've ever met a woman named Charlie."

She chuckled out of politeness. "Charlette is my full name. Charlie was just the nickname my dad used for me growing up. I suppose it just stuck."

Bill's smile had fallen slightly, but it was still warm. "What a nice name. Charlette was the name of my wife. May she rest in peace."

Charlie was startled for a moment. She didn't think that talk about losing a wife would happen with her first conversation with her new neighbor. "Oh, I'm so sorry."

Bill flicked a wrist nonchalantly, but the heaviness was still there. "It was over a decade ago. But I still hear her telling me to sell my cars when we ran out of room in the garage. She never was a fan of them."

Charlie leaned around him to take a look. For being old, they were in pristine condition, shining in the high sun. She had the feeling that Bill handwashed them himself. "Oh. How long have you collected them?"

"They used to be my father's, but I inherited them a while ago. He collected before I was even born. He was the one who taught me the love for the old." Bill turned back and looked at the automobiles fondly.

"That's sweet. My dad used to have an old car like those." Used to, because he'd been driving his precious Mustang when Brandon hit him.

Bill nodded. "Your dad sounds like a smart man."

Charlie could only put on a crocodile smile and nod her head as well. Contrary to what Bill had offered, she wasn't as comfortable talking about family deaths as a conversation starter.

Bill looked over her head at the boxes that had yet to be unloaded. "Do you need a hand with those? Seeing your brother, I assume they're pretty heavy."

Charlie held her hands up. "Oh, no, that's okay. I wouldn't want to make you do that. I'm sure you've got other things to do than waste time moving."

Bill made a noise of disagreement in his throat and stepped around Charlie to survey the boxes. "Nonsense. How about I just help by putting the boxes on your porch, yeah? I can get out of your hair after that."

Once Bill bent down and picked up the previously dropped box, Charlie saw no way out of the assistance without being rude and resigned herself to ducking out of his way. "That's very nice of you, Mr. Forester. I owe you one."

Bill grunted as he set down the box at the top of the stairs and returned. "Please, it's nothing at all. And besides, call me Bill. I'm not old enough yet to be a Mr."

Together, they hauled the significantly heavy to the door (even though she was the one to pack them, Charlie completely forgot about their obtrusive weight), finishing it by Charlie returning to the car to close the back and lock the doors. While Bill was busy making sure the boxes wouldn't fall over, Charlie dipped her head inside of the house for a moment to see if Martin would return. He was nowhere in sight.

"Alright. That looks good."

Charlie brought herself back to the porch. "Thank you again, Bill. I'll admit, I don't think I would've been able to get those boxes over here if you hadn't helped."

Bill clasped his hands together and slowly backed down the porch steps. "Of course. I see you're busy, so I'll quit bothering y'all and head home. Just knock if you ever need anything."

"Will do," she called back. "Same here if you need something."

Bill reached his own porch, pausing right before he opened his screen door. "Have a good day. Stay safe." He laughed. "You never know what's out there at night," he said across the distance, and with a fast wave, he disappeared into his house.

Chapter 3

Supper that night was soggy .99 cent noodles in foam cups. Charlie had managed to secure pillows and blankets and the usual life necessities that would have to do for the next half of the week after a quick trip to the store.

She regretted not having Bill help her with moving the boxes upstairs because her back still smarted from heaving every single box that was on the porch up the stairs and divvying them into the correct rooms. Her right knee pained as well, due to falling down the stairs as a child and denying a doctor to be seen as brave when she obviously needed one. It never did heal right and was always outspoken when she used it too much.

The last comment of Bill's confused her. Of course, there was always danger in the dark. It felt odd for someone to go out and specify it, especially to their neighbor during their first meeting. Eventually, Charlie chalked it up to Bill being nice but messing with her at the same time. It was probably a neighborly thing for people to do here. She wouldn't know much about having new neighbors. This was only the second time they moved, and the first time, they weren't exactly lining up to get to know everyone that surrounded Aunt Mary's house.

"What took you so long?" Martin slurped up another noodle as they sat on the floor in the kitchen. His back was to the cabinets, while Charlie leaned on her side against the fridge. She watched him as he mindlessly picked at the tile's grout. They didn't necessarily *have* to lounge on the ground, but they'd just sat down while the microwave was running and didn't get back up.

She rolled her eyes at him for the second time that day. "Because you unhelpfully decided not to help me unload the rest of the boxes."

Martin made a loud noise in his throat while his mouth was brimming with carbs. "No way was I going back out there. I pushed around all those boxes for no reason, like an idiot! Then there was that weird old guy in the next house over that was watching me the whole time like some weird pedophile. I think he was laughing to himself, too. I bet he's going to tell all his white golfing friends about me."

Charlie picked around in her own supper. "Well, that weird old guy," she threw up a hand in quotation for effect, "is Bill Forester. He had to help me unload the car because *you* wouldn't." She jutted her plastic fork at him.

Martin was not impressed. "That's great. Does he smell like mayonnaise? Because I imagine that he does."

"Oh, my God. He does not—" She sighed. "I will not have a discussion about how our neighbors smell over supper," she mumbled to herself as she stared at the ceiling for strength.

"Hasn't been confirmed nor denied either," Martin sang quietly from his side of the kitchen.

Charlie had to take a moment to process this conversation and change it as soon as possible. "Are you looking forward to school next week?" And then she tutted to herself. "Those poor teachers, being stuck around you."

Martin rolled his eyes at his sister but couldn't hide the tension lining his shoulders.

"Are you nervous?"

"Why would I be?" All of Martin's teenage bravado would never admit anxiety.

"Because we're in a different state and we've literally lived here for a total of five minutes," not including the hotel stays and colleges tours and looking for places to live. "I know I'm nervous about my first day of college."

Martin shifted his back against the cabinets, causing them to knock into place. "You worry about everything."

That was a truth and a lie. Charlie worried about the mundane things in life that everyone else worried about, too—finances, bills, work, more bills. Martin thought she was an over-worrier because she always fawned over him all the time. But in reality, it was a byproduct of basically becoming his guardian after their father died.

"Yes, well, when you're old like me, you'll understand."

"Alright, grandma, we get it. You're oh so mature and wise. You can put away the old card."

Martin was already standing and tossing his plastic dishes into a small garbage can acquired only hours before by the time he finished his sentence. He hopped through the doorway, going into the living room. The creaking of the stairs proved he was heading to the house's higher level. "Make sure to brush your teeth before bed!" Charlie yelled from her position still on the floor.

"Grandma!" The voice was muffled from the walls, but Charlie heard him well enough to chuckle. She would join him in retiring to go to bed that night, although she could see that his leaving was just an obvious ploy to avoid talking about school. Soon, but not yet. For the next uncountable minutes, she would sit there on the old kitchen tiles and take in every crevasse of their kitchen.

Finally, they were away from their mother. Finally, they were free. Finally, in their new home. *Her own* new home.

Chapter 4

"Do you want me to come with you?"

"Does it really matter?"

Charlie checked her blind spot as she merged lanes on the highway. It was the Saturday before the first day of high school. Due to Martin being enrolled so late in the year, he'd missed the chance of open house. Now, a few phone calls later, and a little bit of begging, they'd secured a personal look around the school with the principal.

"Well, I don't want to do anything that makes you uncomfortable."

Martin huffed. "Doing this *is* out of my comfort zone. School doesn't even start till Wednesday. And even then, I'm sure I'll be there long enough to get the picture of where everything is." They'd been over this many times. Charlie had put her foot down when it came to touring the school, but of course, Martin had put up the fact that it was the weekend, and, in his mind, the weekend is for eating junk food and doing nothing.

"I know, Marty. But it'll be helpful to get an idea of what the school looks like. *I* want to get an idea of what the school I'm sending my brother to looks like."

"I'm sure a quick search online will do the trick."

Charlie sighed. She was not going to get irritated over this. "We're already on our way. Now, Mr. Jason had offered to do the tour for both of us, or just for you. You won't be alone. The school will have some of the teachers there because it's so close to the first day."

Martin crossed his arms. "Should I be worried if I'm left alone with this man?"

"You never answered my question." Charlie never took her eyes off the road as she drove—Brandon taught her that much—but could imagine Martin simmering just a foot away from her.

"You never answered mine."

"Martin," she warned.

He flopped his hands in the air. "Fine, no, don't come with. I don't want you to talk to the principal for forever."

Charlie scoffed, lips closing in a faint smile. "What's that supposed to mean?"

Out of her peripheral vision, she could see her brother ticking off fingers. "Store check-outs, hotel front receptionists, nurses, some lady named Maureen at the store yesterday, Bill just before that. Anytime we meet anyone, you talk to them for ages." Martin was winded after his little burst.

Charlie stuck one finger off the wheel to further her point. "I'll have you know that the conversation I had with Maureen yesterday wasn't meaningless. She was just trying to bake cookies for her grandchildren, but the store had moved its stock of sugar. I was simply helping her find it."

"You talked to her for over an hour."

Charlie re-gripped the wheel. "Those store employees need to put their products on better display."

"The sugar was at the front of the store."

"Like I said, weird! You would think the fruit would be there," she affirmed.

Charlie mentally deemed herself the winner when Martin couldn't hold his poker face any longer and burst into a chuckle.

The easy banter between them only eased nerves for a few minutes, because in no time, they arrived at the high school's parking lot and inserted themselves into a space.

"Alright. Mr. Jason said that he'll be waiting for you at the front office." She eyed the glass doors that led inside. "It should be just a little down the hall and to the left."

Pivoting towards Martin, she could see him observing the school wearily. His chest rose faintly, and his legs bounced. No matter how much he didn't want to admit it, attending a new school made him anxious.

Charlie placed two fingers on his shoulder gently. "Are you sure you want to go alone? It would be no problem for me to go with you."

With one final sigh, Martin steeled his joints and put a hand on the door. "It's fine," he said stiffly. "I'll just get it over with. How long is it?"

"About thirty to forty minutes," she confirmed with a glance at her phone. "I'll probably drive around for a bit. Text me when you're almost done, and I'll pick you up."

Martin gave a sharp nod. "Alright." He hopped out of the car, and a moment before he slammed it shut, he stuck his head back inside. "If I'm not back by then, call the police." His smile was only a flash before he was gone from the window and skittering over to the school's front door.

"That boy," Charlie muttered to herself with a shake of her head. She should've known her pervious comment would come back to bite her.

With a curtsy check around her car, she backed up from her spot and drove away as the school's doors closed shut and flashed in the soon-to-be evening light. Out of the parking lot, she surveyed her surroundings. The school was outlined with trees and a neighborhood and a small strip mall only a few minutes away. Because she was still unfamiliar with the area, Charlie decided to head towards the small, connected stores, where she would wait out her time and *not* spend it talking to others mindlessly, contrary to what Martin claimed.

From her car, she eyed what the strip mall held: hair salons, nail salons, even a little fishing store that offered many types of bait for even more types of fishing. Finally, on the very end, was a little convenience store. With the help of some old markings on the ground, Charlie guessed the store used to belong to a gas station, but the pumps were torn down, and other stores were built onto it. Like an only child that went from being all by itself to having eight siblings shoved into it.

Parking once more, Charlie dodged the minimal amount of other vehicles that were placed about and entered the store with a small chime above her head.

To her immediate right was the counter, and the rest of the little store was crowded with fatty and cheap foods that could be swiped easily and eaten on the road. A door that led off from the counter swung open at the sound of Charlie ringing the overhead bell ringing. Chattering followed with it.

"...Yeah, yeah, I know, right?" A woman around early twenties with fiery red hair and deeply freckled skin that spanned all of her visible skin pushed open the door with her back as she held a cup in one hand and a box on her hip with the other. All while balancing a phone on her shoulder to talk with someone. "Yes, exactly. I was thinking the same thing." At the sight of Charlie gawking at her, she gave a quick grin. She stuck one finger that had been wrapped around the cup in the air as a gesture to give her a second. A movement that caused her to dibble steamy liquid onto the grime saturated carpet behind the counter. She clicked her tongue in annoyance and set down the coffee, the woman gripped the phone back into her hand and angled away.

Realizing she was staring, Charlie took to finding the first aisle terribly interesting and ambled around there awkwardly.

"Yes, I bet it's perfect. Alright, I'll see you when I get home tonight. Yep. Alright, love you, bye."

The woman had only been off the call for a second before she was whistling for Charlie's attention. She snapped up at the sound to find the redhead leaning against the counter. "Yes?"

"This usually doesn't happen very often, but I don't believe I've met you before." She spoke with a minimal accent. Bill had the same cadence as this woman, which gave Charlie the idea that it wasn't them who had the accent but her.

Charlie smiled and approached the counter. "I just moved here." She jutted a hand out. "I'm Charlie."

The woman mimicked her look and shook her hand with vigor. "Sam. Charlie Kezben, right? I was hoping I'd run into you at some point. Bill's been telling everyone about his nice new neighbors."

In the span of a few seconds, Martin had been proven right that, yes, Charlie did get stuck talking to someone, and yes, Bill did tell his white friends about them.

"Oh, how sweet of him. I could say the same thing. He was so helpful to help us move it."

Sam flicked a wrist and scoffed. "That's just ol' Bill. Always out being the better person. He makes the rest of us look like monsters." She smiled and shook her head. "Anyway, sorry about earlier. My sister is redecorating her house and I've anointed myself as the appraiser."

"That's alright. I don't need to be distracting you from your job, either."

Another scoff, this one even more dramatic. "You wouldn't believe me when I say that I spend almost all of my time at work talking."

Trust me, I believe you, Charlie thought.

"Besides, I bet you didn't come here just to talk to the lady at the cash register." Sam shooed her away. "You gotta shop. Don't let me get in the way."

Charlie smiled politely and slithered down the aisles, taking in each product one by one. It was unnecessary to give so much mental power to the quick shop, but she had over half an hour to kill. In her meandering of the small store, she stocked up on more noodles and daily necessities. It felt childish, but Charlie grabbed Martin's favorite chocolate bar that their father used to buy them when they'd go out for a treat together on the weekends. Near the back, she did notice a scruffy old man that hunched low enough to be shorter than her. Charlie was never one to make assumptions off of first glances, but the unwavering stare through his ratty hair that was always trained on Charlie, no matter where she was in the store, made her skin crawl. Maybe she should've been the one to tell Martin to call the police on her if she didn't appear.

Charlie unloaded her arms brimming with easy foods onto the counter, where Sam dutifully started to scan them. "My, y'all must really like chow mein," Sam remarked after her little gun beeped on the noodles for the sixth time.

Charlie chuckled. She felt her cheeks warm slightly. "Moving truck unloaded all of our stuff to the wrong house. Then there were some other malfunctions with it, so we're without all our stuff till next week."

Sam put a hand over her heart. "You poor thing. If I had to go without my hair straightener for that long, I think I'd go crazy."

Charlie examined Sam's extremely frizzy and extremely not straight hair. "You straighten your hair?" she asked faintly, eyes glued to the circus of curls.

Sam's laughter was high pitched. "I know, right? If you think it's curly now, wait until you see it when I wake up," she chortled. Charlie responded with a terse smile and crinkled eyes.

"Anyway." Sam brushed a lock out of her eyes as she bagged the last of the uncountable cups of carbs. "Here's your stuff. I hope you and your brother have a good day. Tell Bill I say hello." Sam's winning smile was like a shining sun. Freckles speckled around her face the glimmering stars behind Earth's star.

Charlie nodded, loud plastic bag in hand, and backed up towards the door. "Will do. Have a good day." Or, that's what she would've said, if not for the fact that she ran into the man from the back of the store mid-sentence, making her pause and spin around. "Oh, my goodness, I'm so sorry."

"Did he tell you?"

Charlie looked down at the man in bewilderment as he pinned her with the same stare as before. From their proximity, she could tell he smelled faintly of autumn, cigarette smoke, and sweat. Something that made her inadvertently cringe away.

"Tell me about what?"

Sam huffed from behind her. "Oh, he does this all the time," she grumbled to herself. "Grant, for the love of God, quit terrorizing her. You don't need to tell that dumb old story every time you meet someone." Charlie looked over, seeing Sam had leaned over the counter and was gesturing melodramatically in the air with her hands.

"What story?" Charlie backed up a few paces and swapped her gaze between the two. She gripped her bag as a shield to keep herself further from Grant. She'd never had to use it, but her school had taught a self-defense class that her mother had forced her to attend. If Grant wanted to come closer, she was, hopefully, prepared. "What are you talking about?"

Sam seemed to sigh any time something minor happened. "All the time. He does this all the time," she continued to moan to herself. She leaned her head on her palm on the counter, blowing the entwined locks from her face. "It's an old town story about some guy—"

Grant jutted a gloved finger over his lips, despite the lack of dropped temperature. He shushed loudly. Charlie had a guess that there was a marginal amount of alcohol in his bloodstream. "He's not just *some guy*!" he snapped like a spoiled child.

Charlie looked at Sam for help, who only huffed. "Trust me, he's going to fill you in. This is the fifth time this has happened." Then she turned towards Grant. "Despite *everyone* telling you to *stop*," she pointedly said.

"Do you want to know why we don't stay out late here?"

Charlie looked back to the little man. "Not really," Charlie responded wearily.

"If only that made him shut up," Sam added from the side.

Grant continued anyway, like neither of them had spoken. "They say that after a tornado that hit town some decades ago, a man lost all of his kids and his wife and farmland. Overcome with devastation, he pleaded with the gods for them to be brought back to him. When they did no such thing, he cursed until his final breath. But instead of allowing him to move on, the gods had become sick of his ranting and ravings that they decided that he was not fit for his next life. Instead, they chained him to this world as a spirit, where he was to remain until he was filled with remorse for his actions.

"But the man was not foiled. Instead, he steals children from their parents as an act of malice to show the gods he will never give up. Still to this day, he walks these streets, face covered by a goat's skull, snatching children from under their parent's noses, earning himself the name Misfortune. Some say he comes to those who even dare to speak Misfortune's name."

Charlie had reached her limit of being tormented after Grant said "gods" for the second time. "Of course, he does," she said with an edge to her voice. "Well, that's a nice story, but I have to get going now."

"Do you have no respect for the legend?" Grant's face was overcome with horror.

Charlie gave Grant a taste of his own medicine. Only this time, her gaze was impatient and irritated. At least, she hoped it was, and the cold sweat that dripped down her back didn't give away that she did not at all feel like she had the upper hand.

"Seriously, Grant, you might want to move. She's gonna punch your lights out."

Finally, Grant seemed to have snapped out of his little storyteller mode. He glared at Sam with his yellowed teeth on display. With one last snort and, "Just know there's a reason people in this town don't stay out past sunset," he was gone.

Charlie blinked a few times, bewildered. In the span of a second, Grant had disappeared. Or he had, until she looked around and saw the hunch of a back hiding behind a cardboard cutout of a woman advertising a chip brand.

"Grant, we can see you," Sam said.

"No, you can't," grumbled the 2D woman.

"If you don't get out from behind there, I'm telling Frank you came back here."

Grant spit a hiss and stomped out from behind the cutout, bell jingling as he finally left.

When Charlie looked back at Sam, she only shrugged. "Frank's parole officer," is all she added.

Charlie watched her with wide eyes. "What the hell just happened?" The past five minutes felt like a fever dream.

Sam groaned and straightened her back. "God, he sits there at the back of the store and lurks like some ogre, just to tell some poor soul about a damn ghost story." Sam's eyes were hard as they watched Grant move to where he'd been before, but softened once back on her. "I'm so sorry you had to deal with that. I've called my manager on him, like, eight times to try and get him to leave, but Derek is always telling me to never *deny a customer*."

She frowned and rolled her eyes. "I mean, he never even *buys* anything. It's like he *lives* over there. Honestly, someone needs to report harassment over this. The last person he did that to spit at him when he tried to say that Misfortune would steal his wife." Sam slumped slightly from the intensity of her assertion. "Again, I really am sorry about that. I hope Grant doesn't scare you away. I've found I like you a lot more than him," she added. "And I've known that guy for four years."

Charlie, dazed, creeped out, and owning the high need to get out of there, adapted to her pre-programmed social manners. "All good. I really should get going, though," she added fast. "My brother's waiting for me — and yeah, so… have a good day!" With a quick wave, she was out the store and in her car within a breath.

As she checked the clock to see that she still had some time to spare, Charlie chalked the last few minutes up to be one of the weirdest times of her life. Which she then blamed to be the drunk ramblings of a man that took a town ghost story a little too seriously.

Although, Bill *had* made that odd remark about not knowing what's in the dark.

In the end, Charlie decided that she was too accustomed to living in large towns, and this just must be what it is like to live in a more socially connected town, however off putting it might be. If anything, *she* was probably the only one that didn't know the story.

She slotted her car in the parking lot of the school a few minutes later, only sparing Grant one more thought over how suspicious he made her feel, and this *Misfortune*. And then she proceeded to clear her mind, change the radio, and wait for Martin to exit the school.

Chapter 5

"How was it?" Charlie asked, even though the force that Martin had used to slam his door told her all she needed to know.

Martin's arms were already tied over his chest. He made a noncommittal noise.

She tried again. "Did you enjoy it?"

Martin scoffed. "If by 'enjoy' you mean tortured, then yes, I enjoyed it *very much*." He sulked lower in his seat.

Charlie shook her head in amusement. "Goodness, I can practically taste the angst. Seat belt, please." She checked her mirrors and turned out of the parking space. She was met with a grumble after Martin complied with the road laws. "Why didn't you like it?"

Martin's hands shot out in front of him. "Because Mr. Jason is, like, a billion years old, and, like, three times I thought this guy was going to keel over and die! All he did was stumble through the halls and talk about his cats."

Charlie nodded along hesitantly, like she heard that sentence on the usual. "Okay? Well, did you meet any teachers?"

Martin groaned, but his was followed a grunt of affirmation. "I saw a couple. They didn't really care about what I was doing." His voice lost a hint of bitterness.

"What did you think of it?"

Martin couldn't seem to sit still because he sat up in his seat and leaned forward. "I think that place is going to be my prison for the next nine months."

Charlie smacked her lips and smiled over at her brother. "So good with drama. I knew Aunt Mary was onto something when she suggested you join the club last year. I wonder if this school has one."

"Nothing in this world is making me stay at school longer than I need to," Martin harumphed, which was the same response he gave to Aunt Mary when she had said the same thing.

Melodramatics, Charlie decided, was the name of the game today.

"What do you think?" Charlie held up the slip of paper that was lined with different shades of brown next to the bathroom wall. On the other hand, she toyed with the thin handle of the paint can. Even though they rented house, their landlord had made it clear that he didn't care much of what they did inside, as long as nothing was damaged. Charlie took it as an invitation to personalize the house.

"I think that you've asked me that question too many times," Martin said from his spot on the floor outside the bathroom. He rolled his eyes after being fixed with a withering stare. "The fourth one down. Looks the least like of what will be going on in here."

"Oh my God," Charlie mouthed to herself, unsure if Martin could ever be serious. She relieved her arm of its duty of sitting in the air to scan back over the colors. She placed the paint slip on the counter and moved the paint can off the toilet and onto the ground. "Okay, right now all we have is white, but I can stop by the store tomorrow. Are you sure you have everything you need for school?" She slashed her hand through the air. "Nothing? Are you sure?"

"Yes, Grandma, I'll be fine," Martin reaffirmed for the tenth time.

Charlie mentally marked it down. It was already Monday, and it felt like the days were getting past her. Already, it was a week until her own first day of school. Who knew living as a functioning adult could be so tiring?

"Alright. And remember to take the bus home. I won't be here when school ends because—"

"Because you'll be off stocking clothes and whatever at your new job. *Yeah*, Charlie, *I know*. You've already told me this."

She nodded, exasperated. "Just making sure." She'd already had a job interview online before moving in for a clothing store just ten minutes from their house. She'd gotten the job fairly easily because she used to work retail back when they lived at their old house. That, and it had a high demand for workers. She already had another interview for another job lined up for Saturday.

"Are you sure you don't want me to get a job?" Charlie shoved herself out of her mental checklist to stare down at Martin, who looked up at her with a clear face for once.

"I don't want you to work before you have to," she said, head sure, which was her way of saying no, she absolutely did not want to force him to get a job due to financial situations that weren't his fault. Something that she had had to do at his age. "But you can if you want to, though," she added hastily.

Martin didn't notice her tone. "Nope. I'm living out this whole childhood thing to the fullest." He put his hands behind his head and closed his eyes.

"Have fun with that," Charlie said as she fell back into working mode and left the bathroom to survey the rest of the upstairs walls. To Martin's left was the stairs, and across the hall from them were the bedrooms. At the very end of the hall was hers, but Charlie entered the one that was next to the bathroom: Martin's. "Are you sure you don't want a different color? The green seems a little... abrasive." The bright green that coated the walls of Martin's room was evidence that she wasn't the only renter to take advantage of the freedom to paint. It didn't help that two and a half of the walls were a different shade of green than the rest of the room, like whoever had painted it had run out of their color halfway through and swapped to another.

"I'm surprised you didn't say it looks like the insides of a frog." Martin came to stand beside her, shoulders slumped so his mouth was level with the top of her head.

"I was getting to that," Charlie murmured. As long as paint was in the picture, she was only half there mentally, her mind always whirring.

"I still don't want to paint my room."

"Not even to make the green match?"

"Not even to make the green match," Martin confirmed, voice full of resolve. "I like it. Makes me feel like I'm inside an unfinished painting."

Charlie almost shivered at the ghastliness of it all. "How pretentious of you."

She checked over her own room as well, which was covered in a respectable white, as well as the other walls around the house. The most they needed were slight touch ups that Charlie wasn't going to bother doing. She wasn't here to increase the re-sale value.

That night, they slurped down their cheap suppers and went through a night of wintriness after the heating discontinued function for a few hours and started back up for reasons Charlie couldn't even begin to fathom.

The next morning, after checking and rechecking everything she possibly could for the house's interworkings, and deeming the problem something she was going to deal with later, Charlie skipped down the stairs and into the living room, still zipping up her jacket. "Are you sure you don't want to come with to get the paint?"

Martin, mouth full, stuck the chocolate bar in his hand into the air like a knight would with a sword. "I'm busy," he said through the sugar. Him being 'busy' really meant that he was just slouching on the ground and feasting on chocolate.

Charlie turned away from him to tie her shoes. "Honestly, you can eat in the kitchen. I put the old porch chairs in there." Then she added under her breath, "You look like an animal." Glancing up, she was met with Martin grinning with teeth stained brown. "Lunatic."

She shoved off the stairs after fastening her laces. "Okay, if anyone comes to the door, don't open it."

Martin preened. "And here I was thinking someone would join my tea party."

"The only person that you *could* answer to is Bill, but only if he really needs something." Of the three people Charlie had met in this town so far, one of them she thought was kind of heart, one of them she thought would be a considerate neighbor, and the other was the reason she now had pepper spray in the purse she picked up off the ground.

"Aye, aye, captain." He saluted her with the bar.

"Alright. You're helping me paint when I get back, though. Okay, bye, I love you. Lock the door after I go!" She yelled the last part before the wooden wall could block her voice.

It felt weird to tell her brother she loved him. Not that it was false, it was just that those words were never passed between them before their father died. It was only the thought that every time she disembarked from the house, it could be the last time she saw a family member that spurred her to voice her affection. Martin, being a teenage boy, virtually never affirmed the love for his sister, but Charlie knew that his mock remarks were his way of saying so.

Using the drive to the store as an example, Charlie was able to grasp how large the area was. Understanding that it was marginally bigger than previously thought, she had an idea that the community was more close-knit because no one moved here versus the forced proximity of a small town.

The bright illumination of the florescent lights and sliding doors welcomed Charlie into the appropriately sized general store. This time, the counter was empty, and no one made a move to fill the position at the sound of her. Dodging down the aisles too was reassuring to see she wasn't the only one there. She passed mothers with their strollers and old men hunched over canes and teenagers fumbling around with merchandise to make their friends laugh.

At the back of the store was a general maintenance area, where she retrieved the few small cans that they carried of the least offensive brown that Martin had suggested. She debated changing the color entirely—Martin's lovely comment being the inspiration to do so—but ended up taking the brown in the end. She would just have to not think about what it inadvertently implied.

Back at the front, she waited her turn as the teenagers from before meandered through the line, tittering to themselves as they dealt their crumpled cash to the worker for what looked to be eight different types of mini fireworks and three lighters. They kicked themselves along when it was Charlie's turn, who unloaded the cold cans onto the counter.

"I don't even know why we sell fireworks. They're not even in season anymore. The most it will do is make the local police throw a fit."

Charlie glanced up at the worker that shook his head to himself and began to scan the cans. He had the same pale skin that matched a large majority of the town. He seemed to be around her age, possibly adding a year or two.

She smiled. "I imagine that's one of the reasons behind the purchase."

The worker met her eye and mimicked her look, albeit more reserved. "You new around here?"

Charlie choked with the need to roll her eyes. At least he wasn't in connection with Sam or Bill. It felt odd to meet people for the first time, and they already knew her name. "Yes, only been here for a few days now."

"Lemme guess, that's not the first time you've been asked that," said the worker whose name read *Scott*.

"Right on the dot." Her smile this time was only slightly condescending.

"Trust me, the town's not as tight knit as it seems. It's just that usually only the same four people come around here. That's the only reason I noticed you're new."

She eyed him. "Oh yeah? Do those teens from a moment ago count for three of those spots?"

Scott only smirked. "Tim and Stacy are good kids. It's just Matt that wants to do dumb stuff. They just follow along because he's older. And they only count for one spot because they're basically all stuck to the hip."

Charlie began to move over to the other side of the counter, as all the paint had been scanned. "Well, then I hope that it changes to the same *five* people that come here."

Scott moved to bag the paints. He chuckled slightly. "This might sound odd, but have you heard of Misfortune?"

Charlie groaned halfheartedly. "Not you, too." She hoped store clerks talking about a town tale didn't become a regular thing.

That made Scott chuckle. "I imagine that means you've met Grant."

"Unfortunately," she huffed. Grant was the one exception to her rule of not judging others harshly.

His Adam's apple bobbed again. "What did he say this time? Did Misfortune appear because if aliens, or was it due to his wife taken early from sickness?"

"Actually, it was because a tornado killed his family and he wanted to smite the gods," she answered dryly.

Scott whistled. "Oh, that's a new one. If I were you, I'd feel pretty special."

"It's my lucky day."

"What exactly *do* you know about Misfortune that wasn't from Grant's tale?" He leaned against the counter, interest piqued much more than it should be.

Charlie shrugged. "Not much, honestly. Only that he's supposed to have some animal mask and steal children." She had a feeling that this ghost was deeply rooted in the town's history. Maybe that was the reason why *everyone* seemed to know about it.

Scott began to double bag the paints. "You've got that bit right. Although, no one really knows where the story came from. I know it's not a joke. Kids really *do* go missing here sometimes. Some people here believe that Misfortune is to blame for an actual kidnapping." He opened his mouth again, hesitating, before continuing in a softer tone. "My mom has always been a believer in things like that since she was a kid, and my uncle has some books on him, so I like to believe that it's real, too. The ghost, that is. I don't care for it being the reason kids are going missing. I just... It feels fun just to believe, you know? Like Santa. Everyone knows he's fake, but it's the concept of him that means anything."

Charlie chuckled. "I've yet to see anything that proves Misfortune's real. I'm more of 'see it to believe it.' Although, I'll keep what you said in mind." She picked up her bags and backed away.

Scott nodded, but it was stiffer than before, like he'd said the wrong thing. "Of course. Have a nice day."

Chapter 6

Contrary to what she had previously thought, finding a moment to be on the phone while training in for her new job, all while *hiding* the fact she was on her phone was much harder than previously anticipated.

George, her boss, hadn't allowed Charlie one moment for breath as soon as she walked through the store's doors for her first day at work. He had been chittering nonstop since, and then when her phone had rung, she had to escape to the bathroom to pick it up. She was in the middle of telling the movers, which were a day late, to look under the rock out front for the spare key when George knocked on the women's bathroom door.

"Charlie? Is everything alright in there? I heard talking. You know phones aren't allowed while on shift."

Charlie practically jumped out of her skin when he did that. She had rightfully expected unspoken boundaries of the lady's room to protect her. Apparently, George's obtrusive personality had no concept of boundaries.

She sat on one of the toilets and put a hand over the receiver. "Everything's alright! Just... a family emergency! I'll need a few moments!"

"Oh! What kind of emergency?" George's lovely self had no bounds.

"Umm... my brother... stabbed... himself?" She im-mediately kicked herself as soon as her mouth closed.

"Oh, my! Do you need to go home?"

"No! He's, uh, okay!"

The door rattled. George must have been leaning on the door. "Okay! Take your time, then!"

Charlie sighed, but her quiet didn't last long.

"Ma'am? Is everything alright? Do you need to go to the hospital?" Christ, the mover of the phone had heard her.

"No, no, no. Everything's okay," she said breathlessly. "The key is under the rocks by the front door. Just put all the boxes where you think they should go."

"Alright, then. We should be out of the house by noon. Is there anything else you need?"

A breather, she wanted to say. "Nope. Sounds perfect." With a fast hang up, Charlie exited the stall and washed her hands just to be sure.

When she opened the bathroom door, she had to stifle a scream. There, standing only feet away, was George, with a concerned look. "Jesus, George!" She put a hand on her face to calm her breathing. "You scared me."

"Is your brother okay?" he asked, eyes wide. His wispy frame put Martin's to shame. Although he was more than double her age, George was the most exuberant person she'd ever met.

"He's fine. Martin was just playing a prank." She smiled convincingly, doing her best not to give away how weird she found it for him to be standing outside of the bathroom.

George nodded vigorously. "Ah, I know how it is with teenagers. My Sarah is always pretending to do *drugs* with *needles*." He shook his head. "It doesn't help my ex-wife is encouraging this behavior. Always saying something or other about health. Bah! As if I don't know my own daughter."

Charlie hesitated. "Uh, do you think maybe she has diabetes?" she squeaked.

George only shrugged. "Kids these days, am I right?" he said, ignoring her. Charlie could only respond with a terse laugh that fell into awkwardness. Something George probably didn't even pick up on.

Back on the job, Charlie learned the placements of the clothing items, and demonstrated she had prior knowledge of how to work the checkout till. Minus her boss's complete lack of boundaries that worried her mildly, she could see herself coming to enjoy her new job. By the time she finished her first day of work, she was energized from the change in life but worn out after the labor. It didn't help that she had stayed late into the evening to ensure her knowledge of work, which meant she had to drive home in the dark through the wooded part of town.

And of course, on top of that, Martin decided to call her while she was on the road.

"Where's my skateboard?"

Charlie balanced the phone on her shoulder. "Martin, not now, I'm driving." She paused. "And you haven't skated in years."

"Yeah, well, I wanna make sure I still have it," he huffed.

Ignoring all the flags in her head that told her to put the phone down and focus on the road, as Brandon had taught her, Charlie hiked the phone higher on her shoulder. "Are you home? Did everything go okay at school?" she asked instead. The skateboard had been a present from their father, which made Charlie believe Martin wanted it for sentimental purposes over entertainment. Something he only ever did when he was in a mood.

By the time the question left her mouth, she knew it would've been better to talk about this to his face. "God, Charlie. Everything's *fine*. I'm tired of you worrying about me."

Defending herself would get her nowhere. Martin must have had a *really* bad first day for him to snap at her. "I'm sorry, Marty. I didn't mean to make you upset."

He gave a resigned sigh. "It's fine, just...whatever. Do you know where my board is?"

Charlie thinned her lips and scanned the road. She was in a larger plot of trees that loved to hide oncoming turns and inhibit her brights. She didn't *want* to take her eyes off the road, but the old pain laced through her brother's voice broke her heart. "I don't but give me a second. I think the movers sent me an email of where they put everything." As fast as possible, she pulled the phone away from her ear and minimized the call. Swapping her eyes between the inky blackness in front of the vehicle and her phone, she clicked through her emails until she found one.

"Okay, Martin. They said that they put all the boxes that had your name in the room at the end of the hall. I think they got our rooms mixed up," she said to the loudspeaker.

"Oh. That makes a lot more sense of why the two boxes I looked in had makeup." He tried for a comedic tone, but even Charlie could hear the relief across the line.

She looked away from the road once more. "Did it have a specific marking on it? Like a number or something?"

"Uh, I think I put a one on there."

Charlie dared to look down again to scan the list. "Alright, it says that one is in my room, try—" She glanced back up to the road to correct her position, only to find a person standing right on the dashed line of the road. Their white face reflected in the car's lights as she came barreling towards them at a speed that was much too fast.

Chapter 7

Charlie screamed and dropped her phone, slamming on the brakes. Her tires screeched from the effort, refusing to slow in time. In a panic, Charlie threw the wheel to the right and towards the ditch. Her side mirror clipping the person, flinging off with a pop.

The car jostled and bumped on the unfamiliar terrain. She yanked the wheel to the left to prevent hitting the trees, but one large rock later, there was a large pop from beneath her feet and the airbag was in her face. The car dipped to the left and pulled to an ungraceful stop when it hit the curb of the road.

She breathed hard, her fingers white on the wheel. She peeled them away, knuckled stuck in a claw grip. Her neck smarted from the hard bumps, and the air bags and seat would probably leave bruises, but otherwise she was relatively unharmed. The same couldn't be said about the car.

But what about the person? Charlie's breath hitched, and she spun around in her seat to see if there was anyone lying in the road.

"Charlie! What the hell happened?! Did you just crash?!" The voice buzzed by her feet. Looking down, she saw her phone was still on the line—Martin had heard everything.

She unbuckled herself and snatched up the phone, taking in air fast enough to make her lightheaded. "There was—" she puffed. "A person in the road—I swerved not to hit them—oh my God oh my God oh my God."

She launched herself out of the car, with Martin berating her with questions that her ears didn't pick up on. She scaled the side of the ditch in two steps and desperately scanned the road.

What she hoped she found was a shell-shocked person that was unscathed. What she expected to find was a person lying in the road.

What she *actually* found was nothing.

No one. Not a single soul joined her on the road.

She spun in circles, searching for something, anything, to tell her where they'd gone. Praying that she didn't hurt them. She checked the other side of the road. She hunted the outskirts of the woods. She explored every. Possible. Place.

Nothing. Not even the bright moonlight or her phone flashlight caught a trace.

"Charlie! Jesus! What's going on? Are you hurt?" Martin yelled through the phone.

Charlie put a hand on her forehead and paced, adrenaline coursing through her and forbidding any breaks. "I don't know where they are! There was a person... and... and... *they're gone!*"

"What do you mean they're gone? Who's gone?"

"I mean there's nothing—" She stopped when the still on flashlight brushed over a lump where the person had been on the road.

"Wait, there is something," said the voice that must have been her own.

"Hold on! Where are you? Is anyone hurt? Have you called the cops?"

She didn't answer as she inched towards the lump, which unfurled itself as she got closer. The horns shimmering in the light, and the incisors pointed right at her. The goat skull was dirtied with brown blood, and she could see the maggots squirming inside. Bending down, yet keeping a safe distance, she could see that it was missing its bottom jaw, and the remaining teeth were rotten and chipped.

"Charlie?" Martin asked tensely.

"It's just a goat skull." She sighed. Not something from the person. She hadn't realized the hope had been building in her until her knees fell out from under her and the rocks on the road dug into thighs.

"Where are you?"

Perturbation built in her gut, trying to force her meek lunch break back up. She looked around her, but all she found was an illuminated goat skull, a car in the ditch, and black trees. "I don't know. Somewhere on 18th Street."

"Where's the person?" Normally, Charlie would've felt guilty that her little brother had to walk her through this, but her mind wasn't working right now.

"I don't know."

"It's alright, Charlie. Don't cry. Are you in the road?"

"Yes."

"Okay. Try to get up and out of the way. Then what you're going to do is hang up and call the police. Can you do that?"

Charlie wiped at her nose and sucked up the rest of her tears. "Okay. Okay, I can do that," she said to herself and pushed to her feet. Skittering off the road, she could see the front lights had shattered on the car, and the wheel under the driver's seat had popped. She sighed, doing everything she could to prevent any thoughts of the person from poisoning her mind. "The car took a shot." She focused on the astronomical price that it was going to take to get it fixed. "Lord, the car's ruined."

"That's fine. It's just a car. Call the police, alright?"

"Yeah." She nodded, even though he couldn't see her. "Thank you, Martin. I love you."

"Meh, all in a day's work." Her spirit frayed at the edges when his voice cracked.

He was the first to hang up, because Charlie's fingers were shaking too badly to do so. She hesitated when she went to tap the EMERGENCY button, pausing the glance at the skull on the road.

Even though it was just a skull, looking at it made her skin crawl. She could've sworn that it wasn't there when she was in the car. But she also could've sworn she hit a person, so her mind wasn't something to trust.

With a check in each direction, Charlie stepped back onto the road, morphed her feet with the pavement to make no sound, pulled up her phone and snapped a photo of the skull with a sharp flash, the sight burning itself into her retinas.

That was how she caught three oddly placed lines right under the skull's left eye, like it had been dropped from a high place and landed on a group of rocks. She stared at them for one, two, three blinks.

And then she called the police to tell them she hit a person with her car.

Chapter 8

Even though it was supposed to be her second day of work, George insisted she took the day off when Charlie called to tell him she'd be in late that day. Whether he knew from the compact size of the town, or the shakiness of her voice that had stayed with her since the previous night, she didn't know. His complete lack of boundaries and ability to perceive social cues came in handy though, because he blatantly threatened to fire her if she came in.

And though Charlie should've felt so relieved for the break, she most definitely wasn't. Last night had taken a toll on her.

After frantically dialing the police and spitting out what happened, they had sent a cruiser and an ambulance down. And even with the help of two officers and three paramedics, nothing, not even a trace of human flesh, was found on the scene besides Charlie's.

It had cracked her heart open when the officers had offered to take *her* to the hospital. She *was not* seeing things that weren't there, contrary to what they believed. The image of the person's pale skin reflecting in the car's head beams never left her skull. No way could she imagine something so *vivid*.

Dealing with Martin was even worse. He was all wound up and followed her around the house like a dejected puppy. Not to mention he'd also called Aunt Mary as soon as they'd hung up last night, so by the time she got home near dawn with the help of a police cruiser, her muscles already slithering with tiredness, she then had to weather a berating phone call from her aunt and Martin's questions *on top of that*.

While she appreciated the concern over her safety, four in the morning was not the time to have a conversation about her health.

She managed to get to bed around five, after reassuring Aunt Mary that, yes, she was fine, and yes, her car was in the shop. The rock she had run over had found the bottom of her car, effectively busting everything that it could reach, leaving it indisposed for an annoyingly long amount of time.

The night had fled in a blur. And when her preset alarm went off two hours later, she was frantic to call George to tell him she'd be late. And the wonderful threats he told her led to a quick sigh of relief that wracked her lungs. She still was stuck in the past, but she now had one less thing to deal with.

Her morning was filled with walking around the empty house and holding her phone to her ear long enough to cause her forearm to cramp. Of all the years she'd had a license, she'd never crashed her car before. Not even a tap of someone's rear-end, as Brandon had taught her. Now, she had to talk to a million people at the insurance company and tell them about her totaled car. She probably could've shaved a few hours off of the calls if she actually knew what she was doing. But the only thing she knew was that she would have to join Martin in the club of taking the bus everywhere.

And of course, *of course*, to make her day better, her phone rang again when she was making lunch after missing breakfast thanks to all the previous calls. The caller ID wasn't registered in the phone, but Charlie knew who it was.

She tortured the phone, allowing it to ring until the last second. Only then did she pick up the phone, and answer with a tap, the taste of wariness pungent on her tongue. She sighed hard into the speaker. "Hi, Mom."

"Charlette? Are you okay? Aunt Mary told me you were in a car accident last night," her mother rambled. Her voice wasn't as heavy as usual, but Charlie could tell her mother had already had her first beer of the day. It was probably the reason she called over eighteen hours after the crash she was oh so worried about.

"Yes, Mom, I'm fine," she said, reserved. Stiff. This was the first time they'd spoken since Charlie had moved. And that was a week before she packed up her things, too. Charlie didn't bother with the goodbye because her mother had been at the bar when she was ready to go. "Car got totaled, though."

"Lord, I'm so happy you're alright. I could barely sleep last night thinking about you."

Yeah, right, Charlie thought.

"What on Earth caused it? Was it a deer? I almost hit a deer on the way home last night. Coulda ended up like you."

Charlie sucked on her molars in thought. She'd seen a person. She *knew* she saw a person on the road.

And yet.

And yet.

There was nobody there. Even with the help of five other people, nothing was found. Not a tatter of clothing. Not a smear of blood. Not even a single strand of hair.

And it was something she still didn't know what to think of.

"Yeah, I almost hit a deer, too. Tried to swerve around it, but ended up in the ditch instead," she said, throat mimicking sandpaper. This was her mother, anyway. It's not like she'd remember why her daughter almost died a few hours from now away. Alcohol in her blood stream always meant it was greedy for her memories.

A tut came over the line. "That's what we get for living in such wooded areas. I was always telling your father that we should move somewhere sunnier, like California maybe, or Florida."

Charlie's smile was brittle. She knew her mother couldn't see her, but thinking of her father always brought the same bittersweet feeling. "I know he always loved the trees," she rasped.

Her mother didn't catch on to her pain. "I never did," she huffed. "Anyway, are you sure you're okay? Do you want me to come down and stay with you?"

"No," Charlie rushed out too quickly. "No, Mom, itls alright. I don't even have a scratch on me. We'll be fine." If her mother came to stay, she'd never leave.

"Alright, just… make sure to be safer on the road. And be extra cautious when Martin's with you. I don't know what I'd do if I lost both of you."

Charlie knew where her mother was coming from, but almost spit back, *Oh, so it's okay if only one of us dies?* but she didn't dare. Her mother may be a fragile woman that forced her kids to bear her weight in the world, but she was still her mother. No matter how many times Charlie groaned when she had to interact with her, she still loved her mother. No matter how much it fractured her heart when her mother went and did something that broke her trust. No matter how much she wished it was her that was hit by Brandon, not her father.

Instead, all she said was, "Always."

A clinking sound spilt over the line. Her mother was picking up another bottle. "Alright then, Char, if you say you're okay, I believe you. Is there anything else you want to talk about?"

"Nope. I probably have to go back to calling my insurance company, anyway." She'd already done that, but her mother didn't need to know that.

"Alright, honey. Be safe. I love you."

"Love you, too," Charlie said, even though the line clicked out before she had opened her mouth.

Chapter 9

For the brief second she saw Martin, Charlie could tell something was wrong. He'd come home not long after she'd ended her call with her mother, and the greeting he did was a sharp nod to his sister. And while Charlie knew it was probably common teenage behavior to forgo polite greetings, it was not common behavior for Martin. She was confused even more so when he'd taken the stairs two at a time and went to his room. The last Charlie heard of her little brother was the soft click of his bedroom door.

She ate her sad noodles in a ceramic bowl at the kitchen table without him, and while she thought that using house appliances in her own home would make the weirdness go away, it did not.

Eventually, when she couldn't take it anymore, she braved the steps and rapped on Martin's door with her knuckles. She prayed that her own time as a teenager was enough guidance to deal with her brother. "Martin?" she hesitantly tried. She'd never been one to probe, but with school starting, and being gone for college and work, *and* last night, *and* her being the only adult, she didn't want anything to fester between them.

"What?" came his muffled response. Nothing in his voice told Charlie how he felt.

"Are you dressed? Can I come in?"

"Aw damn," he said in an excessive tone. "And here I was about to have a naked dance party."

When Charlie didn't respond, mostly because she was frozen out of confused mortification, Martin sighed with a tinge of embarrassment. "Yes, you can come in."

Charlie opened the door to find Martin lounging on his bed, phone in hand. "I barely saw you today. How've you been?"

Martin looked away and put his phone down, movements stiffer than they should've been. Something was definitely wrong. "Oh, yeah. I was kinda tired after school. Figured I go to bed early."

"Oh. I just wanted to make sure you were okay. Do you want me to leave?" Charlie knew her brother wasn't sleeping, but wasn't going to overstep her welcome.

"Nah, I'm fine."

Charlie nodded. "Well, I was wondering if you weren't too tired to go out. Figured we play some pool together. We haven't done that since," *Dad died*, she almost said, "we lived with Mom," she said instead.

Martin perked up, but not as much as Charlie had hoped. He used to beg their father every night to take him to the local bar and play a few rounds of pool for a few bucks. She'd hoped doing the same would light whatever weight was sitting on him now.

"Uh, yeah, we can. One issue though, how are we going to get there?"

Charlie smiled thinly. "Ready to take the bus again today?"

The bar was much more packed than Charlie would've expected for a Thursday night. They'd made it after a quick bus trip and short walk. Multiple times, Charlie had tried to engage in conversation, and multiple times, Martin had shut her down.

They weaved by the front bar and a few side tables to the back, where there was indeed a pool table that the bar's website had described, but it was backed into the corner and surrounded by people milling about. Thankfully, it wasn't in use.

Misfortune

"Come on," Charlie beckoned as they stepped through the lingering cigarette smoke and found the green cushioned table. Many pool cues lined the wall, and the wooden covered walls had deep marks. Probably from other pool players hitting the wall from the lack of room.

Martin went over to the cues while Charlie bent down to survey the spot for quarters that would get the game going. Inserting the four necessary coins, the pool balls spit themselves out with a loud rumble. Pulling the old memories of how to play, she placed the rack on the table along with all the balls. Martin was armed with a cue by the time she was done.

And his face was a lot more mellow than she'd hoped.

She let him break the triangle of numbered balls, and he won strips. They went back and forth, leaning on the table and striking their ball. Martin always was a better shot than her. When they had played pool with their father, Martin had tried to explain to her that the game was just about angles, but Charlie had never been good at math.

Which is why she was spurred into even deeper worry for her little brother when she *won*.

She tried for a brittle smile. "Good game, Marty. You almost had me at the end." He did not. "Wanna go again?"

Martin wasn't listening. His head was turned to the side and his eyes were darting which way around the bar, which had only gotten more packed since they'd started playing.

"Marty?" she tried again, to no avail. Setting down her cue stick, Charlie approached him cautiously like he was a frightened puppy. She placed a hand on his arm, and he shrank back, which in turn caused her to startle. "Martin, buddy, are you alright? You've been a little off for a while."

He shoved his hands in his pockets and looked away. "I'm fine," he muttered.

If this was any other time, Charlie might have pointed out that burying hands in pockets and making grumbled responded did not, in fact, shave away the awkwardness to his stance. But the timing of doing that felt inappropriate, instead she said, "Is this about school? Did something happen? Did a classmate do something?" She lay her palm back on his arm.

He wrenched away from her sharp eyes. "This isn't about school," he spat.

Charlie blinked at him. They hadn't fought in years, and now they were two for two in the span of twenty-four hours. "Then what's wrong?" She held his eye, daring him to break the stare.

This only made Martin's internal thermometer rise. "How can you not see?"

She crossed her arms, suddenly defensive. "What are you talking about?" They could barely hear each other over the chatter in the room. It felt like it had reached a crescendo and refused to go back down.

"I thought you died last night!" Martin yelled, overcompensating for the noise.

Charlie, however, froze in her spot, arms limp in their cross. "What?"

Martin waved his hands in the air, eyes looking everywhere but hers. "I was on the phone with you when you crashed, Charlie. All I heard was you screaming and loud banging. And then there was silence. *Jesus*, I thought I listened to my sister die in a car crash." He breathed hard, voice ragged. "I thought you ended up like Dad."

Charlie's mouth hung open. She was mildly aware they had an audience, but her eyes were only for Martin.

Of course, he'd think that. She had the same thought. Martin was so young when they'd lost their father. She'd never even thought of the horror that would be induced if she had to listen to something like that. If their roles had been swapped, she would've probably been calling the cops and telling them her brother was dead once the silence became deafening.

And lying under all these thoughts, Charlie knew she had foolishly assumed that since she was fine, so was Martin.

"Oh, Martin. I'm so sorry. I didn't know it bothered you so much."

He hunched his shoulders, conviction all spent. "You never asked."

And that one sentence shot itself through Charlie's heart, breaking it into an impossible puzzle. She'd made a mockery of what a good sister was supposed to be like. Especially one who shared a deeply rooted trauma of cars accidents.

Charlie watched on pathetically as her brother caved in on himself. "Martin, please. I am so, so sorry. I should've checked up on you. I just thought everything was fine since I was okay. That was so selfish of me. Is there anything I can do for you to forgive me?"

Martin only shrugged and went back to eyeing the room. "It's fine. Can we just get out of here? It's gotten pretty busy."

Charlie was already nodding and putting away their cues and balls. She hadn't realized how stuffy the room felt until they had to master the trudge through it for a second time.

The bus ride home was more awkward than the bar by the tenfold. When Martin didn't respond to her apologies, she forced herself to sit in quiet and stare stiffly at the light-lined floor, any movement away from literally stuffing her knuckles in her mouth.

She'd been so caught up in her job and Aunt Mary and dealing with whether she hit a person that night that she'd completely forgotten about her brother. Not to mention that she had also missed congratulating him on completing his last first day of high school.

Charlie knew she wasn't Martin's mother, but she had promised herself to never be inattentive to Martin like their real mother had. And after only one week of him being under her care did she break the promise.

Back at home, Charlie caught on that her presence wasn't wanted. Ignoring the way it made her feel horrible, she apologized once more and made herself scarce to her brother, escaping into the kitchen. She occupied herself by wiping down the already clean counters, failing to stop herself from mentally rewinding time and thinking of everything she should've done differently.

Martin was still a child. He shouldn't have been forced to swap houses so often and still have the adults in his life be unreliable. Hell, *Charlie* was still a child. She didn't know what she was doing half the time, and nonetheless she would have a full schedule of school and work in less than a week's time. Something that would force Martin to be alone for a majority of time.

Maybe it *would* be better if he went back to living with Aunt Mary.

"You were right."

Charlie gasped and whipped around, finding Martin standing in the doorway. She'd been so caught up in her self-pity she hadn't heard the telltale creaks in the floorboards. "Jesus, you scared me." She put a hand over her head, blinked, then sharpened her eyes at her brother. "Right about what?"

Martin's smile was ridged and built out of his own self-pity. "That I was in a bad mood because of school. And you were right that I had been like that for a while, even before last night." He shook his head right before Charlie could ask for the specifics. "It's not because of a classmate or anything, just... I was thinking about how Dad won't see me graduate."

Charlie felt her lips open in sorrow. She had never even given a second thought to the luxury of having both her parents witness her accept her high school diploma. "And then while you're thinking about that, you listen to me crash my car," she finished quietly.

Martin gave a terse nod. "And then we go back to our lives like the past doesn't matter." He shrugged again, which Charlie now guessed meant that he was trying to downplay the situation. "I didn't want to make a big deal about it, but it bothered me that *you* didn't make a big deal about it either."

Charlie set down the dish towel she had been mindlessly fidgeting with since the beginning. "I'm sorry, Marty. I had the same idea when I was in the ditch. The first thing I thought of was Brandon."

Martin wouldn't look at her, *couldn't* look at her, so Charlie closed the distance between them and hugged her brother. He would've made a wonderful replacement for a wooden board, because he was extremely stiff. "I'm sorry. For everything."

"It's fine, alright? You don't need to hug me, you old grandma," he groaned, shattering the wall that had strung itself up over the past few days.

Martin didn't complete the hug, though he placed his head on the top of hers. With a last light squeeze, she let him go and backed up. "Yes, I do. Before you get too old for your big sister to hug you."

Martin rolled his eyes. "That line came and went about eight years ago."

"So dramatic," she tutted. Though the awkwardness was gone, the knowledge of what happened wasn't. She backed away and surveyed the kitchen. "Did you want supper? I haven't seen you eat all day."

She looked back to see him shrug again, this one more carefree. "Not really. I bet a couple of kids at lunch today that I could eat their lunches on top of mine—"

"Oh, my God." Charlie was already shaking her head to herself before he was down.

"—Let's just say they were down two chicken patties and twenty bucks once the bell rang."

"You are such an idiot."

"You're just jealous you don't have twenty bucks."

"Don't you have something better to do than flaunt money in the kitchen?"

"Yeah, I should probably go upstairs and recount all of my hard-earned cash."

"Two whole ten-dollar bills?"

Martin flashed a shit-eating grin. "I may have made the bet more than one time."

"Jesus," she muttered to herself. "Please stop taking lunches from your classmates."

Martin could only click his tongue and put his hands in the air. "It's not my fault these kids haven't heard about responsible money management."

"You don't—God, just go to bed." She waved him away, hoping that it didn't come across as angry as she intended. The wall between them had disintegrated, but the wound was still there.

Martin left the room with a flourish of a bow, leaving Charlie chuckling in his wake. "Dramatic!" she called out the door.

"Grandma!" he yelled back. "I'll be back with my money doubled tomorrow, and you can't stop me!"

Drama, drama, drama, Charlie thought, smiling to herself.

Chapter 10

On her third day of being employed and second day of work, Charlie finally had a normal shift. George seemed to have caught on that she had a fair idea of what to do and left her to her own devices. That, or he probably forgot he had an employee that might have needed more assistance during her first days.

Either way, Charlie was thankful to be left alone. She had co-workers, yes, but she was usually the only one working during her shift's hours. Scheduling didn't seem to be George's strong suit.

She wandered down the aisles, making herself available to any customer that needed help. The first person that required assistance was an elderly woman that time had almost folded in half. She waved down Charlie with a liver-spotted hand.

"Yes, ma'am. Can I help you with anything?" Charlie politely asked, diverting from the main walkway to her.

"I was wondering which one of these you'd recommend." She gestured to the aisle's clothes, and Charlie took stock of the large amount of flashy women's bikinis.

Charlie held a small smile and did her best not to think about the implications. That wasn't her business. "Is there a specific color you're looking for?"

"My husband likes it when I wear black," said the woman in the warmest voice one might save for their grandchildren.

Charlie nodded. "Of course." She pointed down the aisle to the darker colored bikinis. "You might like those, then. There are many distinctive designs, too."

The older woman nodded. "Ah, yes. Should've seen them before." She waddled off. "I'm sure my husband will love them. Thank you!" she called back.

Charlie's composure could only last for so long. "Oh, that's alright. It was my pleasure to help."

Charlie knew she said the wrong thing when the woman whispered something to herself and cackled. She was a full-grown adult and yet the interaction made her cheeks alight.

Back out on the floor free of workish obligations, Charlie took a moment in the back aisles to herself, which was why she didn't see the person stalking up behind her until they were calling her name.

"Charlie!"

She turned, finding Sam trotting over to join her in the decorative towel aisle that didn't fit the shop's brand of clothing. The familiar face made the memory of the last few moments leak out of her.

"Holy crap! I didn't know you worked here!"

Charlie grinned. "Two days and counting."

Sam finally reached her and puckered her lips. "I supposed that means ol' George is your boss. How is that? Being that him and Grant are, you know, two sides of the same coin."

Charlie bristled for George, even though she had only known him for two days, and in those few hours, he had tried to join her in the bathroom. "George is nice. I believe he means the best."

Sam nodded. "I supposed that *is* better than being harassed with a ghost story in a tiny store." She shook her head. "Grant caught another victim yesterday. A poor little girl whose parents took their eyes off her for a second. I was ringing up their stuff when she comes over bawling. Grant had convinced her Misfortune was hiding in the walls and was going to eat her. Even pulled out a fake goat skull mask for effect," she tutted. "He really is an asshole."

Charlie blinked. The mention of a goat skull caught her attention with a hook that shouldn't have been so sharp. A goat skull was just a goat skull, and a ghost story was nothing more than smoke and mirrors. And yet, the first thing her mind connected the story of Misfortune to was the goat skull she found in the middle of the road.

Glancing around to make sure no one caught her slacking on the job, Charlie decided to forgo other common pleasantries and pulled out her phone. "Hey, Sam, is there anyone that has any pet goats here?"

Sam, oblivious, blinked at her in thought. "While I know this might look like a small town, I don't know *everyone*." She paused. "Although I certainly can't think of anyone near here that has any pet goats. Or wild, come to think of it." Her brow furrowed. "Uh, why?"

Charlie put on her best adult face. "Well, two days ago, I was driving, and found this." She decided that talk of what happened to her car was best to ignore, and she showed her frizzy haired companion the photo.

Sam blinked again, eyes taking a second to adjust to the screen and the jumping of the conversation. Charlie, in her rush, had shoved the phone right under Sam's nose, causing the other woman to lift a hand to push it back. "That, uh…sure looks like a goat skull?" She gasped and backed up. "Charlie, I like you, but I please don't tell me you're one of those people who collect animal bones."

Charlie let her phone drop with a puff from her mouth. "What? No, just—does it look odd to you?"

Sam, after searching Charlie's face to conclude that she did not, in fact, collect bones, resumed surveying the photo. "Um, not really. Although it looks like you weren't the first person to find it," she said, pointing towards the screen. Sure enough, when Charlie turned the phone back to her, Sam had noticed the three gouged out lines under the left eye.

Sam shrugged. "Didn't you say you found this in the middle of the road? It was probably some teenager playing a prank. Matt, if I had to guess. That boy set fireworks off at a park a few days ago," she tutted. "I woke up thinking somebody got shot."

Charlie realized that Sam wasn't going to be much help, especially since she was starting to get off track. She embarrassingly put her phone away. "Anyway, sorry about that."

Sam smiled as an acceptance of the apology. "It's okay. Uh, why exactly did you show me a picture of a goat skull?"

She wasn't going to explain about having a wacky half-formed conspiracy theory to Sam. There was no way one little skull had anything to do with a ghost story blown out of proportion. "Doesn't matter. I bet it was just a prank, like you said." Charlie shoved down any doubts and took Sam's word, or, at least, she pretended she did.

Sam beamed, none the wiser. "Glad I could help."

Charlie hesitated, then remembered where she was. "Is there anything I could help *you* with? I'm sure you didn't come here just to look at pictures."

Sam laughed and switched her weight onto her other foot. "Honestly? I was just in town to kill some time, but I came back here to bleach my eyes because there was some old lady in the changing room trying on bikinis without shutting her stall door."

They may have had only two conversations that had happened when both were working, but Charlie found she was coming to like Sam.

Chapter 11

Charlie decided that since Martin had finished his first week of school (even though it was only three days long) and last weekend had an unwanted school tour, and the whole fiasco with her car, this weekend was going to be dedicated to him.

She originally had an interview for another job that day, but she had walked into the store, taken a look at the checkout lines that were filled with unhappy patrons and irritated workers, and walked right back out the door. She was aware that only having one job while also going to college and renting a house was going to be hard on her bank account, but at least she had more time for Martin.

Well, that's what she told herself when she asked George for more hours. She might also need to plead with Aunt Mary to loan her a little more money.

But she wasn't going to think about that now.

That morning they had decided to give another shot at pool at the same bar. This time, it was much less busy. The only other people in the building were the bartender and day drinkers. And what was much expected was that

Martin completely left Charlie in the dust. (Although, it wasn't hard because she only sank one striped ball, and she was solids.)

They went out to lunch soon after. Charlie consistently chittered to Martin (and everyone they saw) while they waited to eat. She knew that while that may annoy her brother, she didn't want him to fall back into his head. It was something she caught him doing more frequently.

And it was happening again.

"How about we play the 'If You Had' game?" Charlie tried. They had to speak over the clatter of silverware on plates and cooks yelling at each other next to their sizzling stoves.

Martin, who had gone glassy-eyed, snapped back. "What?"

Charlie pretended like she didn't notice. "Do you want to play the 'If You Had' game? You know, the one Dad liked."

Martin softened at the talk of their father, but got a slick look to his eye. Competitive he was.

The game was simple: One person would give the other a situation, and the other person had to come up with the most creative way to use all the items of the situation. All while maintaining a poker face. The goal was to get the other person to laugh, which would earn the other person a point. Three points and the game would find its winner.

"It was my idea, I'm going first. What would you do if you had... a hundred bottles of water? There, I gave you an easy one."

Martin didn't even hesitate. "Obviously, I would take a shower."

"That's a waste of plastic."

"The plastic is included in the shower."

Charlie scrunched her nose. First question and it had already become crazy. "You're showering in melted plastic?"

His face was still completely serious. "Absolutely. Helps clear pores."

Charlie couldn't keep a poker face. A smile cracked out of her. "Jesus."

"You're right, that was really easy. First point of three," Martin quipped. "Next question. What would you do if you had 18,000 crabs?"

"Wow, you're really just *diving* in, aren't you?"

"Do not make puns. Answer the question, sister dearest."

If it didn't cost her the round, she would've rolled her eyes. "Obviously, I would take them to the zoo."

Martin raised an eyebrow. "That's quite boring."

"Bold of you to assume they're going in the tanks, *brother dearest*. I was thinking more of that the zoo could use in infestation."

Martin hummed. "I like that. Two birds with one stone, getting rid of the crabs while also causing ruckus to others. Smart. Although, how are you going to transport such a large bout of sea life?"

"You know me. The crab whisperer." Charlie shrugged like she was surprised Martin didn't think of that answer first.

He nodded. Neither cracked, which ended the second round with nobody earning a point. "What would you do if you had the ability to transport yourself to anywhere in the world?" she asked.

"Can I use this ability multiple times?"

"You can use it as many times as you like."

He had to take a moment to ponder this one. "I would become a doctor, and then travel everywhere and diagnose everyone with diseases that don't exist."

From the strangeness of this conversation, and Martin's fully dead face, Charlie almost lost the game. "That's a twist. What diseases would you tell them about? How would you ensure that you keep your job?"

"Diseases that make them think they need to pay me and only me money, and if the government wants to track me down, it's going to be tough to catch me if I go to the moon."

Charlie nodded like they were speaking business. "Making money *and* a means of escape. Alright. Except, have are you going to survive on the moon?"

"Obviously, I already took a detour to NASA. I'm fully stocked with a ship and food. I just transported them with me."

"So, we're assuming you can just touch things and they come along with you?"

He shrugged. "I think it'd be pretty weird if I popped up in the middle of Tokyo fully naked."

"Oh, I suppose that makes sense. It would be a little hard to get a doctor's degree if you keep getting arrested for public indecency."

"Sorry for the wait. What can I get you two?"

They paused from their game and looked up at their waiter, who was none other than Scott from the store. "Oh, my God. Scott? You work here, too?" Charlie voiced, shocked. She really needed to meet people outside of work hours.

Scott laughed at the sight of who he was serving. "I've worked here for two years. It's nice to see you again. Anyway, can I get you guys anything?"

Martin broke character from their game and leaned on the table to get a good look at Scott. "Do we get a discount because you're Charlie's boyfriend?"

She smacked his elbow off the table. "*Manners*, Martin," she hissed. It was something their mother always did when they misbehaved in public. "I'm sorry about him." She turned her head back up.

Scott only chuckled while Charlie tamped down her mortification. "It's alright. I've got little sisters. I know how it is."

"Can neither confirm nor deny the partnership," Martin murmured almost inaudibly.

Charlie waited for him to continue, but she realized the pause was for her to order. "Uh, we'll take whatever you recommend." And then glared at Martin when he geared up to ask for something else.

Scott's eyes didn't deviate from his notepad. "Got it. French toast sound good?" He pointed his pen down at them.

Charlie slapped Martin's hands when they rose to try and pluck the pen out of his face. She smiled warmly like nothing was happening. "That's prefect. Thank you."

As soon as Scott was gone, Martin smacked Charlie's own hands away from him. "You didn't tell me you got a boyfriend already."

"I *didn't*," she huffed. "I went through his checkout when I was buying the paint for the bathroom."

Martin leaned on the table again, but out of reach of his sister's hands. "Lemme guess, you got stuck talking to him?"

Charlie smiled at her brother. If someone were to look at them from the kitchen, they might be fooled by the sweetness in her eyes. The person looking at her wouldn't be able to hear her harsh tone. "Right on the bell."

Martin wasn't scared of the tone, but soon lost interest in the subject. "Whatever. We never finished the game, you know."

Charlie gestured to the table. "Then go ahead. Unless you don't think you're going to win, Baby Brother."

Martin took the opportunity of not being in the game to roll his eyes. "You sound so stupid saying that." He cleared his throat. "Okay, what would do if you had," the glint in Martin's eye told Charlie she was wrong to assume he lost interest in Scott, "Scott as a boyfriend?"

"That's a terrible question." She frowned.

"Careful. Watch what you show," Martin warned.

"Give me a different question. I'm not answering that." She mumbled her responses. No way was she going to allow Scott to sneak up on with their food and overhear this.

"Deflection will get you booted out of the game."

Suddenly, Charlie wasn't in a playful mood. She leaned back in her chair, arms crossed. "Fine. I quit."

Martin sighed, breaking character again. "It's just a *question*. You've only met him, like, twice, so what's the problem?"

Charlie shook her head. "It's impolite to talk about people like that."

"By that logic, I think you've got about 18,000 apologies to give to those crabs."

"Martin," she warned.

He scoffed. "Fine. Fine, I'm sorry. No more talk about your pretty boy."

She rolled her eyes, but uncrossed her arms and took away her walls. "*Thank you.*" And then she stuck out a hand. "Congrats on your win."

Martin did two fake bows over the table with a flourish of his wrist. Then stuck out his own hand. At the second, like an infuriating child, pulled his hand away, smugly having drawn his sister in for a fake out of a handshake. Charlie was in no way impressed. She dropped her hand, her knuckles loud on the table. "Really? You couldn't even shake my hand? Are you proud of that?"

"Like a parent watching a child graduate."

This boy, was the only thought Charlie could muster in her head.

Two plates clattered onto the table in front of them. "Two French toasts. Can I get you two anything else? Drinks?"

Charlie threw daggers in Martin's direction, but he was too busy already digging into his food. She left him alone, for now. "No, thank you. They look delicious."

Scott smiled at her and lingered. "This is a little off topic, but have you heard the news about Grant?"

Charlie blinked at him, smile faltering on the conversational change. "Er, I heard he's been terrorizing other people with the Misfortune story?" It came out as a question.

Scott dropped his tone. "Sam, I assume you know her, if you know about Grant, said she had to call the police this morning because he walked into the store screaming that Misfortune was back."

Charlie was taken aback, and Martin finally realized that there were other people in the room besides his food. "Wait, what?" he asked through his carb-filled food.

Charlie ignored him. "Oh my God. Is he okay? Why would he do that?"

Scott shrugged. "Sam told me this when I stopped by this morning. It was a little rushed. Just that she opened the store and two minutes later he burst through the door and just started screaming about a goat skull and the kids being taken again. Cops had to be called because he wouldn't leave."

Charlie had nothing to say to that, but Martin did. "Well, isn't that an emotional roller-coaster...except it only goes down. Poor Grant. He will be missed." He put a hand over his heart and then he looked back at the adults. "Who's Grant?"

And her mind shouldn't have gone there first, but the picture of the goat skull in the road was the only thing that sat behind Charlie's eyes. No way did the person in the road have anything to do with Misfortune, and no way was it real. She furrowed her eyebrows. "Kids being taken again?"

Scott raised his own eyebrows. "You haven't heard? Like, four kids have gone missing in the past week. Haven't you seen all the cop cars everywhere?"

"Oh, yeah," she agreed limply. No, she hadn't. A byproduct of no longer having a car.

"Terrible, isn't it?" Scott tutted. "Anyway, sorry about that. Just thought you knew. Have a good day." Scott disappeared from their table in a blink, leaving the two in a daze.

"Well, jeez, that guy really doesn't stick to one thing for a long time." Martin still watched where Scott was warily. "What was that about, anyway?"

Charlie breathed in and out to calm herself and remind her memory that she had nothing to do with Misfortune, and she had no reason to deal with it any longer. "Misfortune's an old town ghost story that describes kids being taken. Grant's a person that really took the story seriously."

Martin went back to his toast. "Perhaps a bit too seriously." He slid the bread on his fork into his mouth with his teeth. "Do you think it's real?"

Charlie blanched. "Do *I* think it's real? Absolutely not. A ghost can't *steal children*. If anything, I think there's some sick person taking those kids."

Martin shrugged, unfazed. "Yeah, I know, but didn't you say you found a goat skull in the middle of the road that night you crashed?"

Charlie was surprised she wasn't the only one to think that skull had some correlation to the story. She played dumb. "Yeah, so?"

"Well," he drawled out, fishing for her to pick up on the thought, too. "Your pretty boy said that dude from the store was also talking about a goat skull. Could they have anything in common?"

She shook her head, but it was stiffer than all the other times she had done it. "The only thing they have in common is people thinking that messing with others is funny."

Martin watched her closely. "Okay. I was just thinking out loud."

Charlie pulled out bills from her wallet, ready to pay and get away from this conversation. "That's a first."

She looked up at Martin to give him a condescending smile. She glanced over his shoulder at the swinging door that led to the back of the kitchen. As it flung open from another waiter, it swung back out. Swung in, swung out. And on the last swing, Charlie could've sworn she caught the glimpse of a goat skull sitting atop of a person's body that was cloaked in black clothing.

Chapter 12

The college felt bigger by tenfold now that it was bursting with life. When Charlie had toured it some time ago, she hadn't given much thought to the spacious areas, as the amount of other people there was kept to a minimum due to her late appearance. Now, it was like they would have to start stacking students to get all of them to fit in the building.

While the town itself that her college was placed in was small, people tended to live some minutes north in a more bustling city. So it didn't surprise her when she got off the bus and didn't recognize a single face. Her need to be polite took over any lingering anxiety, and she greeted almost everyone she passed. She met teachers and shook their hands with perhaps too much vigor, and dutifully listened when they spoke about the aspects of their class. She had already acquired all of her necessary supplies and books, (discounted, of course) and so, despite all her worrying from the previous night, nothing went terribly wrong. Even while at lunch, she didn't have any problems of who she ate with. She just sat down next to a group of people and didn't shut up until class started again. Although, she never did catch their names, only that one of the blond ladies was allergic to peanuts, and another guy was going to be an engineer after getting his bachelor's degree.

It was towards the end of the day that things began to drift off school schedule.

The dean of the college, Dean Mitch Manfree, was jumping from family to family, greeting students and reassuring fussing parents that this school was good for their child when everyone began to empty out of the school for the day. While Charlie didn't know why the parents were there on the first day and not during the tour, she didn't bother pondering on it. It wasn't her business. Although, her personal radar detected someone to speak to, so she couldn't stop her feet from gliding in the dean's direction.

He was just finishing another conversation with a different student when she approached. He was a tall man. Spindly, almost. His brown hair was still prominent, but the thinning white hair by his ears threatened to take over in the years coming. His stature was regal but not stiff, a giveaway that this wasn't the first time he'd done this rodeo. He gave Charlie a reserve smile when he saw her approach.

"Good afternoon. How was your first day?" She had heard him ask that to everyone he greeted.

"It was nice. Thank you for asking." She stuck out a hand. "Charlie Kezben."

The dean obliged in the shake. "Ah, Ms. Kezben." He dropped her hand. "If I'm not mistaken, you just moved to town."

At this point, Charlie wouldn't be surprised if everyone in a twenty-mile radius knew who she was and that she moved. "News sure travels fast."

"Like a cheetah," he agreed. "Where abouts do you live?"

"Just down North Main Street. Some doors down from the restaurant over there."

He nodded. "Do you perhaps live near Bill Forester?"

"Yes?" How deep did this city's roots go?

Dean Manfree warmed a little. "Ah, I thought so. Bill's a family friend. I've known him for my entire life. He's a good man, that one. Looked up to him when I was a kid."

Charlie ultimately just accepted that everyone knew everyone and put it behind her. "I know what you mean. He helped me move in."

"Has he shown you his car collection yet?" Charlie shook her head. "No? Well, consider yourself a part of the one percent of this town that hasn't."

Charlie chuckled. "I've heard about it in passing, but not in person. Although, I did hear about how his wife wasn't a fan of them."

The dean grinned politely, but confusion fell into his eyes. "Wife?" He chuckled. "Ol' Bill never could settle down. He's never been married."

Charlie blinked at him, second guessing herself. What did he mean Bill was never married? She remembered specifically how he had mentioned her in one of the first sentences he said to her, and the slight awkwardness when he told her she died.

Or did he? She was sure. *Swore,* she was *sure.*

But she was also sure that there was a person in the middle of the road that night.

No matter how much she didn't want to admit it, these instances weren't even the only time she thought something was true when it wasn't. Like how that goat skull kept coming back to haunt her thoughts, or that person she thought she saw back at the diner.

Charlie shook herself out of this little crazy spiral. What was most likely happening was that the stress of her new life was catching up to her, and the story of the ghost materializing and thinking incorrect things was just the stress was just her brain's crazy way of coping.

And yet, she had spoken to Bill before the hecticness of her new life even existed.

Charlie chuckled to dispel the quiet that had fallen over them. "My bad. I probably misheard him."

"I bet it turns out he was just talking about one of his cars. I'm pretty sure he names them now that I think about it." Dean Manfree's attention flicked over Charlie's head. Behind her, she heard calls of greetings to the dean.

"Anyway, it was good to meet you, Ms. Kezben. Say hi to Bill for me." And with that, he was gone, and accidentally left Charlie with more questions swirling in her head than before they met.

Chapter 13

The bus ride home was bumpy, like the vehicle's wheels were purposefully locking on to all the rocks and cracks on the pavement. Something that made life a whole lot harder. Her schedule for the rest of the day was sectioned off purely for work, Martin, and sleep. Maybe a meal or two in there. Which meant that if she wanted to look over her classes or her books, it was on the bus.

Which was so lovely to provide no help to holding all the items she had precariously stacked on her lap.

After her books tumbled onto the ground for the third time while trying to finish the class reading, she figured that she would just have to wake up early tomorrow and deal with her stuff then.

Work that day could be described as the least exciting out of her total of three. That was, unless she included the fact that George got the great idea to jump around a door when she clocked in. Effectively making her scream and drop all of her stuff like she was back on the bus. So, no, it was pretty normal.

By the time her shift was over, it was still light out, but Charlie felt like toppling over. She knew she was going to have to do a lot of work for her new life, but she was embarrassed that it only took one day to be tired. Now to do it four more times that week. And then again, the next week. And the next. And the next.

Sometimes being an adult wasn't the most appealing. But then again, anything was better than living in the same house as her mother.

Knowing she shouldn't be tired by late afternoon didn't stop her from yawning all the way from the bus station to her house after getting off with her eyes half closed as she walked, thinking of what food would be easiest for supper. Because of this wonderfully safe combination, she didn't hear the rumble of a car when she crossed the road.

A screech from her left snapped her out of her stupor and she jumped off the road with her heart in her throat. Turning back with jelly legs, Bill was already turning off the car and getting out.

"Christ, Charlie! Are you okay? I took that turn a little too sharp. I'm so sorry!" From his casual wear to the spiffiness of the old car, Charlie guessed he had been out for a joy ride.

She calmed her breathing with a hand to her chest. "No, I'm sorry. I wasn't watching where I was going."

Bill finally came to a stop when he was close enough to ensure he didn't injure his neighbor. "Are you sure you're alright?"

Charlie swallowed and nodded. "I'm fine, really. Just a bit frazzled."

Bill smiled slightly. "I'm surprised you didn't hear me comin'. Ol' Shirley's got a kick to her when she runs."

Charlie perked up at the name. Of course, *of course*, he had been talking about a car. She felt a little embarrassed for the mix-up with Dean Manfree, and the mix-up with herself. "Oh, I was just in my head."

He chuckled. "Please, I've been on this Earth for over sixty years. I know burn-out when I see it."

"Is it that obvious?" Charlie asked sheepishly.

"I remember when I was your age. Let's just say you're handling it a lot better than I did." His smile faded a little. "How about I make it up to you for almost hitting you. I've baked too many cookies. You take some home to your brother."

Charlie shook her head lightly. "Oh, no, that's okay, really. It was my fault."

Bill tsked. "No way. I've got to put my car away, but just come on over to the garage."

Seeing no way out of the neighborly gesture, Charlie smiled politely and followed the car down the street to their houses. Hoping Martin wasn't stalking her from the window to later bombard her with questions as to what she was doing, Charlie stopped in Bill's driveway at a respectable distance. From this angle, she could see that his large garage was even more overflowing with cars than she originally thought.

Bill popped open his door. "Alright. Just give me a second. I hope you like cold treats because I always freeze my cookies."

After he went inside and the door closed behind him, Charlie couldn't stop herself from wandering around the driveway. She never passed the threshold to the garage's smooth flooring, but walked by the cars that sat on the pavemented property.

Her father had also been a connoisseur of antique vehicles, but Charlie herself hadn't really seen the appeal. Mainly because she knew nothing about cars. She thought that one of the cars she passed was a Jaguar something, or a Cadillac. Or maybe it was a Chevrolet?

Yeah, cars weren't her thing. But at least if she had a question about vintage cars, she knew who to go to.

"Here we are," said Bill, coming down the front doors steps and stopping before Charlie. He held a platter of frozen cookies. "I felt like a bag would be impolite, so just take the plate. An old man like me has no use for something so delicate."

Charlie hesitated. "Are you sure? I could just take the cookies and give them back."

"I'll probably break it anyway." He gave a shrug for emphasis, but Charlie had to rush forward to stop the cookies from sliding off when he did so. "See? Like I said. Please, take it."

Reluctantly, Charlie relieved her neighbor of the dish. It's not that she didn't want to accept the gift, it just felt like she was taking too much from him. "Are you really sure?"

"Quite positive. You saw what happened when I held that plate."

"You really are the sweetest, Bill."

He stuck a hand next to his mouth like they were telling secrets. "And it's an apology for when I start my cars in the morning." More than once, Charlie had awoken to the rumbling of an engine since living here. She was too polite to say it really bothered her.

She nodded, but didn't leave just yet. Instead, she looked around at his collection. "So, which one's Charlette?"

Bill blinked at her.

She hesitated at his lack of answer. And mild confusion. "...You know, the one you told me about when you helped me move in...?"

Bill smiled at her, but it didn't feel as sincere as the others had. "Oh! Yes, sorry about that! My old brain can't keep up with the past. Yes, it's that one right over... there!" His hand lifted and his finger drifted over the cars until they stopped on one deeper in the house. "One of my oldest ones, really. It was the first car I bought myself. Isn't she a beauty?"

Charlie watched where his finger went, homing in on a low car with deep navy coloring and fancy adornments that were probably added many years after purchase. "Of course. I'm sure she's very special to you."

Bill preened with the compliment. "Careful now, otherwise I'll be the one with the sweetest neighbor." He sighed contently. "I'm sure you've got to get on to your brother, now. It was nice seeing you."

"Same here," Charlie agreed. "Have a nice day, Bill."

"You too," he called when she departed from his property.

Stepping over their little plot of grass and onto her porch, Charlie breathed out lightly now that she was alone. Today had been stressful, and if she was expected to do it all again tomorrow, she would have to get to bed early. Her time with Martin would have to be cut short. Which meant she would have to make the most of it.

Closing the front door behind her with a foot, Charlie set down the cookies on the coffee table in the living room. "Martin?" she called through the house.

"Why were you at Bill's?"

She whipped around to the staircase, which bore Martin, who was leaning off the railing near the bottom. He must have watched the whole thing, much to her chagrin. Her movement caused hair to fall into her face, so she brushed it away. "He made cookies and gave them to us as a present. Would you like one?"

The look on his face told Charlie her brother was going to say something snarky. "You got *cookies* from our *elderly neighbor?*"

She walked over to the table and snatched a treat for herself. "Yes?"

"That is the most stereotypical thing I have ever heard." Martin jumped off the last stair and pointed in Bill's direction. "And that man plays *golf.*"

"Martin, you don't even know if he *does* play golf."

He obnoxiously walked over to the front window, peered outside through the blinds, and then turned back to her with his face in a pinch. "Trust me, I do."

She rolled her eyes and bit into her cookie.

Martin strode over and grabbed a cookie of his own. After taking off a chunk with his teeth, he pulled back. "Even better, he makes prepackaged cookies," he said through crumbs. This observation didn't stop him from shoving the rest of the cookie in his mouth and grabbing another. And *that* didn't stop him from turning around and walking into the kitchen, saying, "What's for supper?"

"Lamb chops and liver," she shouted back. It was what their mother always said when they asked too many times.

"Wow, you are a terrible cook." A crunch came from the kitchen. "So is Bill. You know what, I'm willing to bet that guy names his cars."

"He does not buy prepackaged cookies," she said instead, and Martin snickered terribly at the aversion.

Chapter 14

The problem with being an extremely polite person with a full schedule was that Charlie's burn-out had no light at the end of the tunnel. Every morning, she felt refreshed and wondered how she could've been so tired only hours before. And then, after she'd go to school and work and see Martin on top of that, she could only think of the sweetness of sleep's oblivion.

That was the full schedule, but the reason that being a polite person fit into it was when she inevitably became a teacher's pet. She couldn't say no when one of them asked for her to run a quick errand for them.

Professor Kess held Charlie's last class of the day, and while she was generally a grumpy person, Charlie to her was like a fresh breath of air. The praise had melted Charlie, so she jumped to the task when Kess asked if Charlie would run a few papers to the dean's office.

She realized her mistake halfway to the office. First, there was a chance she would miss her bus and be late to work. And second, there was a chance she would get stuck talking to someone and increase the odds of being even more late.

Darn Aunt Mary and her teachings of how to be a good person.

Her shoes clicked down the fairly free halls. She passed other stragglers and professors catching up on their work. It also didn't help that the office was on the other side of campus. Charlie was now beginning to understand why Kess had Charlie do the trek instead of herself.

The clock ticked dangerously close to being late when she finally reached the office. She would've walked in and given the secretary the papers and ran out to catch her bus, if not for Scott standing right in the doorway, crowding the way with his back turned. He was speaking with someone she couldn't see.

She stopped, slightly startled and confused as to why she kept meeting him. The need to get going trumped her questions, and she hoped to get around him without making things awkward, but either he was too big, or the doorway was too small, because there was no way she could get through without him moving.

He did the work for her though, taking a step back as he wrapped up his conversation. But as he moved, his step was larger than Charlie expected, and his foot landed right on top of hers. When her shoe became trapped under his foot, she yelped when he obliviously leaned his weight down. She must have startled him, because in their little domino effect, he gasped and jumped forward, spinning around, which knocked the papers in her hand to the ground. The front desk secretary, whom Scott had been speaking to, stepped forward to understand the commotion in front of her. Instead of helping, she stepped on one of the papers, which caught a drift of air on the tiled floor, and took the secretary's foot out from under her.

Charlie shot forward to catch her. She slid her arms under the older woman's and held her up, and somehow, all the trouble that had been going on one second before miraculously stopped.

"Oh, my God," screeched the secretary, even though she wasn't falling anymore. Charlie cringed as she hauled the woman to her feet, Scott rushing forward to assist.

"Is everyone alright? Helen? Er, Charlie?" When he said her name, it was less out of concern, but from surprise that *she* was the one he stepped on.

Charlie, slightly embarrassed at the whole fiasco, bent down and made herself busy cleaning up Professor Kess's papers, which were now lined with crinkles, and one had a rip in it from the secretary's high heel.

"Lord, I'm getting too old for this. This is why I told that uncle of yours to hire more help, Scott!" complained the secretary. Charlie didn't bother to voice on how falling on papers led to a correlation of a staff shortage.

"Uncle appreciates your help, Helen. He's just busy. I'll make sure to remind him when I see him again. I'm sure he'll listen."

Charlie stood and backed up a few paces, as not to intrude on them. That, and to collect herself.

Helen nodded righteously. "Hm, I'll get it through his head if you can't." Helen turned around, eyed Charlie, and brushed herself off. "Watch what you're doing, girly," she said and stomped off, her whole demeanor much more closed off.

Charlie watched her go in bewilderment, but turned back when Scott started to speak. "I'm so sorry about that, Charlie. *I* should've been watching about what I was doing. And I'm sorry about Helen. She's just like that."

Charlie held the papers close to her chest like they were a shield. "No, I'm sorry. Really. I was too close." When Scott shook his head and sighed, she continued. "I didn't know you went here. I've never even seen you in classes."

Scott chuckled. "I don't actually go here. College has never really piqued my interest. I just come down here to help my uncle."

She quirked an eyebrow. "Your uncle?"

"Dean Manfree. You know, tall guy, about yea high. Square face," he said, hand in the air to simulate the Dean's excessive height.

"Yes," she laughed. "I know who the Dean is. Nice guy. I didn't know he was your uncle."

He shrugged. "No offense, but you're probably the only person here that doesn't know that."

She wouldn't be surprised if that wasn't an exaggeration. "Well, that's nice of you to do that. Considering that you have two jobs on top of that."

Scott waved a hand in the air. "It's not as noble as it sounds. Uncle lets me use the books from his personal shelf as payment. I really only come here so I can read his books about Misfortune."

Of course, this town has published books about the ghost, she thought.

"I hope you don't think I'm like Grant," he continued. "But I wasn't lying when I said I believed in the paranormal here."

Logically, Charlie knew she should've agreed that hobbies are a good thing to have and left Scott alone to catch her bus, but the niggling notion that someone could possibly have an idea about her problem gave way to an idea that burrowed it way into her head. Something that wasn't going to leave unless she did something about it.

"Do you maybe have a second, Scott? I have a question about Misfortune."

As soon as Scott's ears picked up on 'Misfortune' he perked up like a dog for a treat. "Of course! What is it?"

She shoved Kess's papers under her arm and pulled her phone out with her other. Shifting over to Scott's side, she pulled up the photo of the goat skull she had found the night she crashed her car. "I know this is just a skull, and I could be crazy, and even though I don't believe in Misfortune, do you think this skull has anything to do with the ghost?"

Scott gently eased the phone out of her hand to bring it closer to his face. The quality of the photo was poor, but whatever Scott saw made his jaw drop open.

Charlie pulled back and laughed nervously. "I'm sure I'm just being dramatic. I probably have to get going anyway."

She reached to take back her phone, but Scott pulled it away from her. "Where," he started breathlessly. "Where did you find this?"

Charlie watched him, wary and concerned. She was unsure whether his behavior was caused from confusion, excitement, or fear. "Um, I found it in the middle of the road while driving?" No one needed to know how.

Scott looked to be tamping down whatever he was feeling, but he looked ready to jump out of his skin. "Are you doing anything right now?"

"Uh, I kinda had to drop off these papers at the office and then—"

Misfortune

Scott didn't let her finish. He pulled the papers she had brandished out of her hand and leaned into the office, tossed them in the direction of Helen's desk, and then reached back to yank her along behind him as he dashed through the front office and into Dean Manfree's personal office. She yelped in surprise, but he soon let go when they passed the door's threshold.

The office was minimal and thankfully empty. A desk sat across from the door, a black chair behind it, and a window behind that. And surrounding everything were floor to ceiling bookshelves.

Scott, still holding her phone that was still brandishing the photo, rifled through the spines on a shelf to the left. "Did you see anyone?"

Charlie snapped out of her survey and looked back to him. "What?"

Scott grumbled when he didn't find what he was looking for on that shelf and moved to the one across from it. "Was there someone around you when you found the skull?" He moved to another shelf. "Specifically, someone you didn't know with very pale skin and black clothes that watched you."

"That's a tall order," Charlie joked. It was like Scott hadn't even heard her. She was beginning to regret showing him the photo. She decided to tell a little bit of the truth, only if it would snap him out of whatever this stupor was. "Well, it was dark, so I could've been wrong, but I thought I saw someone. That was why I stopped in the first place."

Scott's unreadable face broke into a shocked look when she closed her mouth. It soon gave way to a baffled smile. "Are you serious?" he asked giddily. "Jesus, you really saw him! Do you know how lucky you are?"

She blinked at him. "Wait, what? No. No, no, no. That's not what happened. I didn't *really* see anyone. I was just imagining things," she tried, but Scott had found whatever he had been looking for. He slammed a book onto the dean's desk, cutting Charlie off.

He flipped through pages like a wizard looking for a spell, before stopping on one seemingly random. "Here, look," he said, finally managing to calm down. Charlie hesitated, but eventually came up next to him and glanced at the book. It was stuck on a page that had wording on it too small for her to read, but the pictures provided the context; on the bottom left corner was a goat skull, dirtied with browned blood and maggots. A picture not unlike her own.

She would've dismissed it for a different skull, if not for the same three jagged lines under the eye. It shouldn't have made her breath hitch when she saw it. "O—kay?" she said, voice much less sure than before. "This is nice and all, but you've got this whole situation all wrong, and I've got a bus to catch so…"

Scott pointed to the picture, his fingernail scraping on the page. "Barely anyone ever sees him. Like, I can only think of ten people that weren't lying when they said they did. It's like a one in a billion chance."

Charlie suppressed the urge to tell him the number of people in this town wasn't even close to four digits, much less eight.

His large smile dropped. "Or maybe not."

Charlie could only hold her politeness for so long. "Scott, I'm going to be honest with you. I have no clue why you're so excited over this. I get it's your hobby and all but…" She tried to hint that his giddiness was beginning to put her on edge with a flick of her hands.

He must have caught on, because his smile became more reserved, and he took a step back to give her space. "I'm sorry. It's just that you're the first person to talk about a sighting of Misfortune in a long while, at least that I've heard." He blinked and looked back at the book, much less happy than a second before. "I was going to tell you about the skull with the three lines under the eye. It's kinda like Misfortune's calling card. But the last time someone reportedly saw it… Let's say they we're as happy as I am."

"What does that mean?"

He took a breath and his eyes roamed behind Charlie's head, like he couldn't look at her. "Do you remember when we were talking about Misfortune at the store? And how I mentioned that kids were going missing again?"

"Yes?"

"Well, the last person that found that skull with the lines was a woman that had claimed to see Misfortune steal her daughter. She said the police didn't believe her, which was why she came to me. I still don't believe he

Misfortune

takes kids, but even if I did, I couldn't help her. But she said that she found the skull in her daughter's room after she was taken by Misfortune. That was months ago. Have you seen the news?"

The conversational jumps Scott had made had her head spin. "Not really."

"That was the first kidnapping here in a while, and now they're happening about once or twice a month. Ages five to eleven. It's on every station. That's why the ghost is called Misfortune: Usually when you see something that has to do with the story, something bad is probably going happen."

Charlie stared at him, jaw slack. All she wanted was a little background on the picture she took. Now she had a well's worth of information about local kids being taken.

"That's very...uh," she hesitated.

"Intriguing?" Scott supplied.

"I was gonna say terrible."

"Oh."

She finally remembered her phone and picked it back up, looking at her picture. "But what does this mean for the photo I took?"

"Well, from what I believe, you had an encounter with Misfortune, which is absolutely amazing in itself, but I'm gonna take a guess and say that you don't think the same. Either way, something strange is definitely happening. With the kids, and the skull you found."

Charlie definitely did not believe in the supernatural, but she still asked, "Should I be... worried about this?" She gestured to her phone. "Like, with the mask and all that?"

"You're not a kid, so I don't think you have to be too concerned about being taken from your bedroom window by Misfortune, but otherwise the most I think you have to do is be mindful of your surroundings."

"I thought you were supposed to be an expert."

"*Expert* is a little dramatic. I'd say that I'd more of like to *understand* Misfortune. Like where he came from and all that."

Charlie looked back down at her phone. "Good to know. Well, if I have any more strange encounters with the unexplained and then find a skull, I know who to go to."

Scott stuck a finger in the air. "Don't forget to add any strange encounters with tall and very pale people."

"Honestly, that described about half of this town." She kept her head down to check the time on her phone.

"More like two-thirds," Scott chuckled.

Charlie laid eyes on the time right as the hour changed. It meant nothing to Scott, but to Charlie, this was the time her shift started. She gasped and inched towards the door. "Thank you for the time, Scott, but I really have to go."

"Oh? Are you sure? I could—"

"I'll talk to you later if I see anything else!" she yelled back, already out the door. She prayed George would be as forgiving as he had been on her second day working at his store.

And while she ran, she promised herself that she would never talk to Scott about Misfortune again, because if she did, it would get a whole lot harder to deny its presence.

Chapter 15

"Are you okay?"

Charlie blinked herself out of her head and turned to look at Sam, who was perched against the clothing store's counter. "Er, yeah, why?"

Sam raised an eyebrow at her and glanced at the shelf opposite the checkout area that Charlie worked at. "Because you've been staring at the sunglasses rack for the past ten minutes. At some point you've got to get sick of looking at them." She grimaced. "Especially that orange one. Looks like the glasses equivalent of Guy Fieri."

Charlie smiled at her because it got her out of responding. Ever since they had run into each other at a place of work for the third time some weeks ago, Sam hadn't let Charlie go until she got her phone number, claiming that it was just fate that they were to be friends. Charlie hadn't been hard to convince, and they'd gotten along just fine.

Except that they both had full schedules, and so they had no time left over to spend with each other.

Their solution? Visit each other when they're at work and hope their bosses don't catch on.

It was nice to visit with friends, but it also meant that Charlie didn't have very many hours in the day just to herself. Either she was at school, studying for school, working to pay for school, or dreaming about school while she slept. (She knew that last one was a stretch, but it might as well be true at this point.)

But overworking herself for college or her lack of time wasn't her biggest problem. Not even Sam talking too loud or Martin being a minor asshole came close to being the largest.

No, her biggest, most obtrusive problem was that she was going *crazy*.

Ever since she had crashed her car (which was *still* in the shop) and found that skull, it was like she was living in the middle of a reality show and everyone but her knew she was the punchline. She saw the dark clothed person *everywhere she went*. It was always just in flashes, but Charlie had had enough of just glancing in a direction, seeing a goat skull, looking away, looking back in shock, and seeing that nothing was there.

At first, it happened so seldomly that Charlie forgot it was even going on, but after that day of talking to Scott, it was a never-ending nightmare of seeing that thing. And, of course, every time she'd ask Sam or Martin if they had seen a person standing right there just a second before, they'd always say no.

And the best part? If she didn't know any better, she would've thought the little glimpse she caught looked like Scott's description of Misfortune.

"Oh, and we lost her again."

Charlie guiltily snapped out of her head for the second time. She knew they were wasting the little time they had together, but she couldn't stop herself from thinking about those glimpses, and their strange correlation to a story that everyone but her believed. "Sorry, I was just...thinking," she said limply. For her own sake, she wouldn't, *couldn't* believe what was happening to her was anything but a prank or inside her head.

"Well, for the sake of your face, I hope you're not thinking about buying those glasses." Sam reluctantly looked over her shoulder at the sunglasses rack like it was some sort of vile monster.

Thankful for the free out about her spacing out, Charlie played along. "They're not even that bad. I bet the Guy Fieri one would look good with your hair."

Sam whipped back to her, shock written all over her face. "How you wound me, Charlette."

Charlie lifted her hands in the air, palms up. "What?"

"Ever heard of the word 'clashing?' I might as well put on a vest and become a construction worker."

"Who knows, maybe you'd look good as a construction work?"

If looks could speak, Sam would definitely be telling Charlie about how very, very wrong she is. That look alone made Charlie forget about the skull.

"Excuse me, is this the line?"

Whenever a real customer came to Charlie's till, Sam knew it was her cue to skip. She wandered away to the nearest shelf to pretend to browse, which ended up being the blasted sunglasses rack. Charlie smiled quietly at the sight and swapped her gaze to the woman that had come to buy clothing.

Charlie first saw that it was the old woman from some weeks ago that she had assisted. And then the second thing she saw was that the clothes that she had stacked on the counter were a large stack of showy underthings. She had never seen so much lace piled into one place before.

The woman smiled sweetly at Charlie as she began to scan the items. "I believe you were the nice lady that helped me with the bikinis. I really must pass on a thank you from my husband. And probably another for these." Charlie was not going to decipher that twinkle in the woman's eye.

Sam peeked at the older lady's stuff from behind her, saw the stack, then Charlie's face, and snorted.

"Martin! I'm home," Charlie called into the house as she pushed the front door shut with her foot. "I've got Bill's stereotypical cookies!" Bill had greeted her with a fresh plate when she got home just minutes before. Another apology for almost hitting her with his loud cars.

"Martin," she yelled again. Sound bounced around weirdly in the walls, but usually when she announced when she got home, he would greet her in some way, whether it was him commenting that he, too, was home, rudely telling her to shut up (those happened rarely, they were never received well) or stomping from his room upstairs to tell her where he was. But not today. There was nothing.

Odd, but not out of the ordinary. She would survive without addressment from her brother. He was probably upstairs, anyway.

She was relieving herself of the cookies on the coffee table to put down her bag when the rustling came from the kitchen.

Charlie rolled her eyes, even though Martin couldn't see it. "Marty, buddy, I'll make something in a minute. Quit acting like you're gonna starve." It also wasn't out of the ordinary to find him ravaging the kitchen. He must've been really hungry to not acknowledge her. No matter how weird that sounded, it wasn't the first time.

"Come on out. Bill gave us more cookies. Try not to eat them all in a day this time." She crouched down to scrounge through her bag for her phone. The rustling came again, along with footsteps on tile. "And you can't pretend not to like them again. We both know that is a *massive* lie."

She finally found her phone and held the power button to turn it on. She figured that if she used her work hours to talk to friends, the least she could do was turn off her phone to minimize distractions. (That, and the last time she got distracted by her phone, she crashed her car.) (Which then reminded her to call the mechanics and find when the *hell* she was going to get her car back.)

She heard the footsteps again. Martin was walking towards the kitchen doorway. Taking his sweet time, too. "Oh, yeah, don't worry about me. I'll just wait here until you're ready for a cookie like the servant I am." As she waited for her phone screen to go through its powering up sequence, she turned her head towards the kitchen and stuck her tongue out. No, it did not make her feel like an adult, and no, that was not going to stop her from doing it again in the future.

That was how she noticed the lights were off in the kitchen. The most illumination it had were the bulbs from the living room that gave the floor a square of shine when they reached through the doorway. "Hey, buddy, why exactly are you looking walking around in the dark?" Her voice was a little less certain than before, but she was still going to make fun of him when he finally shuffled out.

She shook her head and gave back her attention to her phone. She had a couple of missed notifications from people. One was Aunt Mary, telling her to call again soon to check up. Another was Sam, sending her some funny video that she found online. The third one was Martin, saying that he had a school trip, and wouldn't home until later.

Wait.

Charlie's eyes, which had been skimming over the notifications, shot back to the one from *Martin*. She read it, reread it, re-reread it, and all the while, sweat gathered at the base of her neck where the skin bunched from looking forward while being in a crouch. Her skin felt cold and her mouth dry.

If Martin wasn't home, then who the hell was in the kitchen?

The only thing Charlie could think of were those dramatic police shows that showed the aftermath of a home break-in: Bullets used and people dead on the floor. The mental image was very unhelpful and did nothing to stop her lungs from inflating and retracting rapidly after the realization that someone was in her house.

And that someone was in her house and only the kitchen wall separated them. Now that Charlie thought about it, those footsteps had been heavy. Not as if who they belonged to had been stomping, but as if they were wearing large, military grade boots.

And those same footsteps had been getting closer to the unbarred doorway since she'd started talking. Foolishly, she had told whoever was over there that she was home. Even more so, she must have raised some flags when she suddenly stopped talking.

Charlie had to call the police. She *knew* she had to call the police, but it was as if her muscles didn't work anymore. Turned to stone like a puppet of Medusa. Her heart beat behind her eyes—Lord, if it pulsed any harder, her eyes might be forced out of her skull, brain oozing after it. Her heart *would* make room. Darkness crawled at the edges of her vision with shattered legs and greedy broken-nailed talons because the binder of fear had wrapped thrice around her chest. It refused to let her breath. It refused to let do anything but gaped with lips peeled in terror. It was like if she were to move, whoever was in the kitchen would catch on that she knew and come out and bite. Never in her life had she been so scared. Never in her life had she thought she'd die from a home invasion.

Clenching her muscles to get them to work, Charlie slowly did her best to quietly rise from her crouch and dial to cops. She had yet to raise her eyes to the kitchen doorway, but knew she had to check to see if the person was watching her.

Her phone was to her ear, and her other hand halfway to the doorknob to escape when her eyes flicked to the kitchen without her consent. The operator was asking for her problem when Charlie tripped over her own feet and began to scream her voice raw.

Standing there in the doorway, taking up almost all the room the frame had to offer, was a man drenched in black clothing. Long black coat, black pants that peeked out under, black gloves, black boots.

And sitting on top of all of that was a goat skull. Dirtied with chipped away blood and maggots that crawled through the nose cavity and up into the eye sockets, which were empty, but with the right lighting, a green pupiled eyeball maybe could've been seen.

Charlie focused on none of this, and all of it at once. But what truly made her shriek, what truly made adrenaline kick into her veins, what truly made her heart feel like it would kick itself out of her chest and run away on its own, was that Misfortune was standing only ten feet away from her. And unlike all the other times, he was not disappearing.

Her pants and legs began to warm as he took a step forward.

Chapter 16

"Are you sure you don't want us to call an ambulance, ma'am? Will you be alright?"

Charlie hugged her arms tighter around her body like they would shield her from the people milling around her while they stood outside and nodded with a brittle smile. "I'll be fine." They were the only words her raggedy voice could manage. She had changed out of her piss-soaked clothes, and yet, it still felt like the fabrics were clinging to her sweaty skin.

Somehow, in panic that her mind had blocked out, Charlie had managed to get out of the house and call the police, alerting her neighbors in the process. Bill, to be exact. She must have been a wreck because she had no memory of telling him what had happened. Apparently, she did, because he burst through the house, yelling for whoever was in there to leave.

A surprise to everyone but Charlie, no one was there. No evidence was found of a break-in. Not even a speck of dust in the kitchen was out of place. Although there *were* a few footprints from dirty boots in the kitchen, they started and stopped abruptly, and in no way pointed towards the reality of a robber.

And so, when the police arrived to find a house untouched and a hysterical woman, who had already called about hitting someone with her when she did not, in fact, hit someone, was outside claiming there was, in fact, someone there, they became a little concerned over her mental health.

Charlie would've rather claimed the "break-in" as a laughable ruse than tell police officers about the man with a goat skull that she had been seeing for weeks. She wasn't stupid enough to think they'd let her walk away without a visit to a psychologist. And so, she just stood out on her lawn under the quickly setting fall sun with a few straggler cops, Bill, and the turmoil in her stomach in silence. But what the worst thing about this was the accompanied beat, beat, beat in her chest telling her that Misfortune was *real*.

It was silly, really, to think a town ghost story had a slip of truth behind it, but for the *life* of her, Charlie couldn't come up with anything else to explain what had just happened to her. Not to mention the odd sightings over the weeks of, and if Scott was to be believed, Misfortune and his skull.

That, or she really was going crazy.

But those boot prints spoke a thousand words, even if Charlie was the only one that could hear the speech. If she was hallucinating the whole thing, where did the prints come from? Her feet certainly weren't that big, and Martin never wore shoes that covered his toes, no matter how many times Charlie or the weather told him to.

And so, until she could prove otherwise, Misfortune was haunting her.

Charlie shivered just from the blasphemousness of it all.

"They'll find them, Charlie. You just might need to talk about it to different officers though. Those cops wouldn't be able to catch the criminal even if they ran out of the house right now," Bill said stoically as he watched the police wrap up their stuff and congregate with each other at the curb. He was the only person that still believed the robber still existed. Charlie didn't have the heart nor courage to tell him otherwise. The man had been nice enough to check the whole house after the police did to make sure no one was really there.

She nodded in his direction, eyes a hair-width away from making contact with his. "It's okay, Bill. They're just doing their job," she continued quietly. "I'd say the same thing if I were them."

"Aw, hey, come on now, don't put yourself down." He gently laid a hand on her shoulder. Charlie did her best not to flinch. "You did the right thing. This maniac could've been dangerous. At least no one was hurt. And hey." He paused and pulled his hand away from her and jutted his thumb towards his chest. "If anything like that ever happens again, you know who to come to."

Charlie lips tipped up to a smile from their ground-bound frown. "Thank you, Bill. You have no idea what it means to me to have a neighbor like you."

He shrugged out of her peripheral. "It's what we're for."

A loud, piercing whistle made Charlie's head snap up, along with the officers' and Bill's, too. It was extremely out of place because it was high and blowy, something to show amusement.

"I'm pretty sure all the old white people that live here don't do drugs, so that's not why you're here," Martin said, sidling up to the officers.

The silly smile Martin wore made Charlie's heart break. Martin had no clue about the terrible events that happened at his house. He had no clue how mentally traumatized Charlie was. He had no clue his sister was being haunted.

And on top of that, he hadn't taken her crashing her car too well. She could only imagine that this wasn't going to go over easy with him either.

The cops largely ignored Martin, which Charlie was thankful for. She knew his big mouth was going to get him in trouble at some point, but she didn't want it to be with the police, or *right now*. When he received no answer, he continued. "So, tell me, who died? I mean, this town *is* full of a lot of people that look pretty close to meeting Jesus."

Charlie watched one officer roll their eyes, and another chuckled, but Martin didn't notice this. His mind must have been playing tricks on him, and telling him of false futures, because his back snapped straight and his face dropped. "Where's my sister?"

And when Charlie stepped forward and down the driveway, her guilt of worrying her brother grew so immensely, she felt like her body would burst. When their father had died, an officer had shown up on their doorstep to tell them the news. And now Martin was thinking it was happening again.

"Marty! I'm right here," she called, doing her best to be strong for him and not let her voice break.

From behind her, Bill said he'd head home to give them privacy, but Charlie barely heard him. She was too busy watching Martin's face fill with relief when he laid eyes on his still breathing sister.

Martin left the officers behind and jogged up to her. "Charlie? What's going on? Did Bill finally kick the can?"

She engulfed him in a hug before he could come up with another joke. She needed all the strength (and stalling) she could muster to tell him about what happened.

"What's wrong?" He froze under her. "Did something happen to Mom?"

And she'd gone and made things worse.

She pulled back like he was on fire. "No! No, no, no, that's not what happened! She's fine, I promise," she rushed out. "I—" She sighed. "I thought there was someone in the house.

Martin balked. "Wait, what? Who was it? What happened? Are you okay?"

She calmed him like he was an untamed horse. "Marty, everything's fine. I'm fine, the house is fine, our stuff is fine. I must have just been tired because I came home thought someone was in the kitchen." The lie came out of nowhere, and she didn't even realize she said it until it was sitting out in the open. "I called the police, they came over and checked, and nothing's wrong. I'm sorry I made you upset."

Martin stared at her, wide-eyed. And, worse, like he didn't believe her. "Are you sure? It's a little hard to *mistake someone being in the house*. Did you see anything?"

"I told you, I was tired. All that happened was that I came through the doorway and thought I heard something. I thought it was you, so I started talking, but I saw your text that you'd be home late and believed someone else to be home. My mind must have wandered. Bill came over and checked too, just in case. No one was there." She added Bill to the equation to stop

Martin from digging further. It was best that she told him the truth, even if it was a partial. He didn't need to know about the footprints in the kitchen.

He watched her, gaze swapping between her eyes, then up at the house, to the police behind them who were getting ready to leave, and then back to her. "Okay." He nodded and then tried for a halfhearted smile. "Not the best thing to come home to, but better safe than sorry, yeah?"

Her knees practically buckled from relief that he believed her and guilt that he believed her. "I'm sorry, Marty, really. It was all just crazy, and completely forgot to tell you."

Martin snapped back into his usual persona. "Oh, well, at least it gave us a funny story," he said casually and walked around Charlie. "You should see if Bill will give us anymore of those dry ass cookies of his. They suck, but I think they're growing on me."

"Yeah, he gave us some more when I got home," she answered faintly.

"Sweet," Martin hissed in delight. And when the front door closed behind her, she took the few seconds she had alone to breathe in and out, deep enough to feel her chest contract and expand. She called goodnight to the officers when they left to try and stay on their good side. She didn't know how many supposedly fake calls they could tolerate before they started thinking her a delinquent in it for the kicks.

Before they started thinking her crazy.

Charlie knew nothing about Misfortune, nor did she have a clue of why he—it—he was targeting her. It wasn't like she had anything to do with him, or that she even lived here for a long time.

But something, *something*, must be going on for this to happen, right? She had already checked *not being crazy* of the list of why this was happening, as well as *prank*.

It was a problem that she desperately wanted to fix. She was tired of the flashes of a skull and calling the police on false alarms, and maybe, she wanted to prove to herself that it really wasn't all in her head. (No matter how many times she told herself she wasn't making it all up, she couldn't truly believe it.) But, really, she had no clue what to do. No matter how weird it sounded in her head, how on Earth does someone ask a ghost not to haunt them? Pull out a spirit board and tell it to leave her along?

No, that's not what she was going to do. Better yet, that wasn't the question Charlie wanted to ask him. What she wanted to know was *why*. *Why* was he haunting here? *Why* was he haunting *her*, and not someone else? Moreover, *what* could she do to make him stop?

Charlie had limited knowledge about this ghost, but from what she'd learned, she wasn't the first person to see him, and she also knew someone that researched him in his pastime.

Chapter 17

Charlie's phone rang right as she got on the bus. She sighed when it did, because first, she had just gotten off the phone with the mechanics working on her car, who would need another week, and second, the number was her mother's.

"Hi, Mom," she said quietly as she found her seat, as to not bother the other commuters.

"Are you okay? Martin just called and said someone broke into your house last night!"

Charlie gave another sigh. It was too early for all of this. But at least her mother's words weren't slurred. "False alarm, Mom. I was a walking zombie when I got home and thought someone was in the kitchen. Turns out it was nothing, and just gave myself a scare." She knew Martin didn't do it to be mean, but he really needed to stop ratting out everything that she did to their mother.

A sigh came over the line, this one built with bricks of relief. "God, Char, you gave me a heart attack. You've got to stop putting this old lady in a panic."

Charlie couldn't stop herself from giving a light smile. Her mother had always called herself an 'old lady' ever since they were kids. It was times like these that made her forget the past and think of her mother as someone who would crack any sort of joke just to hear her laugh.

"Sorry, Mom. But believe me, it was very embarrassing to apologize to the police after they found no one and nothing was wrong. I think they either thought I was crazy or messing with them. My neighbor, Bill, even checked for me."

Her mother hummed. "Better safe than sorry, as you know." Her favorite line, and where Martin learned it from. "You know, when I was in school, a friend of mine really did come home to someone robbing her house." She chuckled, a sound Charlie hadn't heard in a while. "Yup. Walked right through the door and ran into the guy while he was walking out with her stuff."

"Goodness." She laughed. "Nothing like that here, Mom. Just a lack of sleep." She hoped that the more she told the lie, the less it would hurt.

"Alright, Charlie. I just wanted to make sure you're safe. Are you doing okay? Is Martin?"

"We're both fine, Mom. Some just need more rest than others."

"Bah, that Martin never could fall asleep on time."

Her heart warmed at the play along. "How are you and Aunt Mary doing, Mom? Got any plans for today?"

"Oh, you know your aunt. Always running at one hundred percent. She'll be out for the day, and I don't have much. I think I'll probably go into town with a friend in a little bit."

And just like that, Charlie's little bubble popped, and she was dropped back into reality. 'Going into town' for her mother meant day drinking. And a lot of it, that is. It wasn't something out of the ordinary, but it never failed to make Charlie's stomach twist. Especially when it was accompanied by the memories of her mother acting this way when her kids lived with her.

"Are you sure, Mom? You know, you could always just *try* and go to the class I talked to you about. You could just go once and never again if you don't like it."

"Charlie, you sent me a link for Alcoholics Anonymous," responded her mother, her voice patronizing. "I do a little drinking, yes, but I'm not an *alcoholic*. You know this."

Charlie blinked away the sting in her heart that begged her to say, *Yes, Mom, you are an alcoholic. You haven't gone a day without being drunk since Dad died.*

Instead, she said, "'Course, Mom. I know. But it doesn't hurt to look." When her mother sighed and geared up for defense, she continued. "Oh, sorry, I'm on the bus and just reached my stop. Gotta go, love you."

She clicked off the call before her mother could say anything else. She put down the phone and went back to looking out the window and watched the world whizzed by in a muddle of green. The bus didn't stop.

Charlie fidgeted in every class she attended. What if Scott didn't believe her? What if he didn't want to help her? What if he wasn't here when she went to check for him at the office?

When Charlie decided that it could go on no longer of being tormented by Misfortune without clear rhyme or reason, the first person she thought of to help her was Scott. He was the clear pursuit: Previous knowledge and easy access to information about the ghost.

But now that reality caught up with her, it was quite self-centered of her to believe Scott would just toss down everything and help her just because she asked. He might be busy, or maybe he wasn't interested in helping her at all. Maybe he never wanted to see her again after she left so soon last time they saw each other. (That thought was a little dramatic, she knew, but she couldn't completely pull it out of the pool of reasons why Scott wouldn't want to help her.)

Dwelling in her thoughts about all the possible outcomes was not helping her situation.

That didn't mean she was going to stop.

At least that since today was Friday, when Scott inevitably rejected her proposal, she could hide at home and pretend it never happened over the weekend, as she had no classes then.

And then she would have the wonderful privilege of feeling mortified when she most likely ran into him on Monday.

Charlie rubbed at her eyes. Spiraling in her Communications class was not the best thing right now.

But she knew that no matter how much she wished she could change how she was going about bringing this up with Scott, she would rather have him reject her a thousand times than continue living her life ignorant to why Misfortune wouldn't leave her alone.

(That was a little dramatic too, but it did make her feel better.)

After weathering through more unwanted scenarios of what Scott could say to her, she finally finished her last class and began to the torturous walk across campus to the front office. She half hoped he was there, and half hoped he wasn't. But it was like the muscles and tendons in her feet had disconnected from the bones, making the trek almost impossible. So, when she eventually reached the office, she was already mentally drained from navigating the journey from her foot related prospects. Sitting at the front desk with a frown plastered on her face was Helen, the not-so-lovely secretary that had fallen on Charlie.

She didn't look up from her computer where she was clacking away from as Charlie walked through the door. "If you're here for the dean, he's not here. Office hours for him are eight to twelve." Her voice was so monotone it sounded like Helen was talking without her own knowledge.

"Um, thank you, but that's not why I'm here."

Helen took half a second away from her typing to stare at Charlie with something that wasn't quite disdain, but *very* near it. "I remember you. You're the clumsy girl, the one that tripped me and Scott."

Charlie put away the barbs that wanted to rise at the jab, but being rude would get her nowhere. "That's me, and, speaking of Sco—"

Helen's tapping of the keyboard drowned her out. "If you have an appointment with one of your professors, just go to their room to speak with them."

"Uh, I'm not here to speak with—"

"If you want to change classes, you'll need to go over to registration."

Charlie took a deep breath. Helen obviously thought she was here for something related to school (and to be fair, that made sense), but it irked Charlie that she wouldn't say anything else. With a shake of her head, Charlie let her eyes wander. They ended up at the desk across the room from Helen. One that read *Registration*.

Charlie squinted at it, turned back to Helen, and decided to play along. "Registration is right there. Why can't you just do it from your desk."

Helen tossed her eyes out of her head with daggers like she had forgotten Charlie was still standing there. "Because I'm at the *General desk*." She pulled a long, sharp nail away from the keys to tap loudly on the sign that read *General*.

Charlie watched her as she went back to typing. "Okay. Then who runs the Registration desk?"

Helen sighed loudly and dropped her hands from the desk. "Do you need something from the Registration desk?"

For all intents and purposes of Charlie's next answer, it was because it was helpful to have more knowledge about Registration just in case she ever changed her courses. (That, and she still didn't appreciate Helen's greeting.) "Yes."

Helen watched her with a look that soured further by the second. She let one long breath out through her nose and rose from the General desk, turning around the sign to say that desk was no longer open. She stomped by Charlie without a glance and her back hunched. Slumping down at the Registration desk, she began to tap at the computer with all her might.

When Charlie opened her mouth, Helen shot out a hand and turned a sign around on the new desk. A previously empty spot now held a *Desk Closed* sign. Charlie blinked at it, looked up at Helen, back at the sign, and then let her gaze roam because it felt weird to stare at her.

"Do you need a class change?" Helen practically spit at her. Her eyes found the desk again, and Helen had removed the closed sign.

Charlie, on her part, was beginning to feel bad for making this lady do work for no reason. "Well, not ac—"

"The dean's hours are eight to twelve. If you need anything else, you'll need to go to the General desk," Helen said, dismissing her with her eyes and went back to clacking.

Charlie slowly turned around to peer at the closed sign that now sat at the General desk. Suddenly, she didn't feel as bad. She gave a resigned sigh. She opened her mouth to ask for Scott again, when she was unsurprisingly cut off.

"Helen! I got the papers! I hope you didn't mind the wait, I picked up coffee, too!" Scott came around the corner to the doorway with folders under his arm and coffee cups filling his hand. He stopped momentarily when he saw Charlie but continued into the room with a smile. "Hey, Charlie."

"Hi, Scott." She responded with only minimal stiffness as he passed her and handed a cup to Helen.

"It's the usual. They didn't have any whole milk, so there's oat milk in there instead."

Helen took one hand off her board to pick up the coffee and loudly sip from it. She pulled back the cup and wrinkled her nose at it, harumphing at it like the cup had personally offended her. "This is terrible. I can't believe they would ever think oat milk is a sufficient substitute."

This did not stop her from then downing the rest.

Scott was unfazed by the secretary and looked back up at Charlie with the same smile. "Are you changing classes? That's always fun."

Helen beat her to an answer. "She's here just to waste breath."

Charlie cut her eyes to the old woman. Helen—more like Hellion—was too enveloped in her computer screen. "I'm *here* because I was actually looking for you, Scott."

He raised his eyebrows but wasn't too concerned. "Oh? Well, speak of the Devil, here I am. What do you need?"

"It's, uh," she stuttered. "It's about Misfortune." Helen's presence in the room made Charlie finish her sentence quietly. It would be a lie to say she didn't feel embarrassed about the problem she had.

Scott's eyes first lit up and when he heard her, but dimmed when he realized that she wasn't as excited as he was. "Alright. We can talk in my uncle's office if you want. And—if you have time."

Charlie was surprised and mortified Scott still remembered her quick departure last time. "Of course, sounds perfect." She had already called George the night before to tell him she'd be in late. Another pompous indication that she had expected Scott to go along with her. But she was already breathing easier that he wasn't pushing her away.

Scott turned around and gestured for Charlie to follow. "Make sure to keep the fort down, Helen."

"My shift ends in five minutes."

Scott saluted to Helen with two fingers, who was now behind Charlie's back as she neared the office. "Appreciate you anyway."

"I'm calling your uncle if you two are too loud."

Charlie ducked into the room to hide the excessive balk she gave. And her embarrassment. She did not like Helen's implication.

"Have a good day, H!" Scott said without a hint of problem over what she said. He closed the door behind him before Helen could say anything other humiliating thing, but Charlie still heard mumbling on the other side of the door.

"Sorry about Helen. I'd give an excuse for how she acts, but that's just her personality." Scott finally showed some humanity and ducked away from the door. "Never mind that. What did you want to talk about Misfortune for?" Scott then gasped before Charlie could open her mouth. "Do you finally believe Misfortune's real?" Charlie had never seen him so happy.

She opened her mouth, closed it, opened it again, and nothing came out. This was going to be a doozy. "Well… sorta?" she squeaked. Technically, she did, in a sense.

Scott literally laughed and slapped his hands together. "I knew it! Once the facts start adding up, belief is pretty much impossible!" His crinkled eyes watched Charlie, waiting for her to follow his feelings. "Er—you aren't as happy about this as I thought you would be."

To that, Charlie did chuckle, one breath of hysteria. She pulled a hand up to her head and mindlessly scooped her hair into it. "Well, the facts sorta added up a little *too* well."

Scott blinked at her. He still had remnants of the outburst but was losing the look each second that Charlie spiraled in front of him. "Isn't that... a good thing? Do you not want yourself to believe in Misfortune?"

"I... yes?" She sighed and braced herself for what came next. "Look, Scott, this is going to sound crazy, but do you remember when you said to come back to you if I ever saw a man wearing a goat skull?"

"...Yes?"

"Well," she began to pick the skin next to her nails. "I did. See him, that it."

Scott's eyebrows raised. Charlie could tell that he wanted to start clapping again, but her demeanor offput his almost credulous excitement. "Oh? Wow, more than once, that barely happens! How many times? Two? Three? I've talked to a few people, and they've never said more than four."

Charlie surveyed the books about the town ghost story over Scott's shoulder. "...Thirty-two times."

When Charlie dared a look at Scott and his only answer was an agape mouth, she suddenly found the floor to be remarkably interesting. "I'm sorry. I know it sounds crazy, and you probably don't believe me, but I see him *all the time*, multiple times a day even. I'm just... so *sick* of it. It's not a prank, and I know I'm not imagining it. Yesterday, uh," that was where her little monologue had a kink. It felt embarrassing to tell someone about what she did. "I saw him. Like, before, it was only glimpses, but yesterday, I *saw* him. Like, I heard someone walking through my house, and he came out of my kitchen. There were dirty footprints and all. I," she laughed self-consciously, "I actually called the police of him. He looked so real, I thought someone broke into my house."

She had hoped telling him about yesterday might spur him to say something, *anything*, that assured her he didn't think she was crazy. But when she glanced up from the ground's carpet, his jaw was still slack like she told

Misfortune

him her plan of mass genocide. Her anxiety and irritation boiled over. "Jesus, Scott, *say* something!"

He shut his mouth with an audible snap. "Holy shit," he whispered. Charlie couldn't tell if he was taking the news better or worse than she imagined.

She shook her head at him and crossed her arms. "I came here because I'm being haunted by a ghost that you research about for fun, and—"

"Oh my God, please let me help you hunt him," Scott butt in. It took him only a blink to step closer to Charlie and stare down at her.

She looked up at him in bewilderment and stepped back to regain space. "I'm sorry, what do you mean by *hunting him*?"

Scott's eyes sparkled. His hands danced in front of him as he spoke. "That's why you're here, right? Misfortune, a ghost you don't believe in, is haunting you, which is driving you insane! So, you came to me, someone who believes in the ghost, to try and get rid of it!"

Now it was Charlie's turn to gape. "That's ... actually spot on."

Scott, giddy in his skin, threw his hands on top of his head and paced the small room. "Holy crap, holy crap, holy crap. You're serious, aren't you? My God, this is the best thing someone's ever told me."

"What? All I want to do is find out why he's haunting me."

Scott balked and turned back to her. "Even better."

His excitement was beginning to make her lightheaded. "Scott, can you just *please* calm down. And *stay* calm. I am *not happy* this is happening."

Charlie hoped this was the last time Scott cooled from an outburst. "Of course, sorry. But Charlie, you have to understand. I've only ever listened to *three* people talk about seeing Misfortune, mind you, it was only a few times, and have had to go off that. Now, here you are, having seen him *thirty-two* times, likely more in the future, and want *my help*."

Charlie wished there were a chair next to her she could collapse into. Not only was Scott willing to help her, but he also believed her, and was finishing her thoughts before she could even voice them. It was literally the best possible scenario, and yet, it didn't make her feel very good. "I'm just so tired of seeing that skull, Scott. I just want to know why he won't *leave me alone*."

Scott finally truly cooled at her admission. "Okay. Okay, alright, I understand. Seeing a person wearing bloody goat skull everywhere you go might not be so fun." He gestured for her to sit in the dean's chair. "Here, let's start at the beginning, yeah? You tell me what you've seen."

"Wait, really? You want to help?"

Scott had already turned around to survey the books on his uncle's shelf. He pivoted his head to look just at her and smiled. "Of course. Misfortune and his story mean a lot to me. I'd love to find out why he is haunting you if it will shed more light on the story." He shrugged and looked away. "That, and you're a friend." He finished, like it was common curtsy for people that have met three times before to just solve ghost story with each other. "Now go on, sit down. Uncle won't mind. What he doesn't know won't hurt him."

For the first time since walking into her house and seeing Misfortune, Charlie held a true smile. It was faint, but still there. Something so warm that when she directed it at the back of Scott's head, she almost expected him to feel it. Silently, she unstuck her feet from the floor and moved behind the desk, sitting in the large leather chair that exhaled loudly when she sat down.

Scott joined her at the desk, setting down a different book than before about Misfortune. He matched her height by kneeling. "Okay, start at the first time you saw him."

Chapter 18

"What do you think?"

"I think you look like a grape."

With the help of the mirror that she faced, Sam frowned at Charlie and pulled the dress away from her body, where she had put it to simulate what she would look like with it on. "Come on, it's pretty, isn't it?"

Charlie stood behind her in, arms brimming with other dresses Sam had tried on and then discarded. "It's pretty, alright, it's just thar purple is not your color, no offense."

Sam glared at her. "You called me a grape. How is that not offensive?"

Charlie put a hand to her chin to reexamine her previous assessment. "Hm, no, you look more like those juice pouches when you blow them full of air."

"That's worse."

Charlie shrugged. "You look like one. Like I said, purple's just not your color."

Sam scoffed. Her frizzy hair bunched up from the movement. "What *isn't* my color is orange." She shivered. "Construction worker," she murmured to her reflection, traumatized, and Charlie fought an eye roll.

It was a few days after coming to get Scott's aid for Charlie's weird predicament, and even though the weekend went by, and they met up after class every day (to Helen's chagrin) Charlie still had yet to thoroughly cover every aspect of Misfortune's hauntings. It didn't help that as the days went by, she was also accumulating another sighting or two, which she then had to relay too, and the cycle kept on going. She was already tired of it and they hadn't even gotten into the physical work of figuring out why this was happening yet.

While George had been accommodating when Charlie told him she would start coming in later in the day, he had sort of started to catch on that Sam wasn't just any ordinary customer, and Charlie never seemed to *truly* help her. So that's why today Sam decided that she had a fake ball to go to and just *had* to try on every dress in the store, while Charlie dutifully waited in the background, accessories in hand.

"You'd look fine in any dress, Sam. Well, any dress that isn't purple. Or orange."

Now Sam did turn around from the mirror. "Oh, Charlie, how you have a way with words. Women must swoon because of your charisma."

"Actually, I like to think they enjoy my virtuousness," Charlie replied, face stoic.

Sam hummed. "No, maybe it's your heroic tendencies."

Charlie cracked first. "'Heroic tendencies?' What exactly did I do to earn such a title?"

Sam gestured to the pile of dresses that lay over Charlie's forearm. "You carry heavy weights so ladies don't have to."

"Oh, so you're a 'lady' now?"

Sam looked behind Charlie's head before flicking a wrist and turning back to the mirror. "Yes. Now be a good gentleman and give me another dress because your boss is watching."

Charlie smiled at the back of Sam's head. With a few steps forward, the mirror helped her see that George was indeed drifting around with papers in his hand and eyes momentarily on them. Their little trick worked, because as Sam pulled another dress in front of her frame, George silently nodded to himself and moved on to another part of the store.

And Charlie's mood was dampened when George moved, because his shadow stayed where it was. She stepped away from the mirror's reach when the disembodied shade grew horns.

"Marty, I'm home!" Charlie called as she entered the house. Reflexes made her eyes kick to the kitchen doorway as soon as she heard noises, but when Martin came out with a half-eaten sandwich in hand, she reassured herself it was just her brother and not Misfortune. "How was school?" she asked as she shrugged off her coat.

Martin finished chewing. "Pretty average. A couple kids got into a fight, and they had to shut down classes so the paramedics could get to them."

Charlie raised an eyebrow at him. "Uh-huh. And what about the bus ride?"

"Driver hit a guy. Spent half the ride running from the cops with us in tow." Martin shrugged as if to say *oh well*.

Charlie crossed the living room to join him in the kitchen and fix herself something. "Wow, eventful day. How did you get home if the cops were chasing after the bus?"

"I jumped out the window."

Charlie nodded as she opened the fridge. "Of course. Shoulda thought of that." She turned back and peered at him for a moment. "Although, you don't look too scratched up for jumping out of a bus during a high-speed chase."

"Meh, you know me. I'm just really good at landing on my feet."

She chuckled. "Okay. As long as you're safe." She pulled out left over mashed potatoes from yesterday and popped them into the microwave.

"Oh, never," Martin shot back.

Charlie had to turn around to show Martin that she was, in fact, rolling her eyes hard enough to make them fall out. Martin was very polite to reply in kind with his own when Charlie went back to watching the microwave.

"Can I ask you a question?" Martin continued from behind her.

"You just did," she answered mindlessly, now digging through the silverware drawer.

Martin bypassed her. "Do you remember that Misfortune guy?"

113

Charlie froze, hand midair as she raised it with a fork and the microwave beeped. "Why do you ask?"

She heard ruffling behind her—Martin shrugging again. "A bunch of people at school talk about the town ghost, and I've just heard about a whole buncha different stories. I was just wondering if people have told you the same thing."

Charlie unglued her hand from the particles of air that wanted to hold it there and opened the microwave, busying herself with her food. "Yeah," she answered, strained. She didn't want to worry Martin with her predicament with Misfortune. He was under enough stress.

Then a terrible thought came to mind. "Why?" she asked. Was Martin being haunted, too?

His nonchalant voice soothed her worries. "Nothing more than curiosity. I just thought it was kinda weird that people are obsessed with a fake story."

Charlie took one deep breath to calm her mind, armed herself with a paper plate full of semi-warm potatoes, and turned around. "I know what you mean. I've met people that are like that, too."

It's better he doesn't know it's better he doesn't know it's better he doesn't know, she told herself. Like the lies didn't hurt.

Martin grinned at her. "Psychos, am I right? Who the heck would think some guy wearing a goat skull is real? Hmm, someone really crazy, that's who," he answered himself.

Charlie swallowed and looked away. "Have you done your homework?"

Martin lost a hint of his beaming look and eyed her, not oblivious to the conversational change. "Don't worry, *Grandma*, I'm not slacking in school."

"Good, then. Otherwise, you'd have to go and sleep with the cows outside."

Martin scoffed and left the kitchen. "That is such a lame joke, and you know it is."

Charlie didn't bother to follow him. "Quit being dramatic and go feed the cows!"

"You have to take you dementia meds, Grandma! You don't live on a farm anymore!" he called from the living room.

"What?! You have to speak up, my hearing isn't like it used to be!"

"Oh, really? Well, I said that I'm too tired to feed the cows! Looks like you're going to have to do it!"

"Darn kids these days. Don't know how to respect their elders," she muttered to herself.

"Whatever," Martin answered. She hadn't spoken quietly enough. "Will you grab my water from the counter? I forgot it."

Now Charlie really was a little annoyed. "You should be careful what you wish for. You never know if I'll fall and break a hip one of these days."

"If only I could be so lucky," Martin snickered in the other room.

Charlie's mouth made an audible click as she opened it to scoff. "Jesus." But she did turn around to grab Martin's water. He was definitely going to get an earful about her *hard labor* when she gave it to him though.

Charlie picked up the sweating glass by the sink, and then dropped it, glasses shattering on the floor. She made no noise as she found Misfortune's empty eyeholes staring up at her from less than a foot away. The thin glass of the kitchen window the only thing that separated them.

Chapter 19

It was getting worse.

Charlie was beginning to see Misfortune at a minimum of four times a day. No matter where she was. Misfortune was standing next to her professor as they taught. Misfortune was a passenger on the bus. Misfortune was the inky shadow of a building. Misfortune was standing above her bed when she woke up in a sweat at night.

It was like her life rotated around her constantly checking over her shoulder, searching for that skull in the dark, always feeling like invisible eyes were playing over her skin.

It was when these feelings, and the terrible instance of seeing Misfortune over her bed, were told to Scott that they finally moved on from just laying down the base work of the information they had about the ghost to the lettuce of their terrible sandwich.

"Are you sure this is a good idea?" Charlie fidgeted in the passenger seat of Scott's car. She had been relieved when he told her that today they were finally going to start getting to the bottom of Misfortune, but after Scott drove them away from the school and stopped at the outskirts of town, Charlie was beginning to think that maybe there had to be a better way of going about things.

"I told you. Lidia came to me for help a while ago. She has had an encounter with Misfortune, too. There's a chance she might know something about him that we don't."

Which is a tall order, Charlie wanted to say. Instead, she eyed Lidia's run-down house through the car's window. "How do you know she even wants to help? If I was her, and people came knocking on my door about some ghost, I wouldn't want to talk to them."

Scott's door popped its suction, and the car began to ring before he turned off the engine. It drew Charlie's attention. His eyes twinkled at her. "We both know that's not true." He turned and hoped out. "Now come on, Scoob, we've got a mystery to solve."

Charlie hesitated a moment longer, watching Scott walk around the car and wait for her on the sidewalk. The car's roof cut off his head, but she knew he was waiting for her to get out.

All the bells in her head that told her this was a bad idea, that showing up on a stranger's doorstep to speak with her about a town ghost, which was borderline inappropriate and, frankly, rude considering what happened, rang without submission. And it would be a lie to say she didn't wish she was at work right now, and not out *hunting ghosts*.

Nevertheless, Scott's patient manner and knowledge (and the problem of Misfortune was highly unlikely to absolve on its own) spurred her on to pull down the sun visor to check her make-up and hair. If she was going to slot herself into this poor lady's day, she might as well look presentable.

Charlie snapped open the mirror, and then immediately slapped shut the whole visor itself and got out of the car and smiled reassuringly at Scott, pretending like she hadn't looked into the little mirror and saw Misfortune sitting in the backseat.

Scott was on his thrice round of knocking when the doubts in Charlie's mind came back in full force. It had been presumptuous of them to not even consider the fact that this Lidia *might not even be home*.

"Do you think she's home?" Charlie asked, voicing her thoughts.

Scott pulled his hand away from the door and listened for any signs that someone heard them.

Nothing told them so.

He sighed, defeated. "I don't know. She'd visited me around mid-day, so I was hoping that meant she didn't work around this time." He frowned. "Now I feel bad knowing she probably took time off of work to see me and I couldn't do anything for her."

This was not making Charlie feel any better.

"Hey, at least we know she probably takes Misfortune seriously, then," Scott added with a little bit of hope.

Charlie nodded but couldn't met his eye. "Yeah," she conceded.

Scott knocked again, absentmindedly at this point. "Do you have any other leads?" Charlie asked.

Scott scrunched up his nose in thought. "Honestly? Not really. The most we have is my uncle's books, and you."

Charlie hummed in self-pity. "That's reassuring."

"Hey, don't worry. I'm sure we'll find out why—"

Scott, still whacking his knuckles against the door, stopped when stomping starting inside the home. Both of them stepped back when the yelling started.

"For fuck's sake! Can't you take a hint to leave! Fucking reporters." The voice cut off as it neared the door. It was feminine and deep, like a smoker that hadn't taken a break from their addiction in years. The door whipped open to a woman dressed in a dark uniform and greasy brown hair tied behind her head. Her white skin was dotted with old acne scars and crow's feet permanently lived at the corners of her eyes. If her voice didn't give it away, Charlie definitely knew Lidia smoked after nicotine wafted out the door and ran for the street like a dog.

Charlie hid her reaction to the strong scent and was thankful Scott stepped up to Lidia. She didn't think her sociable nature could handle this one.

"Good afternoon, Ms. Thompson. How are you doing?"

Lidia sneered at him. "I've told you reporters that I'd call the cops if you come here one more time. Now either get the fuck off my property or I'll get you arrested for trespassing."

Charlie blinked dumbfoundedly at Lidia's hostile approach, but Scott watched her like he was speaking with Helen—blunt yet open. "Good thing we're not reporters."

Lidia's sneer dropped a hint, but she didn't lose her irritation. "I don't want whatever you're selling."

"Not salespeople either."

"Then you better start telling me why you're wasting my time." Lidia leaned back into the house like she was about to shut the door.

Scott spoke fast, finally showing hints that he, too, was a little put off by how Lidia acted. "I'm Scott James. I don't know if you remember me, but you visited me at the college some months ago to talk about your experience with Misfortune." Lidia's face gave no indication she remembered Scott, but she didn't look so close to closing the door anymore. "We were actually hoping that you'd like to talk about Misfortune with us."

And just like that, Lidia snapped out of her listening mode. The sneer she now gave put the first one to shame. "I don't give a shit who you are or what I told you. You're here because of some conspiracy theory, aren't you? Or better yet, I bet you came here because you thought I was crazy."

Charlie softened a little as Lidia spoke. Instead of seeing the words as insults, all they did was tell Charlie that more than once, people had come to her door to harass her about her experience with Misfortune. Pity welled in her.

Scott shook his head. "No, ma'am. Nothing like that, I promise. We're here because we have a similar problem."

That caught her off-guard. "What's that supposed to mean?" she asked warily.

"It means I saw him, too," Charlie cut in.

Lidia shot her eyes at Charlie. "And who the hell are you?"

Charlie wiped her hand on her shirt and hoped they didn't leave a sweat stain behind. "Charlie. Kezben. What we mean is that I saw him, too. Well, see him," she amended, like that made things better. "A lot actually. Multiple times a day."

"I'm not a medium," Lidia said with narrowed eyes.

"No," Charlie agreed. "But you know what it's like to see him. To look into the skull's eyes and see that nothing's looking back." She stepped forward, hoping that putting her heart into the conversation will make Lidia see their side. "And I know what that's like because I see that skull so many times a day. I saw just a few minutes ago, really. When we were getting out of the car. All we want to do is find out why he's here, and why this is happening. And we just need your help."

Lidia started at her. And with each second gone by, her gaze hardened. "You're talking about some delusions, girl," she spit, voice steel. "You come to my house and say we're alike, just because we both saw that damn ghost. But we're *not* alike. My daughter was stolen from me by that *fucking* thing. That is not ghost, that is a monster." Lidia was vibrating with bitter anger. "You have no right to compare what I've gone through to your little hallucinations. Now get off my porch, before I really do call the cops."

The door slammed in Charlie's face and rebounded in her heart. Not only did she cause them to lose their one and only option for more information, but she'd also brought the poor lady near tears.

Scott sighed from behind her. "Time to move on to option B."

Charlie stepped back to peer at him just as he walked up to the door with his fist raised in the air and a hand in his pocket. "Ms. Thompson?" He knocked lightly. "We'll pay you if you tell us about Misfortune!"

The door opened fast. Lidia hadn't moved from her spot. Her face was still splotched from her outburst, and she wouldn't look at Charlie. "How much?"

Chapter 20

"Whadu ya' wanna know?" Lidia eyed them both as they settled at the kitchen table. It was obvious who Lidia liked more, because the table only had two chairs, and Lidia offered the other chair to Scott after sitting down, forcing Charlie to stand regent behind Scott.

"Would you mind telling us about what happened at the time of your encounter with Misfortune? We understand if you don't want to go into detail, all we need is information about the ghost." Scott, ever prepared, pulled a miniature notebook out of his back pocket like a waiter would once sitting down. Quietly, Charlie nudged herself off to the side and tried to make herself as small as possible.

Lidia was already armed with a little glass briming with a dark liquid that made Charlie's nose burn from her stance some feet away. Lidia shrugged. Numb, almost. "It's fine. I had made supper for my daughter, and when I called her over to the table, she didn't leave her room." Lidia's hand constantly swirled her drink. In the few sentences that she spoke, Charlie could feel grief pouring out of her. "And when I went to go check on her." Her face contorted into agony and hate. "That... monster had her." Those few words made her shiver. "The last time I saw my daughter was almost a year ago, sitting in the arms of a fucking monster wearing a goat skull."

Scott nodded along, not speaking until Lidia was done. "That's terrible. I could never imagine what you're going through."

"That's right," Lidia's eyes cut towards Charlie. "You can't."

Scott cleared his throat to get Lidia's attention off Charlie, who was eternally grateful. She could only find the floor oh so interesting for so long. "Was there anything odd leading up to that night? Something that stuck out to you?"

Lidia took a moment to answer this question. She was still winding herself back up after the last one. "Maybe? Depends on what you're looking for. Stuff around the house would be in various places than where I put them, but," she shrugged, "I also have a toddler." She stared at Scott, waiting for the next question, then peered into her glass and cleared her throat. "Had," she amended, so quietly Charlie barely heard her.

"So, basically," Scott scribbled in his little book, "no warning. No incentive. You were just living your life, and then this happened."

"I think taking my fucking daughter from me is a pretty damn good incentive for freak like him."

"Of course. Now, that night, did it feel different? Like your gut was telling you something was wrong?"

Lidia swallowed hard. In that one moment, Charlie could tell that Lidia's body made her look much farther along in years than she really was. "At the time, I had a very demanding job. The last night I had my daughter, I was too busy thinking about how tired I was…"

Scott scratched at his paper some more. "You don't have to go on if you don't want to." Everyone could see the guilt for not thinking about her daughter had been eating at Lidia terribly.

Lidia dabbed at her eyes with her sleeve. "No, I'm fine. Anyway, to answer your question, no, nothing felt off. It just felt like another late night."

"Now, when you saw Misfortune, did your daughter see him, too?" Charlie could see where Scott was going with this.

Lidia chuckled wetly. "Sure did. My sweet baby thought he was there to play with her."

Scott cut in just this once to stop her from crying. "Can you describe what he looked like?"

Lidia nodded. "He wore all black." She used her hands to reference her own body. "Thick coat, thick gloves. I couldn't see much of his skin, but I'm pretty sure he's white." She guffawed. "And then that goddamn skull on his head. Bloodied and had maggots crawling all over it. It wasn't even complete either. It had some lines under the eye. Disgusting thing," she spit.

Scott and Charlie shared a glance. Three lines. Misfortune's supposed mark for his mask. Or, in some cases, his calling card.

"Did you ever see him again?" Charlie piped up. She couldn't help herself. This was the part she had really been waiting for.

Charlie had never seen a side eye so irritated and dismissive before. She knew she earned it, but she still felt defensive afterwards. Lidia talked into her glass. "God, I wish. All he ever did was show up and take my daughter."

"Not even in a glance? A feeling? A shadow in the corner?" Charlie mentally begged, pleaded for Lidia, anybody at this point, to help her understand what she was going through.

For the first time since standing at the door, Lidia held Charlie's eye for more than a second. "*No*."

"And that's alright," Scott added, middleman. "We understand that this was a tough time for you."

Lidia sighed. Seemingly pulling herself out of storyteller mode and finally looking around. "I don't have anything more, really. That was the only encounter I had with your little ghost. Is that all you wanted?"

Scott pulled out his wallet, seeing the invitation that their visit was coming to an end. "What we want is to find out why Misfortune is doing what he does."

"Why he took your daughter, and why he haunts me," Charlie added softly.

Lidia hummed as Scott began to pull out a few bills. Charlie jumped to attention and fished out her own wallet. No way was she going to let Scott pay for this, too.

"I'm not the only one, you know."

Both Charlie and Scott stopped mid-way for their wallets. "What do you mean?" she asked.

"I'm not the only one that has had a child taken by that *thing*."

They shared another look again. Charlie recalled one of the first conversations they had with each other, where they both said they didn't believe Misfortune was the cause of the kidnappings. Yes, Charlie had been wary about the truth to Lidia's story when Scott talked about it briefly before they got here. They hadn't said anything aloud about the whole Misfortune-kidnapping-thing, but Charlie had yet to believe it was true.

Although, with what she'd seen and the strain in Lidia's body as she talked, she wasn't too sure she'd walk out of this house with that same belief.

"Do you know anyone else that experienced the same as you?" Scott prompted.

Lidia sat back in her chair and flicked a wrist. "Just look it up online. You'll find a whole buncha people like me. Kids gone. Besides, no matter what you or the cops believe, people see your Misfortune all the time."

Charlie took the moment of Scott pondering over Lidia's words to pull out some bills from her wallet and passed them to the other woman. "Of course. Thank you for your time, and sorry for what I said earlier."

She heard Scott grunt in discontent behind her as she pulled away from the table. She ignored him.

Lidia nodded absentmindedly as she counted the bills. She spoke as she flipped through them. "Y'all can leave, unless you planned on staying for supper, too."

"Nope." Scott pushed from the table and started towards the door. "Thank you for what you've said. You've helped us more than you could imagine."

"Sure, I did," she grunted sarcastically.

Scott tipped his head in the direction of the door, telling Charlie to follow, and started towards it. Charlie made to tow herself behind him, but Lidia stopped her with a hand grasping her forearm. When Scott turned around after failing to hear her steps, Charlie waved him on with a face she hoped conveyed that she would only be a minute.

"Yes?" she asked after the door closed behind Scott.

"I don't like you," Lidia said into the money.

Charlie blinked at her, taken aback. She knew this, yes, but goodness, Lidia didn't need to rub it in. "I'm sorry about earlier, really."

Lidia took a deep breath and waited a moment to let it out. "I don't like you," she said again. "But I believe you." She turned her head up and peered into Charlie's eyes. "I believe that Misfortune is hurting you every day like he hurts me every day. And I believe that you are going to find out why he did this to me. To us." She didn't bother to hide the tremor in her voice, nor stop the rogue tears from finding the ground. "Find out why he took my baby girl." Lidia's hand squeezed Charlie arm hard enough to bruise. She shook it for a point.

Charlie gently used her other arm to peel her off and took Lidia's hand between her palms. "We will, Ms. Thompson. I promise you. We'll do everything we can."

Lidia nodded along with her. "And you tell me what happened to my baby. My darling Genevieve. I need to know what that ghost did to her."

Charlie's heart broke in two at the implication that Lidia no longer believed her daughter was alive.

"I promise you'll be the first to know." She squeezed Lidia's fingers reassuringly.

Lidia swallowed hard and pulled her hand away like Charlie's hands were rocks and her palm had been stuck. Charlie took her leave and made for the door. Right before she put her hand on the handle, Lidia left her with one last parting gift.

"If… if you need another person to talk to about Misfortune, someone who's like you, you might want to visit Kyle Fortic."

Chapter 21

"What was that about?" Scott asked before Charlie was even fully seated in the car.

Charlie was still blinking herself out of what Lidia had told her. "Well, she told me she didn't like me."

Scott started a car and gave Lidia's house an odd look. "Dang. I could tell she wasn't too fond of you, but I didn't think she'd pull you aside to make sure you knew."

Charlie kept replaying the conversation in her head, the anguish of Lidia's voice, the pressure of her hand on her arm. She shook her head like she could shake herself into the present. "That's not all she said. She... told me that she believes we'll find out what's going on with Misfortune. That— we'll find out what happened to her daughter."

Scott took a moment to peer over at Charlie. "Wow, no pressure or anything."

Charlie was not in a joking mood. "She's in pain, Scott. She thinks her daughter is dead because of Misfortune."

"Jesus." Scott tapped at the steering wheel. "I know I'll never understand her pain, but I really do feel bad for her. When she visited me those few months ago, she told me she had her daughter at sixteen. Believe me, I felt terrible when I had to tell her after that I couldn't help her."

The pity hit Charlie with brass knuckles. *Lidia was younger than both her and Scott.*

"Anyway, at least she was very helpful," Scott said, steering them away from Lidia's well of parental guilt and misery. "First of all, she said both her and her daughter had seen Misfortune, which means that it's not just you that can see him when he appears."

"He just appears at a time when only *I'll* see him," Charlie finished. "Like in my room, or when no one else is around."

"Did you really see him earlier? In the car?"

Charlie almost laughed. "You know I did."

Scott sighed. "Anyway, I'm starting to believe that these child-taking stories might have a little more truth to them."

Charlie nodded. "I believe Lidia, and I believe that there's a chance she's not the only one. But what I can't get by is *why* he'd take kids."

He hummed. "*Why* is always the name of the game, my friend."

"We have to at least look into those kid's disappearances, Scott." She sighed. "I know we're no cops or teenagers with a talking dog, but I can't take the guilt of lying to Lidia."

Scott turned down a street. "Let's take it one step at a time, yeah? Let's figure out what Misfortune's deal is first before we tackle that. We'll need to find people more like you and then focus on that later. All we need is time."

"Oh!" Charlie exclaimed. She'd almost forgotten one of the best things Lidia had told her. "Lidia gave me a name. Someone she said that we should talk to because he was like me."

Scott grinned over at her. "See? There ya go. We'll understand him first and then the kids. It'll all work out."

Charlie felt bad that they were here talking about kids being taken like it was some math problem that had a simple solution and not life shattering events, but like Scott had said, people had gone to the cops for these kidnappings and been brushed off. She hoped that more people were willing to believe them when they say they are literally ghost hunting.

Misfortune

"All she said was that his name was Kyle Fortic, but I imagine this town is small enough that someone will know him."

Scott sighed contently. "The wonders of having a close community and the ability to search anyone up at your fingertips."

"Here, I'll see if I can find him," Charlie said, pulling out her phone.

"Alright." Scott slowed the car at what Charlie assumed was a stoplight. "I do work late this week, so we'll have to go see him in a couple of days. Sorry we won't be able to meet in the office."

Charlie absentmindedly nodded along. "Honestly, I could use a break from Helen."

She expected Scott to drive off at some point, but when they'd been sitting at the light for a while, she did a curtsy check of their surroundings. She openly gaped when she saw they were sitting outside her work.

"I thought it would be easier to just drop you off, rather than go back to school to wait for the bus."

Embarrassed she had been distracted by her phone, Charlie beamed as convincingly as she could at Scott and unbuckled herself. "Thank you," she mouthed, and Scott sent her off with a mock salute.

Charlie tucked her phone away in her pocket, content to pick up her search at a later time, and got out of the car. She paced the small journey built out of the sidewalk, listened to Scott drive away, and stepped around a pedestrian that was slightly in her way. She walked into her work with the facts weighing on her mind and pretended the hair on the back of her neck didn't stand up like dead eyes were on her.

Chapter 22

"What would you do if you had a bobsled full of huskies?" Charlie asked as Martin broke the triangle of pool balls with a hard smack that made her ears ring. It was their seventh time at the bar's pool table (not including the miniature disaster of the first time) and so far, Charlie had yet to win a single round.

"How bland, sister," Martin tutted. "Why not give me a hundred bobsleds?" He bent down over the table and aimed up a shot after Charlie missed her chance at the free table.

"You should see the logic behind the question, *brother*. Then you'd understand that you have to take creative control on this one. It's basically a freebie."

The cue ball whacked into the blue painted number two, sending Martin into the lead. He never took his eyes off the table. "Then I would breed the huskies, teach them the ways of humans, and then when we inevitably rise into power that rivals Earth's biggest nations, we will, obviously, take over the world." And then he raised his cue to strike another ball.

Charlie nodded along like a solider talking strategy. "Now, these huskies, do they have free will? Or are they enslaved to a teenager, bent on world domination?"

"They're loyal to me." He paused to survey the table. "They want whatever I want."

"Ah," says Charlie. "Indirect manipulation. I like it."

They eyed each other to see if one of them would crack, but neither laughed, and no one earned a point that round.

Martin was already four balls down, and Charlie had yet to touch her assigned strips. "What would you do if you had an army of rats that had super strength?"

Charlie took a second to think on this one. She leaned on her cue, as she really had no use for it anymore. "How big is my army?"

"'Bout a thousand."

"And do they listen to me?"

Martin looked over to her, and if it wouldn't have cost him the game, would've smiled sweetly at her, eyes off the table for only a moment. "They listen to you like I listen to you."

"So, no," she sighed out. "Great army."

Martin snapped in her face as he rounded the table to take *another* shot. "Get to work, sis. You don't want to forfeit the round, do you?"

If it wouldn't have cost her the round, she would've smacked his hand out of her face. "Then I would use food as an incentive to listen to me, because that always seems to work with you. I could do a lot with their strength."

When Martin surprisingly missed a shot (only because the ball bounced out of the pocket) Charlie lined up to make her own shot. "Let's just say that some people would go to bed in their house in Atlanta, Georgia, and then wake up in the same house now in Augusta, Maine."

When she enviably missed, Martin took her place. "Hmmm. Bed-moving prank taken to another level. It's good, but it could use some work. How would the rats remove the house from the ground? How fast do they move? Do they follow the highway? The back roads?"

"Obviously, they would just chew their way through the wood and pipes of houses with their strength, and because of that, they can lift it up and run with it like it weighs nothing. And no, they don't need to follow a road. All I gotta do is string up some cheese in the front of the house like some fisherman and have them drive for me."

Martin missed once more and turned back to her, a thoughtful look on his face. "What kind of cheese?" The seriousness in his face fought to make Charlie lose.

Her lips were crooked as she spoke, something she quickly amended. "Mozzarella?"

Martin stuck up a finger and mimicked an incorrect buzzer. "Wrong, that's bad for them. You shoulda said cheddar. Honestly, you can't go wrong with it."

Charlie had to take a moment to breathe. "And how do you know that?"

Martin stared her dead in the eye. "Ever since I became the Lord of the Rats."

"Oh my God," she breathed out, heavily annoyed.

Martin sucked in air between his teeth. "Oops. Somebody broke character." He tsked, persona borderline condescending.

She opened her mouth with a click and pushed him away when he leered his win at her. "Shut up, Marty."

He snickered at her, and before lining up at the table that held all strips and one eight ball, his eyes glanced over her shoulder. "High blood-pressure alert on your six."

Charlie furrowed her brows, thinking it was a startup to the next round. But when Martin eyed what was over her shoulder for a little too long, she joined him in the stare. Behind her was the rest of the small town bar. Just sitting down at the counter on the wall to the left of the door was a group of white men getting on in their years. Charlie examined the back of each man's head until she landed on a familiar one. One that wasn't facing the bar, instead peering back at her with a polite smile.

Charlie perked up and smiled back at Bill, who was raising a hand to wave. Bill nodded her way and leaned back to tell his friends something. And when they nodded back to him, he pushed off the seat and made his way over to them.

"Charlie! Martin! It's good to see y'all again. I didn't know you played pool," he greeted. Charlie hadn't seen Bill since he'd approached her a few days ago and asked in the nicest way possible if it was okay if his car's bled a little bit onto their lawn. Charlie, in a fit of neighborly politeness, offered that he could use the driveway that led to their garage. It went unused anyway.

Despite Bill being one of the best well-known people to them and in general, Martin, ever the socialist, was suddenly concentrating awfully hard on making the shot to win the game of pool. Charlie knew it wasn't that he was being rude, or disliked Bill per se, but that his pride probably still smarted from Bill witnessing him fail to pick up the boxes all those weeks ago.

"Been playing pool since we were in diapers." She laughed. "Though I'll be honest, I've never been quite good."

"You never even sunk a ball," muttered Martin, having already smacked the eight ball into a hole. He was right, the table was still full of her assigned balls.

Bill chuckled. "I was the same growin' up. Took me a long while to really learn the game. Are you folks staying around some more? I came with some buddies of mine, but can I play a round of stick with ya?"

Martin came up beside Charlie. "Do we have to?" He sighed.

Charlie elbowed him hard enough to cause him to grunt and step away from her, pride and side both smarting.

"Of course, Bill." She stuck out her cue to him, barely used since she picked it up. "You can play Martin. You wouldn't have much competition with me."

Bill gripped the cue lightly and tossed it in the air to spin it around. "Always a generous one, you are. Y'all'll need another batch of cookies in the comin' future."

Bill moved to chalk up the stick, (something Charlie had completely neglected to do, mainly because she hadn't even need it) while Martin gave an exaggerated sigh as he moved to across the table.

Charlie frowned at him a pointed to Bill's turned back. "Be nice," she mouthed, accompanying it with a pointed stare. When Martin only frowned back, she added a mimic of dialing a phone and holding it to her ear. "Hello? Aunt Mary?" That worked to make Martin straighten his back.

Bill turned around, confused. "What was that?"

Charlie just let her raised palm fall forward like she was brushing something off herself. "Nothing. I just hope you win."

"Hm, maybe two batches of cookies are in the future instead."

"Traitor," mouthed Martin.

When Bill turned around to set up the balls for the break, Charlie did another mime of calling their aunt.

In the end, Bill had lost, but only by one ball. Martin hadn't acted humble with his win whatsoever and was only a step short of pretty much parading himself around the entire bar. Charlie had to apologize to Bill when he went to go reconvene with his friends. Bill, ever himself, had been proud of Martin for doing so well in the game, and even offered a rematch at any time.

Martin had shrugged at the time, but as soon as they got to the bus, he had chuckled impertinently and said, "Hell no."

Charlie smacked him again on the arm. "Be nice. Honestly, you were very rude to Bill. All he wanted was to play pool with you."

Martin groaned. "Believe me, the only thing I want from him is those terrible cookies."

Charlie was still a little annoyed on the side at his behavior to their neighbor, but sighed with a shake of her head, "You like those cookies, Marty. They're good and *not prepackaged*. I don't even know why you deny it."

Martin scrunched up his nose. "Because he's an old white guy that's probably gonna sneak a roofie in a batch when he thinks we trust him."

Charlie recited the Christian Lord's name in full in response. "Sometimes I don't know what to do with you."

He shrugged and looked out the bus's shaky window. "Meh, just water me three times a day and leave me out in the sun. Ground dirt will work just as fine as potted soil."

Charlie couldn't even begin to understand how he thinks of such weird responses and didn't think she could try. She watched him as he looked out the window, studying the same nose she had their father shared and his eyes dancing over the passing building to focus on each one from less than a second. Suddenly, she was very, very thankful he wanted to come with her when she said she was moving out. She didn't know what she'd do without her little brother.

Chapter 23

Since Scott was unavailable during the period of time Charlie had taken off her work schedule in order to meet with him, it meant that first the first time in a long while, she had time dedicated to herself.

To be more specific, *pamper* herself.

Charlie wasn't big on the whole concept of being overly feminine, but when Sam had called and more or less forced her into a stereotypical 'girl's time' she had no choice but to say yes.

She had yet to decide if agreeing with the plan was the correct course of action or not, but it had led to them getting a manicure, (something Charlie also hadn't decided was the best thing to do or not) and then shopping at the nearby mall.

Just like what they did when pretending at Charlie's work, she carried the items while Sam popped in from store to store like some clothes-addicted fiend. Charlie had no qualms against helping her friend. She enjoyed seeing Sam fawn over different types of clothes. And besides, it wasn't like she could afford any of them anyway. At least helping Sam deviated the attention off her if anyone was wondering why she didn't buy anything.

"Any ideas of what we should start with?" Sam asked as they wandered into but another store.

Charlie rearranged one of the many bags she held. They were starting to imprint themselves on the tips of her fingers. "Well, we both know orange and purple anything are off the table."

Sam walked ahead, sticking a finger over her already frizzled hair. "Correct you are, my friend."

"And you have no use for dresses."

"It's not like this town is brimming with parties."

"And the season's coming to an end, so no billowy clothing."

Sam stopped at a rack and flashed a smile at Charlie. "My pupil, how far you've come."

Charlie rolled her eyes. She had learned the prospects of clothes from working for George, but Sam liked to pretend that Charlie's new cultured intelligence over clothes was because of her. She eyed the waterfall of orange that sprayed down Sam's head. "How about a bandana?"

Sam stopped and turned around, open wander on her face. "Really?" she asked, falling out of their oddly found game.

Charlie shrugged. "It's in season, so a lot of stores should have them. And besides, I don't think you need the other reason."

Sam hummed and raised a defiant eyebrow. "My mama always said that I should never be ashamed of the space my hair takes up. But I like your thinking." She twisted around with a valorous finger jutted in the air. "To the bandana aisle, good gentleman."

She marched off towards the back of the store while Charlie followed along with a chuckle.

While that store failed to have a proper selection of bandanas, another valiant march to a different store led them to discover a full rack of them.

"It's like a dream come true," Sam whispered, stars in her eyes.

"You're being dramatic," Charlie replied.

Sam flicked a wrist and returned to her normal self. "Yeah, I am. Now come on. Time not spent shopping is wasted."

Back out into the shop's main halls with another bag in tow, Sam finally seemed to be coming to an end.

"Hey, we've probably got another fifteen minutes before we gotta go," she said, checking her watch. "I've been running around the whole time for myself. Let's go somewhere you want to."

Ah, the last thing Charlie wanted to hear. "No thanks, Sam. I don't need anything."

Sam guffawed. "And I don't need another four pairs of pants and yet here we are. *Come on.*"

"It's okay. Really."

"Charlette Kezben. Screw your head on straight."

"Sam, I—" Charlie stopped and let out an involuntary gasp as they turned a corner and Misfortune appeared in front of her. The breath fell out of her when she stared and stared into those soulless eyes, and they failed to disappear.

"Charlie?"

Charlie broke away from watching her nightmare. "What?"

Sam watched her dubiously. "Are you okay? You keep staring at that ad."

"The ad," Charlie repeated, glancing back over to where Misfortune was. Expecting him to be gone, she found a large screen advertising a perfume with Misfortune as the cover. Now that she really examined the features, she could see the proportions of his face were off, and there were no lines under the eye. In fact, it was more of a cartoon character with a goat mask than anything.

Sam followed her gaze again. "Honestly, I could see why you'd act like that. It is really weird to have a ghost as the spokesperson. I know I wouldn't want Bigfoot to be the sponsor of my make-up."

When Charlie didn't answer, still reeling from her supposed encounter with the damned ghost, Sam put her hands on her hips and shifted her weight. "That's it. I'm not letting you walk out of here without getting something for yourself."

"Sam—" she started.

She lifted a hand. "Zip it. You carried around my bags. The least I can do is pay you back."

"Please, I don't want charity work."

"This isn't charity work. I'm spending an afternoon at the mall with my friend. Now let's go before I start buying you bandanas, too."

Charlie sighed as the guilt swirled to join the perturbation already in her gut. She wanted to tell Sam that no, she wasn't going to use her money, and Sam must have seen this, because she lifted a hand and made a slicing movement over her throat.

Charlie never thought she'd feel her heart expand after being threatened by someone.

Sam turned back around and twirled a finger. "Now hurry up, my good gentleman. Our chariot awaits. Choose a way to spend the shillings and fast."

Charlie sped up to hook an arm through Sam's. "Thank you," she whispered.

Sam shrugged next to her. "Meh, I'm just making sure you don't want to get rid of me."

Charlie was so overcome with thankfulness for her friend that she was almost lucky enough to miss the goat skull that peered at her from the window that led to the parking lot.

Chapter 24

So far, Charlie hadn't found much on Kyle Fortic besides that he lived not too far out of town and that he had some work issues. Or, she assumed so, from the magnificent amount of links she found online to his resume.

It was a start, of course, having an address, but she didn't appreciate that she didn't have anything further than a name. No pictures, no idea if he lived alone, no clue if he would even be home or willing to talk to them (she didn't feel too inclined to have a repeat of last time).

Charlie still had another two days to work out the schematics of how they would approach Kyle. It did help that George had called her to say he'd be out of work for the day, so the shop was closed (or, at least, that's what she thought he meant, for all she'd heard was George rambling on over the line about cats, of all things, and a large bang of a dresser falling over cutting him off. Charlie was a little too scared to find out what he was even talking about or what had happened).

So, after she got home, she found it was nice to take a breather and focus on her work in peace. The past few days spent with Martin and Sam had really cooled her nerves, but she couldn't dedicate all her free time to outings.

She hummed along to the quiet radio on her phone as she worked at the kitchen table. From where she sat, the front door could be seen through the kitchen doorway, so Martin could see she was home when he walked in without having to distract her. Although, it was probably wishful thinking he'd do such a thing. Charlie liked to think she was good at keeping up with her work. She wasn't the most eye-catching student with her grades, but definitely not something to scoff at.

She had just gotten up for one second to grab a snack when the front door opened.

"Doing school right now," she called, head half buried in the fridge.

When Martin didn't answer, and heavy steps landed on the dampening carpet, Charlie froze. Her hand was still midway in his journey towards a package of cheese, but her original goal had been forgotten by the time she realized what was happening.

Her breath hitched and her eyes stung with the need to blink. It was like the world had sucked itself down into a hole and specifically only taken her with it. Her heart beat, beat, beat in her throat, and she believed herself a second from passing out when the thought of Lidia hit her head.

I believe that Misfortune is hurting you every day like he hurts me every day. And I believe that you are going to find out why he did what he did.

Lidia was so spot on it almost made Charlie laugh right at the moment. She had never really let on to anyone about how no matter how many times she'd seen Misfortune, he always made her heart clench and her mouth dehydrate itself.

And she was no fool to know this didn't help her case. How was she supposed to understand why he was tormenting her? How was she supposed to find out what happened to Gen or the rest of the kids if she couldn't even look him in the eye?

With the deepest, hardest breath that made her chest ache, Charlie slowly released herself from the fridge. She was shaking and impossibly terrified, no doubt, but just imaging Lidia's wet eyes after retailing the taking of her daughter pulled her out of the fridge, and the thought that Misfortune could possibly turn his attention towards Martin propelled her feet towards the kitchen door. Their placement swapped from the last time Misfortune gave Charlie's house a visit for longer than two seconds.

As she silently stalked towards the door, the steps started again, and he began to climb the stairs one by one. By the time Charlie had reached the threshold to the living room, she had just missed the ghost. His stomping up the carpeted stairs were separated just by a thin wall. They climbed to the top and turned the corner towards the bedrooms.

Charlie followed and stood at the bottom of the stairs. Yet again, Misfortune was just out of view. While she hadn't seen him, the dirty footprints that displayed themselves on the carpet told her all she needed to know.

It took every fiber of her body to will herself to put a hand on the banister and go up those steps. Her breathing came in puffs, as if the radiator had stopped working like it does periodically in the night. When she reached the final step and peered around the corner, she saw the dirty prints led down the hall and to her room.

She clenched her fists to keep herself in the moment and placed her foot on the grimy evidence of Misfortune. While she already knew when he was, she still cracked the bathroom door and Martin's door open with a hiss of the hinges, just in case. Whether it was to make sure he wasn't messing with her or to stall for time, Charlie couldn't answer.

Like the world had stopped just for this moment, Charlie could hear no sound as she came to a halt outside her closed bedroom door. She regarded the ground once more to ensure Misfortune had led her here, and the cutoff print under the door told her all she needed to know. Like a million eyes watching her that knew an answer she didn't, Charlie placed a hand of the bitingly cold knob and turned.

Whether it was good or bad, Charlie opened the door to find Misfortune in her room. He wasn't facing her, instead his black covered back was to her—he was gazing out the window. The prospect of a ghost looking out her bedroom window almost made Charlie laugh. Bubbly, unkept laughter.

What immediately crushed her psychotic laugh was when he turned around. Misfortune, while a ghost, had the build of a relatively broad man.

Not in the way of being overly fit, but in the way that when he had his back to her, his chest could conceal the child that lay limp in his arms.

Her legs were draped over one elbow, and her shoulders on the other. The little girl's skin, which was probably a smooth warm on another day, was pale and slick with sweat in Misfortune's arms. She had no physical injuries, her chest rose without inhabitation, and her face looked peaceful, but Charlie's stomach still clenched at the sight.

She could recognize the slim nose and big brown eyebrows that Lidia shared anywhere.

Charlie swallowed and opened her mouth. "What did you do to her?" she asked quietly, her broken voice almost unheard by her own ears.

Charlie didn't miss that Gen didn't move in Misfortune's arms. He had no problem with her weight, nor did his chest move to breathe. Despite this, he pulled Gen closer to himself while shaking his head.

Charlie watched the daylight reflect off his mask, eyes set on not blinking. From the angle of the light, it was almost as if she could see a face behind it.

"No?" she interpreted breathily.

He did nothing. Seconds ticked by, and every nervous glance at Gen spurred her on. "You... hurt her," she stated simply.

Another shake of his head.

"You... didn't hurt her?"

This time, she was rewarded with a nod. This was definitely the most horrifying yet oddest things she'd ever done in her life. And she willingly liked Martin.

She was losing it.

"Then why did you take her?" She dared a step forward.

While he had no movement in his chest that indicated breath or a heart, Misfortune stiffened at her slight approach. She had a feeling she was walking an exceptionally fine line. Easing back to where she was, she peered at Misfortune, examining him, almost. Of all the terrible things he'd done to her, Misfortune didn't seem to do anything for no reason. For all the times he'd shown himself to her, it was for her attention. Maybe he'd brought Gen here to show her another thing. If she was going to find out why he was changing tactics, open-ended questions weren't going to work if he didn't talk.

"You took Gen," she prompted.

A nod.

"You hurt her."

A shake of the skull.

She paused. "But you took her for a reason."

Another nod.

"Are your intentions with her bad?"

Another shake, this one jerkier. *Hard no*.

"Are your intentions with *me* bad?"

Same sharp decline.

Charlie knew he wouldn't answer, but she cracked anyway. "Then help me understand why you took Gen. Why you're haunting me. *Please*," she begged.

In response, Misfortune turned his back on her and went back to peering out the window, Gen's legs swaying lightly and out of sight.

"Please, *please*," she started, but jerked her head back when the front door slammed again.

"Charlie?"

Martin. He was home, and Misfortune was a single story away from him.

Charlie turned her head to yell down at him. "Marty?" Her stiff breathing was back, but when she shot her eyes back to Misfortune, he, and Gen, were gone.

"Gen!" she near shrieked.

"Charlie?" Martin worried from the bottom step.

Charlie panicked and jumped away from the door, bolting to the top of the stairs with a look that didn't indicate that she was shaking uncontrollably.

Martin was halfway up the stairs when he caught glance at his sister at the top of the steps. "Charlie? You good? Why were you yelling?"

"What are talking about?" It was like the guilt of lying to her brother had carved a hole in her heart to ensure it always had room to make permanent residence.

Martin blinked at her. "You were yelling, just now. Weren't you?"

In no way would Charlie ever be able to fill the hole, especially as it was dug deeper. "No? I was just working on school, my computer's in the kitchen. I was just using the bathroom." Martin's face furrowed in thought, and Charlie continued. "Maybe it was the pipes that you heard."

He watched her for a moment longer, sniffed, and then pivoted on the steps. "Alright then, good chap. Carry on."

And as Martin tossed his weight down the steps and disappeared into what Charlie assumed was the kitchen, she allowed herself to be supported by the wall. Her heart still throbbed from the adrenaline of *speaking* with Misfortune and seeing poor little Gen, too.

She eyed the dirty prints that led themselves into her room. She followed them back to the window where, sure enough, they disappeared. Almost as if Misfortune was jumped out the window. But of course, with a curtesy glance into the wanning day, there was nothing outside the window that indicated a ghost and a little girl were nearby.

The only thing she could see was the setting sun, the roof of their barely used garage, and one of Bill's cars, which was putting that barely used garage to use.

Chapter 25

"You're kidding," Scott whooshed out.

"Scott, I wish so badly I was."

Charlie kept her eyes on the road and hands firmly on the wheel as to keep them from quivering. It was one of the first time she'd driven her car since getting it back from the mechanic, inside successfully replaced and bank account effectively drained.

Because of this, she designated herself to becoming the driver when they decided to finally visit Kyle because Charlie felt guilty Scott had been chauffeuring her around for a problem that barely concerned him. That, and that she'd have something to do instead to awkwardly staring forward when she inevitably told him about her interaction with Misfortune.

Scott leaned back in his seat with a hand on his forehead. So far, he was taking it a lot worse than she'd hoped. He tended to overreact whenever it came to the ghost.

"Holy crap, Charlie. This is crazy. You *talked* to Misfortune! Don't you realize how great this is?"

Charlie shrugged. "'Talked' isn't the word I'd use. More like I communicated with him. I more of just asked yes or no questions and he shook his head."

Scott nodded along like a child listening to a bedtime story. "But that's the best part! Not only are we dealing with a ghost, but he *sentient*. He's aware of the things around him, and he understood you!" Scott put a knuckle to his lip. "I wonder... Perhaps if we can isolate him somehow, we'll be able to ask him a few more questions."

Even though she wanted to, Charlie didn't flick her eyes in Scott's direction. But she did give a small smile. "Slow down there, Fred. We don't even know what makes him show up at what time of the day. Nor even if he wants to communicate again."

That popped Scott's bubble, but he patched it quickly. "And what about Gen? You said she was breathing. Do you really think she's alive?"

She sighed. "I was close enough to see that Misfortune didn't move. As in, his chest didn't have a heartbeat, but Gen's did. I assume he brought her along to show me that she was alive, and that he didn't hurt her." She tapped at the wheel. "But *why*? Somehow, he must understand what we're doing, right?" She brought up a hand for emphasis. "Of all the kids that have been reported missing because a goat skull-masked figure took them, Misfortune brought Gen. First of all, that means that he's been appearing around me and I haven't noticed, and second—"

"Do you think maybe he wants to help?"

Charlie balked hard enough to *almost* take her eyes off the road. "What? No, I was gonna say that he's taking children for no reason."

"But what if he's actually trying to help us?"

"Help us do what? Find out why he steals kids?"

Charlie could hear fabric rub against itself as Scott shook his head. "No, think about it. You move to this town without any prior knowledge of Misfortune, and then all of a sudden, he starts haunting you. So, then you start going on an investigation to try and find out why he's doing this, but instead, you *learn* more about him. What if he's trying to show us something?"

Charlie watched the road in silence for a full ten seconds. "You've lost me." And Scott sighed dramatically. "What would he be showing us? Gen? How she's still alive?"

Scott went still. "That might be absolutely it."

Charlie blinked at his decisive tone. "Okay? But what about all the other kids?"

She watched him with her peripheral vision as he stuck out his hands and shook his head with his eyes smushed shut. "No, not that. Well, maybe sort of that, but the fact is that you saw that she's *alive*. But this also proved that *he isn't*."

"Hmm, well, I sort of thought this was a by-product of being a ghost." Scott bypassed her. "Assuming he's not a malicious entity, *he's a ghost*." Her internal timer was ticking down. "Believe me, I'm aware."

Scott sat up far enough to truly be in her vision. He spoke soundly. "Charlie, if he's a ghost, that means that he was a person at some point."

She eyed him for a moment. "I suppose it's a possibility. But it's a little hard to interview someone's who's dead."

"What I'm trying to say is that, what if he's not trying to hurt anyone but get our attention?"

She thinned her lips. "Attention about what?"

"His death."

And her timer over Scott's absurdness reached its end. She looked over to him, but only for a blink's worth of time. "Scott, really, it's a nice theory, but—"

She stopped when Scott gasped and sat back in his chair like he fell. Charlie turned her attention to the road, which was in the middle of two woods in-between the towns. Like an enlightened version of the night she crashed her car, Misfortune was standing right in the middle of the road.

Charlie almost screamed from fear, shock, and the annoyance of *oh sweet baby Jesus not again*.

Instead, she learned from her mistakes and hit the brakes not a moment too soon. The tires screeched and Scott and she pitched forward with hands on the dash to brace themselves, but miraculously, the car came to a stop.

And still standing there in the middle of the road was Misfortune. Skull promptly on his head, and coat draping itself over his body.

"Oh my God," Scott whispered from the passenger seat, voice full of wonder. Charlie, on the other hand, was beginning to get fed up with Misfortune's uncalled-for appearances. They didn't move a muscle as the ghost peered into their car. Nor did they make a sound as he slowly turned to the side and drifted off the road, into the ditch, and disappeared into the impenetrable trees and out of the sun's reach. The only parts of his body that ever moved were his legs. The wind didn't even ruffle his coat. Wouldn't dare touch something that wasn't in their true, living world.

Charlie and Scott blinked in unison at the last spot they saw Misfortune. Scott was the first one to turn away to look at Charlie, face building with a giddiness. "If he appeared at your house to show you Gen was alive, what do you think he'd do to communicate that I'm right?"

Charlie could only stare at the part of the trees and replay Scott's theory in her head.

While knocking multiple times on Lidia's door did the trick then, the strategy fell short on Kyle's door. Charlie was really beginning to believe he wasn't home.

It was like she was living her life through a plane of glass. Not the type that she felt when she was overcome with grief for her father, but that she was so far in her head thinking about this change of game for Misfortune, she was oblivious to her surroundings. She could hear Scott tapping on the door repeatedly, but all she could think about was that a ghost might be haunting her just because it wanted someone to know about something that happened to them when they died.

What kind of Scooby-Doo plot was this?

It was all too much and made total sense at the same time. If Misfortune was haunting her because he wanted her to learn about something, then she had her answer for the *why* he was doing it. She had yet to comprehend what the children had to do with it, who Misfortune even was in life, or why he chose her, but if he showed himself to Scott as a way of communication, Charlie was inclined to believe that was that he wanted.

But still, they only had one piece of the puzzle. And she was really hoping Kyle would fill in any blank space.

"Maybe he's not home," she said at least.

"You know, I'm starting to think you're right." Scott leaned back and eyed the house. The building itself was in better condition than Lidia's was, but the yard was horribly overgrown. "Do you think he still lives here?"

The answer appeared itself to be a large blue truck grumbling down the road and stopping behind Charlie's car. "Only one way to find out," Charlie replied in a muted tone when a middle-aged man with tanned brown skin hopped out of the car with a not-so-welcoming look on his face.

Scott took initiative and strode down the front steps to meet him. "Hello! Are you Kyle Fortic?"

"Who's asking?" replied Hopefully-Kyle-And-Not-Some-Random-Guy.

Charlie joined Scott. "Last week, we spoke with Lidia Thompson. She pointed us here when we asked her about—"

"I'm not paying the damn child support," spat Hopefully-Kyle.

The two blinked at him. "What?" Charlie sputtered, confused. "No, we're here to talk about Misfortune."

Hopefully-Kyle approached them, hostility written all over his face. "I told Lidia that she was crazy. Just because she took some mushroom and thought that fucking ghost took my kid, doesn't mean she gets a penny out of me. She couldn't even keep her, either."

Okay, that one needed a moment to unpack. It took Charlie a couple of second to put together that yes, this is Kyle, who was probably Gen's father, and also doesn't believe in Lidia's story.

"We're... not here over child support," Scott said. "We talked to her about Misfortune, yes, but that because we want to learn about him. She directed us here because she said you see him." That's not exactly what Lidia said, but Charlie hoped it's what she meant.

Kyle glared at Scott, sizing him up. "Well then, you've come a long way for nothing. Lidia lied to you. I've never seen that goddamn ghost in my life." He waved them away from his door. "Go bother someone just as crazy as you."

While it might be based on how she interpreted their characters, and she could be totally wrong, Charlie didn't think Lidia would lie to her, and she definitely thought Kyle would. She moved to try and placate him with raised hands. "Sir, please. If we could just have a moment of your time. All we want is information about Misfortune."

Kyle turned his razor gaze on her, hand on the doorway. "How about I give you information about the nearest crazy house," he sneered.

Scott frowned and blocked in his other side. "Lidia said you've seen him. We promise it'll be confidential if you tell us what happened." His voice was no longer as welcoming as it had been.

The fire was aimed at him in turn. "How about you kids *leave me alone*."

"You'll never seen us again if you tell us about him," Charlie offered in what she hoped was her most forgiving tone. Her pride wasn't appreciating how Kyle was treating them.

Walled in like a stray dog fleeing from catchers, Kyle edged towards the door and scrutinized them furiously. He stood next to the door and Charlie and Scott joined back together so they could both look at Kyle. "You wanna know what I have to say about Misfortune?" he seethed. "I think he's a fucking hoax. Just because Lidia had delusions, doesn't mean that she, nor you two, get to drag me into this pathetic cry for attention. Now get off my lawn and find something to do with your lives that actually benefits society." His eyes were distracted by something to the side.

While Charlie was discouraged, Scott didn't bat an eye. "That's a pretty poor way to describe an encounter."

Kyle started forward. "Listen here, you little s—" He paused when his eyes were taken by something behind them again.

Charlie came between them with assuaging hands. "We're sorry, Mr. Fortic. I see we've pushed our welcome." *Or lack thereof.* "Thank you for your time. We'll see ourselves out." She elbowed Scott lightly in the direction of her car.

"If you come back here again, I'm calling the cops," said Kyle as his parting gift. His eyes flicked to something behind their heads again and came right back to them just as fast. Charlie looked behind them, but it was just trees, trees, trees.

Charlie pushed Scott towards her car and did her best not to feel dejected. Her resolve withered once they were in the car, and she watched Kyle's silhouette fade into the background.

"That guy was an ass," muttered Scott.

Charlie sighed. "We did kinda show up on his step unannounced."

"That doesn't allow him to insult anyone like that, though."

Charlie agreed vehemently, but it benefited no one to sit on another's rudeness. Although, she didn't miss that odd glance Kyle did. She didn't think he'd be distracted by something. "Do you think he saw Misfortune?"

Scott snapped out of his little fit. "What?"

"He got weird at the end and he kept looking at something behind us. So, I assumed..." She, of all people, could recognize when another was distracted by a supposed ghost.

Scott hummed. "Maybe. Honestly, this has been a pretty weird day. I mean, I've researched Misfortune for years and I *finally* saw him in real life today, and I'm too tired to be excited about it."

Charlie shrugged. "Pretty normal day for me, really."

Scott chuckled. "Seeing Kyle was kind of a waste of time, I'll be honest. But I think we're going at this wrong. I really do believe Misfortune is trying to tell us something."

"About his life?"

"Or maybe his death." And just like that, Scott was back on his roll.

"Yeah," Charlie said quietly as she glanced out her side window and caught the tail end of a skull in the woods. "Maybe you're right."

Chapter 26

Turns out, researching the life of a town ghost story without knowing anything about them prior to their death was harder said than done. Who knew?

Charlie felt like the college's dean as she sat in the office chair. She'd spent so many hours in that chair that it might as well have been hers as a part-time. She'd used up most of her time allotted that day to research Misfortune using the books in the office, every time she closed her eyes, they still continued to go from left to right. It didn't help that she was days into this endeavor, and they didn't allow people into the office on the weekend, so she had to continuously use the time before work. She wished that they could talk to at least *one* of the people that published these books, but about all of them were in the same position as Grant: Deemed crazy or a social outcast.

The most they had to go off of was when the sightings started, which was around forty-some years ago, but they couldn't determine the day because they didn't know if people were lying, or if he died a different day and didn't appear immediately. Long story short, Charlie was losing her marbles with the craziness she'd caught herself into and didn't think Scott was far behind.

Charlie wondered to herself on why Scott could be so upbeat while witnessing something out of a nightmare, but then again, his pastime was researching the ghost, so she supposed it made sense.

Speaking of him, Scott had left to grab her coffee before she had to leave, but she had an idea that it was also to get a break from Helen. And Helen just so happened to work late today, and as the time ticked on that they sat in that room together, she continued to sing practically lewd comments through the door. She thankfully stopped those comments when Scott left.

However, that didn't mean she shut up completely.

"Have you solved who Bigfoot is yet in there?" she called from the main office. She had learned to taunt her ever since Charlie had forced her to swap desk for kicks.

"No, Helen. I haven't." If she responded, maybe Helen would quit her taunts.

"For the last time, it's Mrs. Johnson to you, girl," spat Helen's raggedy voice.

Charlie rolled her eyes. Suddenly, she was missing Grant. He was a lot to deal with, but at least she'd learn from him now. "And my name's not *girl*. It's Charlie."

"Mmm, I'm not calling you that. Sounds too much like a boy's name."

Charlie rubbed at her eyes to give them a break and not yell back something inappropriate like *Bring it up with my parents*. "Thanks for the input, Helen."

"It's Mrs. Johnson!"

Despite herself, Charlie chuckled quietly.

The distraction of Helen only worked for so long because Charlie had to eventually go back to working on Misfortune. Going back to the assumption Misfortune died around forty years ago, was male, and lived in this town, her investigation wasn't going so hot. Yes, it was a shortened category thanks to the characteristics, but this town, Charlie realized, was a lot larger than she originally thought.

She started out first pulling out her computer and researching town deaths around forty-six years ago, because that's around the maximum amount of time Misfortune could've gone back to, and then working up the years from there. She referenced men in their twenties to thirties, assuming Misfortune took on a form in the afterlife that mimicked his living one, but surprise, surprise, since Charlie, nor anybody, had never actually seen Misfortune's face, she didn't really know who she was looking for.

She referenced males with average build and relatively broad shoulders, but that barely cut down the population.

It did, however, help that since the town was close-knit *now*, everyone was tethered by the wrist *then*, so death records were pretty well kept. But still, Charlie hadn't made much more progress that day (similar to all the other days), and by the time she only had a few more minutes, Scott had returned.

"Anything new?" he asked after giving her his coffee and sitting down on the extra chair they'd brought in for him.

Charlie gave her computer's track another mindless scroll. "Well, if Misfortune could give us a hint at who he was, that'd be great, but so far, I'm willing to give up if it means he was some old guy named Bentley Green that worked in carpentry if it means I don't have to look up dead people anymore." She'd picked a random name.

Scott gave a conservative smile. "Sounds wonderful." He leaned back in his chair, thumbing through pages of a different book. "I asked my mom and uncle if they knew anyone of importance that died around that time, but my mom was too young, and my uncle didn't have much of an answer." He sighed and made a face. "Although, it was a really weird way to learn I had an uncle that died around that time."

Charlie leaned on her hand with her elbow on the desk. "Your uncle didn't happen to be within the twenties to thirties range, did he?"

Scott shook his head. "Nah, I think he was like seven or eight, actually. I never even heard about him before because my mom didn't know either."

Charlie sipped from her piping hot coffee, ignoring the blaze on her tongue. She focused on the mild pain when the shadows changed behind Scott. The glimpses of the ghost were beginning to bother her less. And she didn't want to rile up Scott right now. "Your grandparents never told her?"

He shrugged. "My grandparents were already divorced by the time my mom was born, which was also around the time my uncle died. They're long dead. The only thing they left behind was an old bakery my uncle sold, but from what my mom's told me about them, they weren't the best people."

Charlie hummed. "That's too bad."

Scott only made a face as if to say *all good*.

She went back to studying dead people on her computer. "I was really hoping Bentley Green would fit the category for Misfortune, but now that I look at him, he looks nothing like Misfortune."

"Lemme see."

Charlie turned her computer to Scott. As he regarded the picture, he peered at her with a raised eyebrow. "He looks nothing like Misfortune."

Charlie yanked back her computer with a puff of air and a hidden smile. "You think I don't see that now?" She checked the time on the bottom left corner. "I should go."

Scott checked the clock on the wall, too. "Yeah, probably. Make sure to stay safe. From the sound of it, Misfortune really likes to play in the road."

Another shift of the light, this time behind her. She knew Scott saw the inevitable flash of a skull and didn't bother to turn around. His widened eyes told her all she needed to know.

"See ya, Scott." She loaded her arms with the computer and the few books Scott had borrowed to her that his uncle wouldn't miss. She pretended not to notice he didn't send her off with a goodbye, too enraptured with the wall that had now gone back to normal.

Charlie felt herself wither a little bit when Scott got excited about Misfortune that time. While she had been miserable and thinking herself crazy the first and second time she saw Misfortune, Scott had a grin building on his face. He was so, so *happy* to see this ghost, while Charlie had wanted nothing more to do with it.

No, not wither, *jealous*.

It was wrong to feel that way, yes. Her father had always taught her never to want what others had, but it just felt a bit unfair when Misfortune chose *her*, a person who had never heard of the story, over *him*, someone who was obsessed with the story.

Scott was a good person, helping her out of his own kind accord. She knew she shouldn't feel a little resentful of his ease to the situation.

Charlie mentally slapped herself and walked out of the room. Why Misfortune chose her, it didn't matter now. This was a problem for both Charlie, Scott, and all the people like Lidia and Gen. She was looking into this story for herself and those kids, and she was above these petty thoughts.

Charlie had forgotten all about her inessential thought process by the time she reached the car. And for the first time since before she crashed, she drove without Misfortune present on the road.

That ghost showed its abilities when she entered the backroom at work to find George and instead found a raggedy blue bear sitting next to his skull.

Chapter 27

"Hey, Charlie," Martin said near the door.

"What?" Charlie grunted out, busy fixing her hair for the day at her vanity. It was a newly added fixture to her room because she needed something to put in front of her window. Otherwise, all she'd do every time she saw the glass was picture Gen's limp body in Misfortune's arms.

"Aren't you a little old for teddy bears?"

Charlie stopped fussing with her hair to gaze at Martin through the mirror. She didn't need to look at what he what referencing. Sitting at a side table by the vanity was the little blue bear she'd found at work. She'd taken it home because that goat skull she'd found next to told her all she needed to know about it. She'd taken the skull too, but when she got out of her car after getting home yesterday and went to grab the bear and skull, only one item remained.

Undeterred, Charlie took the bear to her room, whereupon further inspection, its left black beaded eye was barely attached and there were years old stains dotting its once aerial blue body, dying it to a color near blacked navy.

What really made the bear stand out, though, was the three jagged lines under the eye. Similar to Misfortune's skull.

Charlie had yet to determine if this little bear was the biggest clue yet, or one of the most disturbing things she'd seen. Her main theory was that this was another hint that the children kidnapped were still alive. Like how Misfortune had wanted to tell her about Gen.

That didn't mean she knew what to do with it.

"Since I found it at a garage sale," she answered, lies about Misfortune coming to her easier.

Reflection Martin leaned against the door and crossed his arms. "And since when do *you* shop at garage sales?"

"Since I saw the sign and got sidetracked."

Martin hummed. "Lemme guess, you went there, found the person selling, got stuck talking to them, and they talked you into taking this little haunted bear."

It hurt that he would've been right, if not for the story being complete fabrication. "You know me so well, it's as if we live together."

Martin made a *phew* gesture near his forehead. "Good thing that'll never happen. Got me worried for a second there."

Charlie chuckled. "You all ready for school? Lunch money? Backpack? Shoes?"

"Actually," he said with a dead face. "I don't have any of them. I think I'll forget my pants, too."

"'Think'? Are you planning on forgetting your pants?"

"Life is full of surprises."

She snorted at that. "Sure, if surprises are called 'counts of public indecency'."

Martin's military face cracked, a blink's worth of a smile. "The police'll have to catch me first."

Charlie rolled her eyes and leaned forward to focus back on her hair. "Get to school. I don't want any calls home because you were streaking down the halls."

She heard him walk away. "Great advice, Grandma! Don't let the dementia make you forget we're playing pool again tonight!"

"Oh, really? Well, I'll have to check with my secretary to make sure I have time."

She heard him enter his room. "Be honest, Char. Nobody likes you enough to hang out with you besides me."

Charlie leaned back from her vanity and swiveled towards the door. "Martin Johnson Kezben," she warned.

Martin poked his head out the door. "Yes? You called my name. Do you need something? I'm busy getting prepared for my school day that may or may not contain pants."

Charlie had to cover her face to stop laughing when he exited the room, fully dressed, but with an extra spare pair of pants in one hand and shoes in the other.

This boy.

She worked on finding Misfortune's name that day, the next, the rest of the week, the weekend included, and the Monday after that.

Nothing. She couldn't find a single person that fit her categories. Not in any of the year's spans. So, when she moved onto women and added a few ages to mix in motion with the search, no face nor body shape really hit the right angle to be Misfortune.

Sure, there was a chance that Misfortune took on a body that didn't represent who he was in life, but that gave her a momentous headache just thinking about it.

Not to mention that little bear had thrown a wrench into their plan's gears. She had showed it to Scott, but he had been just as clueless for its origin. So far, they both agreed it was most likely just another clue like Gen. Charlie decided to expand her research on the kids to see if any of them had a specific teddy bear they liked.

One thing she did appreciate was Martin's like of pool (borderline obsessive, if she was to be honest) because it gave her life a pop in color every so often. Especially when Bill jumped in to play a game, too, oblivious to Martin's sudden grumpiness when he came by. Although Charlie could tell he was warming to their neighbor. Martin only made half the rude comments about Bill nowadays, which was astounding personal growth on his part.

But this didn't mean Martin had emotionally matured enough to go to the store with his sister without a fit.

"Why, pray tell, did I need to come with?" he grumbled as he trailed behind Charlie, who was surveying the store's many aisles with a noisy cart under her palms.

"Because you need to get out of the house."

"I *do* leave the house."

She scoffed. "Going to school and standing around a dimly lit pool table three times a week don't count, Marty."

As she paused to examine a shelf, he put himself in her vision and raised a pristine finger. "Uh, actually, I sit on the bus too. Don't sell me short."

"Would never dream of it," she said sweetly, and tossed a can of beans in the cart, which rattled in protest.

Martin made a face as they continued, and he fell behind her. "Ew. Beans, really?"

Now it was her turn to jut a finger into the air. "Hey, you know what they say about beans."

"Charlie, I swear to god, if you start singing that song, I *will* go to the customer service counter and tell them you're trying to kidnap me."

Charlie peered back at him. "Good. Finally, someone will take you off my hands."

He stuck his tongue out at her.

"Why don't you go to refrigerators and grab the milk for me?" She could tell that he really was feeling a bit restless.

Martin barked a laugh and jogged ahead of the cart, turning around to talk for a moment. "Screw that, I'm going to the toy aisle. I'm getting water balloons, dude."

Whatever made his boat float, Charlie supposed.

She wandered down a couple other aisles, content to mindlessly waste time over truly shopping. It felt nice to take a mental break, even if she had to do it in public while pushing around a can of beans and off-brand cereal she'd picked up earlier.

She turned into the frozen aisle after snatching a few different items to prepare for the days she was too tired to cook when she froze. Down the aisle, holding the door open with his hand buried in the freezer, was Kyle. The lovely man who had ever so kindly talked to her about Misfortune.

He had yet to see her, but Charlie got the idea he didn't want to, ever again. As much as he wasn't fond of her, she wasn't fond of him.

She tried to pull back her car as quietly as possible, but of course, her screeching wheels amplified in sound when she banged the side of the cart against a rack of cheap toys that definitely weren't there a second ago.

Drawn by the sound, Kyle glanced at her while letting the now fogged freezer fall shut with a snap of the resealing suction. They stared at each other, unmoving. Kyle blinked at her, hands full of frozen dinner, as Charlie was mortified that her cart was momentarily stuck. If they were annoyed and irritated with each other the last time they met, everything was just so *awkward* now.

She gave a smile with too many teeth, tugged her cart once, twice, thrice to get it unstuck, dragging the dangling stack of toys along with her, and bolted away.

She kept her head down as she shoved along her jostling cart, recollection of the very inglorious moment playing over in her head. Charlie wasn't one to be embarrassed easily, but it felt weird to see the man that told her she belonged in a psych ward just because she believed in ghosts at the local grocery store. She had the half-mind to rip the stack of cheap toys off the cart and deposit them on another shelf. At least she knew her head with still working right, because then she had the guilty thought that a poor store worker was going to have to deal with the relocation of those toys when it was found in that odd spot.

She figured that she had enough in her cart, and of all times, it was a good time to go, which only left one more problem: Finding Martin. That would be fine; she knew where he was, but the toy aisle was on the side of the store that she had seen Kyle. She'd have to go around where she hoped he still was a retrieve her little brother.

With more effort than she cared to admit, Charlie retraced her steps and peeked around corners to check if the coast was Kyle-free. She did this at every corner there was, and sure, she got stared at by child and parents pivoted away from her, but it was worth it, because she avoided Kyle Fortic in a whole.

Dancing down a few aisles colored blue and pink, she did indeed find Martin in the water balloon section—an aisle two down from where she was. Martin had yet to notice her, too enraptured in pondering the latex. Charlie backed her cart up a few inches to turn in his direction and started down the aisle towards him.

She was one aisle away when a person cut through the front and Charlie, in her haste to reach Martin, rammed her cart right into their midsection. The person grunted hard and held their stomach. Charlie had hit them hard enough that they'd dropped their items. She sputtered an apology and jumped around the cart to retrieve their products for them.

Charlie was bending down to pick up the items when realized too late they were frozen dinners. Too late, she noticed the jeans that stood in front of her look too familiar.

When Charlie stood, she couldn't make eye contact with Kyle as she apologized.

"I'm so, so sorry. I wasn't looking where I was going. Are you okay?"

Kyle grunted in response and tucked his dinners back under his arm, mouth downturned and cheekbones sucked in. Charlie took it as a dismissal, so she began to back up and return to the front of the cart, pretending she wasn't using it as a barrier. She could feel Kyle's gaze on her cheeks.

"You're that girl that showed up at my door last week."

Charlie's eyes flicked to Kyle, but when his gaze was unwavering, she found Martin, who she could see right over Kyle's shoulder. Martin was watching them, but when Charlie tried to silently call him over to save her, the boy had the *audacity* to throw the bird in her direction and twirl off to another aisle.

Kyle peeked over his shoulder when Charlie failed to respond. "Er, yes, that's me. Small world, huh?" she sputtered.

"You and that boy," Kyle added.

Charlie could see Kyle was still harboring some feelings over their last encounter, his slouch in the shoulders and stiffness in his chest giving it away. "Yes, me and Scott." When she paused, the awkwardness gobbled it up and begged for more. "I just wanna say, I'm sorry for how we treated you. It was very rude, and we should've have shown up like that either. I—"

"How is she?" Kyle cut in.

Charlie stopped her apology and looked at him fully. "What?"

Now it was Kyle's turn to find something behind her head very interesting. "Dia." He cleared his throat. "Lidia, I mean. You, uh, said you talked to her. How was she?"

Charlie watched him for a moment. Where was the man that swore at them and cussed out his ex? Charlie had assumed Kyle and Lidia weren't fans of each other, and having a child together made things worse. But now, seeing him without vindication in his features, Kyle looked hollow, sad, almost.

"She's..." Her voice cracked, and she had to start again. "She's holding up, I guess. Not—not the best." It felt weird to talk about Lidia to the father of her child. And yet Charlie, someone who'd only met Lidia once, knew her better than Kyle, apparently.

"The, uh..." These next words she would say would have to be picked out carefully. "*Kidnapping* had taken a toll on her. She's having a hard time." She knew Kyle believed Gen wasn't taken at all, but thought the foster system owned her.

Kyle nodded, still not looking at her. "Thank you. For telling me. I'd been worried about her. Your little stop by reminded me of her, that's why."

Charlie smiled lightly. She was unsure why Kyle felt the need to explain himself to her. When he didn't continue, she nodded at him and pulled her cart away, internally frantic to find Martin and simultaneously hide behind him and whack him for leaving in an inappropriate way.

"I'm sorry."

Charlie paused, cart halfway cleared by Kyle. She peered at him incredulously.

Kyle noticed. "About that day at my house. I was in a bad mood. Laid off from a job and all that." He shrugged. If Charlie knew Kyle better, she would've thought he looked guilty. "It's just that—" He sighed hard. "You two came up to me to start talking about Misfortune. And I—I can't go through all that again."

"What do you mean?" she asked before she knew how insensitive that question was.

Kyle continued anyway, voice turned bitter. "I thought I saw that retched ghost too. Local news heard of it, made it a stupid story, and I people showed up to my fucking job to harass me about it."

"Oh," is all Charlie responded. And now she could see how terribly insensitive they'd been. He must have thought they were another bunch of people there to give him trouble. She knew if she'd been in his place, she'd probably act similar (more or less cussing). "I'm so sorry. We didn't know."

Kyle shrugged as if to say *meh*.

"But," she started, "did you really see Misfortune?"

It was the wrong question, or at least the wrong formatting, because Kyle eyed her out of the corner of his eye.

"I don't mean to be offensive," she amended. "I just—I have the same problem." She spat out the rest like a patient reliving trauma in therapy. "I see him *all the time*. When I drive, when I sleep, when I make supper. That's why we went to go visit Lidia. We were trying to figure out why I see the ghost. She pointed us in your direction when I told her what we were doing."

Kyle inspected her for a second, looking for the lie. He ended up looking away first. "That ghost is what broke us up, you know," he instead said.

Charlie learned to keep her mouth shut, for Kyle would answer in time. "We'd been dating for about a year at that point." He sighed. "Dating's the wrong word. We have a daughter— you can guess why we were together. But me and Dia never really got along that well. Hot and cold, we were. Then I started seeing that damn ghost everywhere, finding goat skulls and seeing it watch me." He shook his head. "I thought I was going crazy, and then there were those people who believed I was. Then Dia got pregnant, and I couldn't handle it anymore."

"Oh," she breathed out. She listened intently, not bothering to point out they had only met once and were in the middle of a grocery store aisle.

"I love my daughter, and I cared for Dia, but that ghost brings no good. And I wasn't lying when I said I don't believe the ghost took my daughter. I don't believe any of those kidnapping stories, but I don't think he's fake either."

Charlie nodded solemnly. "I promise I won't tell anyone the specifics, but what was it like when you saw Misfortune? How many times did you see him?"

Kyle rearranged his hold on his dinners, which were going soggy under his arm. "God, I saw that fucker everywhere I went. What was it that you said? Driving, sleeping, making supper, all that, too. I could barely go anywhere without having a panic attack over seeing that goat skull."

"Did it stop for you?"

"Eventually, yes. It was after I left Lidia. I'd stopped leaving my house at this point. You can imagine why. But when I had to go to the store one day, I'd left the house, and he wasn't there."

"Really?" she gasped.

Kyle shrugged again. "Thought the monster was playing a trick on me. But I never did see him again." Then he blinked and centered his focus on Charlie. "Until you came to my house. He stood behind you, you know. Almost everywhere that you were, he was nearby."

To that, Charlie had no response.

"Look, kid. I don't know what good it does knowing this, but the best thing I can say is that whatever you're doing to get his attention, stop. I only got him off my back because I did everything I could to keep his attention away. I'm sure these visits to people like me don't help. You'll be much happier when you do."

Charlie watched Kyle physically, but mentally, she was creating more pieces for her puzzle.

It made sense, really. If they assumed they were right that Misfortune had unfinished business in life, and he wanted someone living to fix it for him, it *made sense* that Charlie wasn't the first one. All the people that claimed to see the ghost must have been Misfortune's chosen advocate, but when they failed to understand what he wanted, he lost interest and chose someone else. Kyle, for example. And Hell, probably Grant, too.

"Okay," she responded instead. No way was she going to stop this, but she didn't want to explain that to Kyle.

"Okay," he repeated back to her. He began to inch further down the aisle. "You stay safe out there. Stay away from that ghost."

She smiled at him. "You, too."

Charlie watched Kyle leave for a moment before heading in her respective way. Finally, *finally*, they had an answer to why Misfortune chose her. The answer was that he didn't. Specifically, that is. He just chose people randomly and hoped they had it in them to solve his mystery. He'd picked her, and technically Scott, later on by proxy.

Scott. He had to know about this as soon as possible.

But first, she had to find her delinquent brother.

She searched the toy aisle for him again, but found nothing. When she went back through the rest of the store, she had the late mercy of no Kyle, but no Martin either. Sweeping to the front, she found him checking out the cheap kids' toys they sold by the check-outs. She walked up to him with an unimpressed look.

Martin smiled back at her, brandishing two bags of water balloons, and dropping them into her cart with a thud. "Took you long enough. The workers were beginning to think I was lost due to the sheer amount of time I had to spend studying this stuff."

Charlie whacked Martin on the arm, not hard, but definitely not lightly either.

"Ow! Charlie, what the hell?" He pulled his arm back and cradled it.

Charlie rolled her eyes. "Quit with the drama. You know what you did."

"Oh, really?" he mused. "And what, pray tell, did I do to fall out of your good graces, Dear Sister?"

"Marty, you flicked me off and ran away like a child."

His arm must have suddenly healed because he raised it to make his point. "First of all, I am still legally a child, and last I checked, that's how teenagers behave. Second, I was flicking off the guy you got stuck talking to. I could tell you didn't want to, so I was being a supportive brother and told him I didn't like him from behind his back."

"Martin Kezben, that makes absolutely no sense."

"Have you ever thought that maybe it makes sense to everyone but you?"

That earned him another whack.

Back on the hunt to leave the store, Martin (was more or less forced to) unloaded the items in the cart onto the check-out counter, while Charlie dug in her wallet. As she did so, she saw movement out of her eye. Believing it to be Misfortune, she flinched a look, but it was just Kyle, raising a palm in goodbye. Charlie smiled and raised one too, and as he walked away and out the door, Misfortune stood where Kyle had been, face directed at watching Kyle. He stayed like that for a moment, before directing his skull to Charlie.

When he began to take a step back and fall into the shadows the store florescent lights failed to reach, she looked away.

Chapter 28

Despite the reinforcement Kyle gave to their theory, Charlie was stumped at Misfortune's identity. They had little to go off of and had to trust old records. She wished it was like a detective movie, where she and Scott had a list of suspicious people and could track them around inconspicuously. Unlucky for her, they couldn't spy on dead people.

Scott, usually on the joyous spectrum of emotions, was starting to feel their train begin to slow as well. He chittered less when they researched, and he cracked less jokes. Either to focus on his work or because he was losing faith, or both.

Charlie had long ago stopped looking into the bear. She'd found nothing and didn't think families of the stolen kids would appreciate it if she showed up on their doorstep and started asking about their kid's toys (Lidia excluded).

Nowadays, when they sat in the office for two hours and started at books until their eyes went blurry, Charlie brought along the bear. Not for educational purposes, but to just prop it up on a sweaty water bottle and allow it to watch over their work. Why? Because Charlie wanted to.

That, and she was tired of Martin making fun of it. The last time she'd left that bear home, he'd walked into her room and told her it was probably possessed by a little Victorian child. And Charlie, with her now unnecessary excessive knowledge of ghosts, told him that's not how possession works. Martin only shrugged and told her the black, beady eyes don't lie.

Charlie wouldn't be lying if she said she couldn't not think about that conversation every time she got bored with her book and mindlessly stared at the bear instead.

"What are you thinking about?" asked Scott from his side of the desk.

"The bear has some weird eyes," she answered truthfully.

Scott released a puff of air through his nose in amusement. "They are pretty creepy. It's like wherever you go, they're always watching you."

To test the theory, Charlie sat up and swayed back and forth in her seat. Scott was technically right, because the overhead light bounced off the black beads, making a small point of light always follow her.

"Anything new on your side?" she asked when they had been staring at the bear for a few seconds too long.

Scott eased back in his chair and flipped through his book. "Unless you want to count Bentley Green from before, I've got nothing new."

Charlie let a hand flow through her hair. "What could we possibly be missing? We've got the records of names, we've got the years he probably died, we've even got proof of his first sighting." She didn't mention that last one was debatable.

"Not to mention the bear's wonderful moral support," Scott added.

"I don't know what to do. We don't have any indication of who he is. He's only ever given us stuff about the kids and that darn skull."

Scott shrugged. "Maybe he was a goat farmer in life?"

Charlie wasn't in a joking mood. "You know he wasn't." She'd already gone through every dead goat farmer in the area.

Scott deflated a little at her hard tone. "Or maybe he didn't live here? Or Misfortune wasn't male? Or older or younger than we thought?"

Charlie only sighed. It'd taken this long for them to research all the middle-aged men in the town (and some women). She could only imagine how long it would take to do that again for *everyone*.

"Come on, Charlie. Don't lose hope. We'll find him."

She looked back down at her computer and scrolled through an article she'd already gone through a million times in order to not look at Scott. "This isn't a movie, Scott."

"Well, why shouldn't it be? Two super awesome main characters with a crazy problem go on an adventure to solve the impossible. Sounds good to me."

She rolled her eyes, the heavy feeling that had hooked its talons into her chest loosening their hold by a little, initially having been placed there by the lack of new information for Misfortune. "I think you're overselling it just a tad."

"I think I told it perfectly." He grinned back at her.

Footsteps outside the door told them someone was approaching.

"Thanks, Helen. Yes, I'll look into hiring another secretary. No, no, I can't hire someone right now."

They both leaned back to look at the door when it opened. Helen's squawky voice filtered through. Standing in front of them with his hand still on the knob and face directed towards Helen was Dean Manfree.

He sighed at her. "Because I haven't interviewed anyone, Helen. No, I can't just hire someone off the street. Helen—" Another deflated sigh and the dean turned around and shut the door on Helen while she was mid word about how qualifications don't matter. Dean Manfree startled when two sets of eyes stared up at him from his own desk.

He put a hand to his chest. "Goodness, you two scared me."

Charlie made to stand. "I'm sorry, Dean Manfree. We can leave."

He waved her down, unbothered she was sitting in his chair, and slid over to the bookshelf to the right of the door, their left. "No, that's alright. Scott told me you two are here all the time. It was my fault, I forgot."

Scott did jump up. "Do you need help?"

And he, too, was waved away. "Honestly, I just came by to grab my badge from the office out there." He pulled the lanyard off his buttoned shirt for proof. "I only came in here to get away from Helen," he whispered, like she was lurking by the door. Then again, Charlie wouldn't put it past her.

Scott chuckled, which gave Charlie the idea this wasn't the first time this had happened. "Here," he said, reaching for one of their many books spread out on the desk. "Take one of these just in case."

The dean grinned and accepted the book graciously. "Thank you, Scottie. I knew she'd have a fit if I—"

When he stopped with his mouth still open for the next word, Charlie and Scott looked on, waiting for him to continue. When he didn't for a few seconds, they shared a worried look.

"Uncle?" Scott voiced the concern.

Dean Manfree's mouth shut with an audible clamp. The skin around his jaw and eyes now stretched tenser than a ratchet strap. Just when Charlie worried she was watching a man have a heart attack, he spoke. "How do you have that?"

Charlie followed the dean's unwavering stare down the desk, over the books, and up to her water bottle. No, not the bottle, the bear propped up on it. Scott saw it at the same time, and when she looked to him questioningly, he only shrugged.

"Um, I found it?"

"Where?" Charlie had only ever spoken to the dean once before this, but his voice had been soft and kind, so she flinched at his hard tone.

Scott did his best to put his body in between the dean and the bear. "Uncle, what's wrong?"

The dean kept his eyes right where they were like he could see through his nephew. He spoke low. "Where did you get that bear?"

"I... found it at my work."

When the dean didn't move, and the hair on the back of Charlie's neck began to stand, Scott put a hand on his uncle's shoulder. "What's wrong?"

Finally, the dean snapped out his stupor. He looked up at Scott, dazed a little, and backed up, clearing his throat. "My apologies. That was very unprofessional. Please, forgive me."

"Are you okay?" Scott continued at the same time Charlie asked, "Do you know something about this bear?"

It was as if the dean hadn't even heard his nephew. His eyes shot to Charlie. He opened his mouth, and then his eyes cleared, and it snapped back closed for the second time that day.

"Uncle?" Scott prompted.

He swallowed, doing his best to maintain proper posture. He shook his head. "It's nothing, really. There's too low of a chance of them being the same."

"What's the same?"

Dean Manfree eyes were directed at Scott, but it was like his body begged his to gaze his glazed eyes upon the bear again. "Scottie, do you remember when I told you about your other uncle?"

Scott blinked at him. "Yeah?"

The dean smiled weakly at him. "I just... That bear looked a lot like the one he loved. Callen carried it everywhere with him. Again, I'm sorry. I just got caught up in the past when I saw it."

Charlie suppressed a gasp when the lights above them flickered hard, but neither of the men noticed, too consumed by the bear and the story.

"No, we're sorry. We shouldn't have brought it."

The dean swept a hand in Scott's direction. "No, no, you couldn't have known. I was just stuck in memories of my brother." The lights jumped again.

"Mitch! Did you forget to pay the electricity bill?!" screeched Helen from outside.

The dean cleared his throat again, taking a few steps towards the door with a smile that didn't quite reach his eyes. "Truly, forgive me for how I acted. I won't bother you two any longer." He turned to the door, braced himself with a breath and twisted the knob. "Helen, I believe it is *your* job to pay the electricity bill."

"This is why you need to hire another secretary today!"

"Helen, please—" Dean Manfree's response was muffled when the door closed, leaving two sets of bewildered eyes in his wake.

Chapter 29

Charlie had already been at work for three hours now and had yet to get the conversation with the dean out of her teeth. Why would he react like that? It was just a bear, and yet, it was a bear she had received from Misfortune. Did that mean Scott's other uncle was taken by Misfortune? If it did, that opened a whole can of worms she didn't think she could deal with.

First of all, if this was the case, then their timings for when Misfortune was alive were incorrect, which then meant they had been researching those previous time periods for nothing. Second, the period for kidnappings was now also messed up. Previously, they would come in margins, preferred to just random takings. But then that would also be incorrect because this child would have been taken, yet no other child was taken within five years of this.

But the main reason to why none of this made sense was because Scott's family had a body.

As to not upset the dean further, they had turned to looking up the dean's brother online, which led them to the terrible story of his death. Apparently, according to a sketchy news article, the dean and his brother, Callen, ages nine and seven, had come home from school to find their parents arguing at home. Callen had supposedly been in a bad mood that day, so when he saw their parents, he couldn't handle their yelling and ran back outside. The last time Callen was seen alive was when he was caught by a security camera running through alleyways and around streets in a panic. The cameras didn't catch it, but that was how Callen was connected to a hit-and-run. The worst part was that he was first identified by the blue bear he was holding.

It was terribly traumatic, yes, but also had nothing to do with Misfortune.

And yet, the bear fit into the story. It even had pictures that matched their own blue bear, something that made Scott and Charlie shiver.

So, what did it mean? Misfortune obviously wanted her to do something with it, but the bear wasn't like the skull, or Gen. It had no obvious place in the puzzle.

Did Misfortune already have something to do with Callen? Scott's family? None of it made sense. Hence the whole being distracted on the job thing.

"Charlie?"

Charlie perked up from where she'd been staring at the counter for the past ten minutes. She was happy Sam had to work that day, too, because she wouldn't have let Charlie get away with sitting in her head so much.

George was second in line for forcing her to get back to work, too. She smiled conservatively at him where he stood at the other end of the counter. "Yes?"

"Are you alright? You look like my ex-wife every time I start talking," he said with the most honest face.

Charlie shook her head lightly. "Sorry, George. Just zoned out for a little bit."

George nodded along. "Ah, that makes sense—Both for the slowness of the day and my ex-wife."

Charlie looked away when the shadows behind her boss began to shift and twist into a body. "Say, George, do you mind if I do some cleaning instead? It's not like there's too many people looking to check out right now." She gestured to the completely empty store floor.

"Go ahead. Try not to act like my ex-wife though." He laughed at him own joke. *"That'd* be terrible for everyone you'd meet."

Charlie smiled politely because that was the only thing she could think of.

Escaping to the back of the store, Charlie raided the cleaning closest and set to work of avoiding everyone, which included customers and her boss. But if she was honest, only one of them applied.

She contently sanitized shelves and the backrooms. It was easy to find alone time in the employees' lounge when she was the only one on the clock (scheduling still wasn't George's strong suit).

When she got bored in there, she moved onto the bathroom. Was it fun? No. Had it been cleaned before? Also, no. Was she going to do it again anytime soon? Absolutely not.

She backed out of the further of the two stalls in the women's restroom, having finally finished in there, moving to wipe her forehead with her triceps, then thinking better of it. She may not of enjoyed the job, but she also didn't half-ass it.

When Charlie turned around to discard of her filthy gloves, she left out an involuntary gasp. Standing a few feet away between her and the door and a young boy, hair a cross between brown and blond, skin paler than the moon, and eyes unblinking as they bore into Charlie's.

She placed a hand on her chest after cooling down from the fear, then jerked it off and hoped she didn't soil her shirt, too. "Hello," she greeted softly. "Do you need help?" She assumed he had just gotten lost.

Instead of asking for his parents or who she was or anything at all, the boy continued to watch her, unmoving.

Charlie hesitated. Was this something to do with Misfortune? The boy looked familiar, yes, but not like one of the children that were reported to be taken by Misfortune. So what was going on?

"Buddy?" she tried again. As they stared at each other for longer, Charlie noticed more things about the boy, how sunken his cheeks were, how chapped his lips were, how his shoes were too big for his little feet. How his chest didn't move.

Charlie sucked in a breath. This child wasn't alive, but what made her stumble back and catch herself on the stall was realizing why the boy looked familiar. He had the same nose and dule green eyes as the dean and Scott. Callen Manfree was standing in front of her.

She swallowed. It wasn't the first time she'd had to deal with confusing situations that included ghosts, but usually Misfortune was there in some form. Taking a moment to glance around, no skull or black clothing was in sight. When Charlie brought her gaze back to the boy, he was gone. Charlie should've felt relieved. Instead, her heart clenched. Something about Callen made her hair stand up and warning bells go off in her head. Whatever he wanted, he was not like Gen.

She twisted around in the bathroom, searching. She couldn't see him, but she could *feel* him. Her stomach threatened to show Charlie her lunch again, and she felt lightheaded. She was unsure of what was happening, but she was sure of one thing: Callen was *angry*. She could feel the ripples in the room of his fury, his outrage, and his deeply rooted resentment. It was more overwhelming than if Charlie were stand in a room full of smoke.

Her eyes burned, but she clenched her fists, refusing to be cowed by Callen. She turned around for the third time and there he was, standing in the same place as he had been before. Charlie had drifted while seeking him, so they had only two feet between them.

That wasn't why her jaw dropped her and her stomach gave another punch to be freed of the food it held. Peering at her with his green eyes was Callen, but he looked nothing like before. His moon skin was covered in bloody gashes and red rashes. His eyes were bloodshot, and maroon liquid pooled at his feet. The skin on his left cheek was ripped like a tiger had taken a swipe at it. His left arm was bent in the most terrible way, but he didn't seem to notice, as his arms now held items.

He took a step forward and closed the distance between them. Callen may have been half Charlie's size, but he might as well have been as tall as the ceiling. He handed her one of his two items with his broken arm. It was a little bear, blue and red matted its fur, and one of the eyes popping out by a thread. The bear the dean had identified as Callen's. Charlie, obviously out of her right mind, accepted the bear without problem.

The second, and possibly more terrifying one, was the goat skull. *Misfortune's goat skull*, she thought, as if it belonged to someone else. When she reached a hand towards it to grasp it, ignoring the slickness of the bone, Callen's mouth opened. It made no sound, but his lips first touched together and then his purple tongue pushed towards the roof of his mouth. He was saying one word, but Charlie couldn't make it out.

"Time?" she guessed quietly. "Mint? Grab?" She blinked at him, confused. She glanced down at the skull, eyes catching on the jagged lines under the eye, and then back to Callen. She tilted her head. "Mine?"

Callen gave no affirmation to if she was correct, but his mouth ceased movement immediately.

"Yours?" she continued. The skull was Misfortune's, but she wasn't about to argue about that with a dead child. Was he showing her the skull? Charlie guessed so and assumed she wasn't to take it. She let go of the skull and stepped back, cradling the bear.

For the first time, Callen's face showed a hint of emotion. His brows furrowed and his mouth ticked down so fast that a blink would've lasted longer. He followed Charlie's single step and raised the skull higher. "Mine," he mouthed again, and shoved it towards her.

Charlie raised an eyebrow of her own. "Yours," she repeated again but made no move to grab it again.

Callen held it up even higher, but when Charlie still didn't meet it with a hand, he pulled it back to look her deep in the eyes with something that was borderline malicious. Without warning, he thrust it forward at her. Whether he did it purposefully, the horns jut into her stomach and Charlie's breath caught with pain. She dipped forward with the moment. She grunted with wide eyes, hand shaking when she went to pull the two mini knives out, and Callen backed up. It didn't take long for blood to peek through her shirt. An unhappy surprise added to the dousing cold shock she felt when she shot her eyes back to the ghost boy. She hadn't expected him to hurt her. As she gaped at his blank, unfeeling eyes, Charlie felt the creeps and tremors of fear for Callen build in her chest. If she didn't understand what he wanted, would hurt her again? Callen gave no indication to if he felt sorry, just watching her deal with the two little holes in her stomach. He took another step forward and Charlie flinched back, trembling hand plastered over her stomach to hold back the blood and hold back the pain for now—but he didn't care. He took his snapped arm and pointed at the lines under the eye and parted his lips again. At first, Charlie believed he was saying "Mine" again, but his mouth opened once for the first letter, and stayed opened for the rest of the syllable.

"Down? Key? Elf?" she tripped over the words; her legs just as broken in this verbal marathon as his arm, but whatever Callen was saying, she couldn't tell. She nudged the bear into the crook of the elbow of the arm that held the skull. Squeezing the lifeless items to keep her breath even, to not give Callen the hint that her stomach burned with every mindless rise of her chest. She guessed a few words, but with every wrong one, the sick feeling progressed further. Callen had a short temper, and he was already *very, very* angry. In the craziness, Charlie dimly wondered why.

"Pill?" she spat out as her legs threatened to topple her from the persuading of Callen's feelings.

And just like that, the pressure in the room and in her head paused. She watched Callen, who did the same, mouth no longer trying to tell her that word.

He opened it again, at the pace of a snail. But when Charlie looked at him warily, he closed it. Raising his still intact arm, he curled his middle, ring, and pinky finger, using his thumb and forefinger to straighten into a pinching motion.

She blinked at him. "Almost?"

He nodded his head vigorously.

She caught on surprisingly fast. "Will? Ill? Mill?" Callen continuously shook his head to every one. "Till? Quill? Kill?"

His face twitched at the last one, so Charlie paused. "Kill?" she repeated, looking for confirmation. Callen gave none. "Kill. You… were killed."

If Charlie believed his rage from before was terrible, she had no idea what came next was possible. The skull slipped through her gloves fingers and dropped to the ground with a crack. It was only a wave of anger, but it took the energy out of Charlie. Callen wasn't affected. Instead, he slowly ducked his chin and raised it again.

Note to herself, Charlie knew not to bring up a ghost's death to them.

Callen continued to nod, lifting his hand, and pointing at the lines for the second time. He mouthed the word again, but with his nodding and Charlie's booming headache, she just couldn't figure what he was saying.

"I'm sorry," she whispered.

She expected more rage from the child, but instead, the florescent lights that hovered in the bathroom flickered and went out for a moment. She caught flashes of Callen backing away from her. He stood in the middle of the bathroom for one, two, three jumps of light. On the fourth, there was no one there. On the fifth, Misfortune stood in his place, face blanked out from the lack of light, but his black clothing was illuminated enough. On the sixth and final flash, the room emptied itself of both ghosts, and the sickening feeling they brought.

Charlie wavered and dropped on her butt from fear, exhaustion, and just pure bewilderment as her mind processed at what the heck just happened to her.

She clutched the bear under her arm because it was the only thing she had to comfort her. When she went to look at the goat, her hand closed around thin around, and found Misfortune had retrieved his mask during the jumble of the lights.

She lifted her shirt to find to little holes where the horns had punctured her stomach. They had already bruised terribly from the force, but the bleeding had long stopped.

George opened the bathroom door right as she let her shirt fall in a daze. "Looked like you were having a party in here," he greeted sweetly.

"Yeah," she sighed out.

George didn't look bothered in the slightest that his employee was sitting on the ground in his bathroom with dirty gloves and cradling a grimy bear.

"Just came in here to say I needed some help at the front. Feel free to join me when you're ready." He gave her one last grin and then parted with the door. Charlie was too confused and stunned from her conversation with Callen that she wasn't even bothered George had opened with women's restroom without a second thought.

Charlie didn't make a move to stand. Didn't bother wasting the rest of her wanning energy, which was all deviated to purely making her chest rise and fall. Her thoughts overcame the moment, because one thing became abundantly clear: Callen Manfree, Scott's dead uncle of forty years, was, in a way she couldn't begin to comprehend, connected to Misfortune's case.

And beyond that, the tremor-inducing fear she felt for her safety. She'd long stopped worrying for her life once Misfortune turned from a haunter to a familiar face.

He never hurt her.

But Callen did. If they were working together, what would stop them from using more forceful methods to get whatever they wanted?

Chapter 30

Charlie didn't go to work the next day. Nor college either. She wasn't skipping without reason—she was sick. Likely a byproduct of swinging around those nasty gloves without moderation. That, and she was sort of still in a daze from yesterday.

Charlie had thought that, while they still had a lot to learn, she and Scott had a proper line to follow while they investigated Misfortune: Take note of what Lidia and Kyle said and then use their data to research young-to-middle-aged men from forty years ago.

Then, like a spear thrown from the opposite boat, Callen Manfree shows up and throws all of that off the deck.

What on Earth did he have to do with Misfortune? Why was he so mad? What was he trying to say? And even though it didn't connect to Misfortune, who killed him?

Would he hurt her again?

The only thing Charlie had put together with Callen and Misfortune was that Callen happened to die around the time they had originally thought Misfortune first appeared. But with their influx of theories, Charlie had no clue when Misfortune first appeared was any more.

Maybe it was a blessing that she contracted a sickness from those gloves. Working at her job and on schoolwork and Misfortune's case was taking a toll on her.

With her mind in a jumble, Charlie did her best to remember all the things she *knew* about this ghost business.

First, Misfortune was dead.

Second, his time of death was no less than forty years ago. Possible to be much before.

Third, he was not Bentley Green, nor any other male within the previously assumed time period.

Fourth, something either happened to him during his life or death, and Charlie was randomly selected to figure it out.

Fifth, Misfortune either couldn't talk, or preferred not to.

Sixth, Gen was alive.

Seventh, Callen was not.

Eighth, Callen can, and perhaps will, hurt her.

Ninth, Callen was connected to Misfortune.

Tenth, Charlie was losing her marbles.

Okay, maybe this list wasn't helping her as much as she thought it would. Then again, maybe going crazy was a byproduct of being holed up in her room all day, per 'guidance' from Martin ("If you infect me with your nasty germs, I *will* move in with Bill," he'd said when she'd told him that morning). To prevent her brother's threatened abandonment, she stayed in her room. *You couldn't do that. You're still in school*, she'd told him. *I'm a legal adult*, he'd snickered, *you couldn't stop me.*

One mercy she had was that she had the house to herself. It wasn't that she didn't enjoy Sam or Scott or Martin (debatable). She meant it as in there were no ghosts in her room. For the first time in quite a few weeks, Charlie woke up, stayed awake for longer than an hour, and didn't see Misfortune. No shifting of shadows, no flickering of lights, no skull lying on her bedside table.

It gave her a prescription of weird comfort and terrible foreboding.

Did she do something wrong? Did she handle Callen's situation wrong, and Misfortune didn't like that? Did she hallucinate the entire encounter? No, she wasn't going to fall back into *that* spiral again.

Besides, she couldn't have. The two angry welts on her stomach surrounded with high tides of black bruises made for compelling proof.

Long story short, as she had previously assumed, they were at an impasse. Leaving Charlie to silently worry for her safety.

Solution? Don't think about it until Misfortune eventually shows up again and forces her thought back to the matter.

So, doing her best to pivot away from the little blue bear propped up on her vanity, she called Sam, chatted with her until she had to pry herself away from the phone to work her shift. Next, she dialed Aunt Mary and checked up on her. She then reluctantly followed that up with one to her mother, who was, unsurprisingly, drunk. That phone call didn't last long.

By the time she heard Martin come banging through the front door, she had dialed herself out and was now rereading a book she used to be obsessed with as a teenager.

"Haveth the maid still locked in her chambers?" Martin called from the stairs, voice muffled from the walls.

She wished he could hear her scoff. "I'm not going to get you sick, drama queen. You can go to your room."

"Better being safe than sorry, you fart," she heard him mutter when the stomping on the steps continued. He acted like she had the plague. She had a runny nose and a cough.

"Did you call me a fart?" she said exasperatedly. "Aren't you a little old for such insults?"

"Would you rather I call you something else?"

"Martin Kezben, you are lucky I'm staying in my room right now."

He laughed, hiccups echoing near the little walls of the bathroom. "God, trust me, I know I am."

"Little sh—"

"What was that?"

"Nothing, dear brother," she crooned. "I just hope you had a good day. Oh, by the way, I may or may not have just used the bathroom."

No response came, but she did hear hurried steps run from the bathroom and end at the bottom of the stairs in a matter of two seconds.

The call of attention back to Misfortune came in the form of the bear being tossed off her vanity and onto her book. Charlie lifted her book so the bear could slide off her and onto her bed comforter. She glanced in her vanity's direction, but there was no evidence of Misfortune or Callen.

She sighed. Of all things, she was inconvenienced, but one of the ghosts haunting her probably was fed up with her avoidance.

But she was alive, and they were dead. This was *her* house. So, she did the sensible thing. She tossed the bear back onto the vanity and went back to skimming over the ink on her page.

The bear landed with a thud back on the book, beads in its butt settling loudly.

Charlie frowned, not bothering to look up, and threw the bear off the bed, uncaring of where it landed.

A second later, the bear smacked her upside the head.

"Seriously?" she grunted, examining the room for the culprit. But, of course, when the room was empty. Charlie wasn't even surprised. After yesterday, she didn't think she had the ability anymore.

She stopped procrastinating when the bulb in her bedside lamp began to buzz obnoxiously loudly.

"Excessive much?" she wondered at the lamp when it stopped shaking. She waited for another fit to come, but nothing happened.

Charlie shook her head and looked down at the bear, which laid spread eagle onto of her forgotten book. Instead of tossing herself into research immediately, she picked up the bear gently and gazed at it. She was reminded of the dull pain on the skin on her stomach, but otherwise, the bear stumped her.

She assumed that this bear was like Callen—connected to both ghosts. She had first found it next to Misfortune's skull, but that article had told her this bear was found next to Callen's dead body. Sure, she felt a little queasy thumbing over the threads with she now knew were matted with a child's blood, but she wasn't going to think about that.

Another question to add to her over filling pile was that she didn't know why she still needed it.

She had already put together that Callen and Misfortune were working together, so now what? Was the bear supposed to signify something else about the other stolen kids, or something else entirely?

To kick start her thought process, Charlie tossed the bear in the air by a few inches and caught it easily. She used the weight of the beads to counter the unbalance of the bear to cast it further towards the ceiling. Over and over, she slung it upward, eyes tracking its movements so she could tell her hand where to place itself so she caught it every time.

Around the twenty-third toss, she threw it a little too high into the air, and when she snatched it to prevent further decent, she did so by its face. She had used quite a bit of force when doing so too, which led to the eye that had been dangling on loosely to snapping and falling off.

Charlie stopped and reached for it, but the shift on her mattress made it sink towards the side, which then caused the eye to fall off and land on the ground buried somewhere like an ant in tall grass.

Charlie mentally berated herself. Not only was it disrespectful to the ghosts that could obviously cause her harm, but she also now had to find the damned eye and fix it.

She left her book where it was and gripped the bear in her right hand as she slunk down to the floor. She gave the carpet a curtsy glance over, but she could already tell this was going to be a nightmare. She passed a hand over the knotted flooring, but the only thing she got from this was knowledge that she needed to vacuum more often.

Maybe it drifted under her bed? Charlie backed up and moved to her knees and elbows to peer under her bed. She only learned even further that cleaning was a very important part of owning a house.

She sat back on her hunches, and grasped the bear between both her hands, its little arms falling over the skin that connected her thumb to her forefinger.

A hand appeared between her eyes and the bear.

"Oh, thanks, Martin," she said automatically, way before her mind could comprehend that she hadn't heard her door open. The hand was half the size of her brothers, had white skin, and was covered in blood.

She sucked in a breath and shot her head up to Callen, who was kneeling next to her, so close she probably would've felt his body heat if he was alive.

She froze. Peering at Callen's face so near hers made her inwardly cringe; all she could think of was the guiltless way he'd harmed her. Callen didn't care about her. He wanted to use her, even if the reason was above her. A hand strayed to her healing stomach, the memory of being thrusted back when the horns stabbed her blazing in her mind. And his face. Child he may be, it horribly disfigured. It was difficult not to focus on the skin on his left cheek that wasn't connected to his face.

Wait.

Charlie gripped the bear tighter and made no move to retrieve the bead. Her realization of what she had missed sucking her breath away.

Callen didn't catch onto what she was going through, because he shoved the bead toward her in the classic inpatient style of a child. Charlie flinched hard, seeing the skull in his hands again with in an off-timed blink.

Charlie's lungs begged her to breathe. And when she did, needles picked at her sinuses. This didn't stop her from taking the bear in her left hand and raising it up to Callen's face. Shivering from her personally offense to get closer to him. She held the toy right under the ghost's chin, careful not to touch him.

Callen watched her like he was held captive by her eyes. When his own hand lowed with the bead, she knew he was making the same connection as her.

Comparing the bear to Callen's face, Charlie could see they both had those three terrible lines under their left eye, but that wasn't what made her heart stop. It was the fact that not only did they had the lines, but she knew that Misfortune's skull had the same print.

"Oh my God." It was a whisper, but her voice broke on every single syllable. In the shock of what was going on, she didn't miss that. Had Callen been alive, her breath should've shuffled his unruly hair.

In a blink, Callen was gone, replaced by Misfortune. He was in the smaller ghost's place, but because he was much taller, he sat on his heels, ducking his head. It did the trick, because Charlie was able to equally line up the bear to his face without moving her hand. Sure enough, it matched what she had suddenly discovered.

Charlie's lips wavered as she opened them and peered into the hazy green eyes that peeked out through the skull's holes, only able to be witnessed due to their proximity.

"You're the same person."

Chapter 31

If Charlie hadn't learned from Brandon Fredricks that she should always obey the traffic law no matter what, her wheels wouldn't have even been touching the pavement as she raced down the highway towards her college.

She had wasted no time bolting out of her room, unbothered that she was still in the clothes she slipped in or Martin's confusion, and landed in her car, fusing herself to the gas pedal. All the while her left hand gripped the bear in a vice so tight it wouldn't have been able to breathe if it needed air.

Her free hand was shaking in the wheel. Not out of fear, but of what she now knew. It was crazy, impossible, and true at once.

She reached her college's parking lot without slowing down, which caused her to slam into the wheel when she jammed her foot onto the brake. She didn't even notice.

Charlie didn't remember how she got to the office, but one second she was opening her car door and the next she was frantically asking Helen, who was cleaning up for the early evening, where Scott was.

"I may be a secretary, but I'm not his," she responded in turn. She didn't bother to look up from her desk.

"Helen, please, I need your help," Charlie begged.

Helen said, "I think you can help yourself out the door."

"Please, Helen—"

"Mrs. Johnson," Helen corrected.

"Do you have an idea of where he is?"

Helen finally brought her eyes to Charlie. "I have an idea where security is, and I'm feeling very inclined to give them a call."

Charlie was too distraught to be bothered by Helen's usual personality. "Charlie?"

She whipped around to the door, where Scott stood, hands brimming with his and Helen's usual coffee, and his face painted in confusion.

"Scott, it's Callen!" She rushed to him immediately.

"Callen's what?" He cocked his head, unbothered and ignorant to the breakthrough.

"I'm calling security," Helen mumbled. "She's drunk."

"Hold on, Helen." Scott set down both coffees on her desk and met Charlie halfway. "Callen? As in my uncle? What about him?"

"He's who we were looking for," she shot out. "*He's* Misfortune."

For the first time since coming to him for help, Scott was actually baffled. "I'm sorry, what?" he sputtered, lifting a hand. Either to calm her, himself, or perhaps both.

"Scott, either you get her out of here or I call security," Helen huffed in the back, oblivious of the momentous moment.

"*Give us a second.*" Charlie didn't know if it was a good thing that Scott still wasn't coming to his senses, because she'd also never heard him snap at Helen.

"Come on," he said much quieter. "Let's go to the office. You can explain in there." He used his still raised hand to gesture towards the room.

Again, Charlie was standing in one place and a blink later, she was in another. As soon as Scott closed the door, it all came spilling out.

"So when I was cleaning the bathroom at work yesterday, Callen appeared—"

"Wait, *Callen*? As in, my uncle? *He appeared*?"

"Yes," Charlie said in a huff, beginning to pace. "Just give me a second to explain. So, then he appears, and had injuries, ones I assumed killed him.

He had Misfortune's skull and the bear with him, too." She lifted the bear, which she still gripped for effect. "He gives me the bear, but when he gives me the mask, he said 'Mine.' Which then I didn't understand." She sucked in a breath, forgetting to breathe, her words jumbled to near nonsense. "But now I realize he was telling me the mask, which is Misfortune's, is also *his*. Which is the first reason he and Misfortune are the same person.

"Second, he had three lines under his left eye. Look." She held the bear higher. "So does the bear!"

"And so does Misfortune," Scott finished for her, voice barely above a whisper.

"Yeah," Charlie said breathily, suddenly unknowing what to say next. Scott's paling face making her panic. *Scott didn't react badly to anything. So why this?*

Scott breathed out of his mouth as he stumbled around her and the desk, dropping into his living uncle's chair. "How is this possible?"

"I don't know, but everything about the past few weeks feels a little unbelievable, too. But Scott," he looked up at her with his head leaning on a hand when she paused. "This isn't a ghost mystery anymore. Your uncle was in a hit and run. This is about a murder."

Scott did his best to compose himself. Charlie could see his fragments fusing back together. "That's want he wants people to solve, right? Who killed him?"

She nodded. "I'd assume so. When I talked to him, he was terribly angry. I wonder if that's why he has moved on or whatever. He's too resentful about what happened to him."

Scott took a composing breath, and he was back to about eighty percent of his usual personality. "But why is he a grown man? Why does he wear a mask?" He paused, eyes sharpening. "Why didn't he go to my uncle? Or my mom? Or *me*? He obviously still has his memories of when he was alive, so why wouldn't he go to people he knew?"

Charlie could only shrug. "Your guess is as good as mine. Maybe he chose strangers that be thought would be the best, and your family didn't fit?"

199

"Well, then why did he pick Kyle? He obviously didn't have the capabilities to solve anything. Why not pick an officer that worked on his murder?"

Charlie shook her head. "I don't know."

They paused to sit in their own heads, mulling over the newly added questions. Sure, they'd solved one of the biggest questions, but they'd multiplied by tenfold.

"Did he say anything else when you saw him? Give you anything else?"

Charlie mentally sunk down. "He said told me something else, but he only mouthed words, so I couldn't make out what it was."

Scott nodded mindlessly. "You know, I gotta be honest. Of all the people I expected you to say was Misfortune, Callen wasn't even on the table."

Charlie tried to laugh, but just didn't feel up to it. "What do we do now? Solve a cold case from forty years ago? Convict the person that killed Callen and, I don't know, set him free?"

Scott opened his mouth to answer, but the flickering of the lights and churning of the shadows beat him to the punch.

"I think we have our answer," Scott said solemnly as they peered at the lights conspicuously.

And with the connection between Misfortune and Callen made, Charlie suddenly had a terrible thought.

If the two were one, what was stopping *either* of them from harming her?

Chapter 32

Solving a murder, it turns out, is a lot harder than the movies make it out to be. Not to mention an unsolved one from forty years ago that the town buried in sorrow it placed in itself rather than the family that lost the child.

Charlie could barely find any background information on Callen save the one article she used to reference his face to Scott's when she first met him. Sure, she found one newspaper that had details, but most of the paragraphs were filled with ads, and the part that actually held information held both old news they already knew and other parents that didn't even know the Manfree's worrying about themselves. Charlie was getting really tired of rereading quotes like, "We were so scared when we heard the news. My husband and I worried for our son. What if the monster that killed the Manfree boy saw ours?"

And she thought Martin was dramatic.

She worked relentlessly with Scott like they had done for the past weeks, but it was like everything they did was held down by weights. The entire ordeal swapped from being a crazy ghost story to a crazy ghost story with personal attachment. Charlie didn't think that knowing Callen was the ghost would shake Scott so much, but she supposed if she found out the ghost was Aunt Mary, she'd have been just as baffled.

They decided not to include Scott's family. Mainly because the only person that was still alive that knew Callen was the dean, and just from the one interaction they had with him that included Callen, it was obvious he wouldn't be able to deal with it properly.

And surprise, surprise, Charlie and Scott hit the end of the road for the eighth time. Charlie had hoped that her confusion would bleed into Misfortune's (Callen's?) conscious, and he would give her a hint like the other times. Instead, Misfortune suddenly formed an aversion to her. He didn't show up, not even a jump of electricity or anything, ever since she found out his identity.

Callen's child ghost, however, didn't have that problem. He'd stalk her from corners and push her books off her desk, but he was more into acting like a poltergeist than handing over anymore tips. The only thing she got from him that meant something to the case was that after she found out who he was, the little blue bear disappeared. Looks like its only purpose was to inform her of who he was.

When neither form of Callen seemed inclined to assist her, Charlie decided that maybe taking a break from the case would do her good. Scott scrambled to join her on that boat when she proposed it. Which led to Charlie joining him while retrieving and Helen's coffee run. That led to Helen peering at her down her nose when Charlie produced her coffee at her desk instead of Scott. Which then led to Charlie secretly stick her tongue out at the older woman. Helen's gasp was so sharp, Charlie thought she had induced a heart attack.

They went back to work, yes, but it produced nothing. And when Charlie went to leave, she knew she wasn't the only one disheartened over their lack of progress. Sure, in the past, they'd gotten stuck, but they always managed to remove their tires from the dirt in some wacky way or other. After another week, it became obvious this wasn't going to happen.

Charlie's disappointment must have started to bleed into her personal life because Bill hailed her down after she parked her car outside her house.

Charlie, head down and bag in her arms, snapped up at the call of her name and found Bill standing next to one of his many cars. One hand filled with a polishing rag and the other raised in greeting. "Oh, hi, Bill!" she called back. "How are you doing?"

He lowered his arm to throw in forward. "You know me, Charlie. I'm always in a good mood."

She smiled and stepped closer to hear him better. "I'd love to be like that. Just always happy about everything."

Bill beamed at her. "Looks to me like you're nearly there." Before Charlie could offer her polite thank-you and escape, Bill sobered. "I don't mean to be disrespectful or probing, but are *you* alright?"

Charlie's mouth tipped down. "What do you mean?"

Bill leaned off his car to give her his full attention. "It just seems like you've been sad lately. I worried something was wrong is all."

Charlie felt her chest buzz. It'd been a while since she'd had a male figure bear concern for her. "Sorry, Bill. Just some stuff going on that isn't working out. I didn't know I'd made it so obvious."

Bill chuckled. "No, I'm sorry. I was just thinking the worst and my old heart can't take that." He calmed. "Would you like to come in for tea?" He raised a hand like someone might be listening in. "I tried my hand at a pie today to change things up. Not too bad, if I do say so myself. You can have some."

Charlie glanced at her own house. Martin was home, she knew, so she didn't have to worry about his arrival. She was still in her work clothes, but she didn't think Bill was the type of person to mind.

She must have hesitated too long because Bill continued. "It's alright if you have things going on. I should have been more mindful to remember you have a life, too."

"No," she said hurriedly, turning back to him. "I'd love to come over. Lemme just drop my bag off."

With a short detour to her door to change shoes, shuck her bag to a living room chair, yell she was home for Martin's sake, Charlie was soon back out and crossing over to Bill's car-covered driveway. "Who's this one?" she asked, siding up next to the car Bill had been polishing.

Bill must not have enough people in his life that asked about his beloved cars, because he slapped a hand on the hood and beamed at it with a pride like a parent watching their child graduate. "This one's Walter. Named after my dad. It was the first one I bought myself after he gave me the collection."

"Aw, Bill, that's so sweet."

Bill brushed off her compliment with another run of his hand, but his pleased smile gave away his true feelings. He walked back towards his house and waved her on. "Enough about me and my obsession. Let's go inside before the pie gets cold."

Charlie had never been inside of Bill's house, nor Bill in hers, but it was exactly as she pictured. His house was a copy of hers but swapped in the mirror. That's where the resemblance ended. The living room would've made a great example room of peak furniture style of the '80s, and all along the stairs wall were pictures of Bill and others of who Charlie could imagine was his expansive family over the years. The rest of the wall space was either covered in curtains that mimicked bus seat designs and many, many framed pictures of cars over the years.

"You have a seat. I'll only be minute."

Bill rushed off while Charlie took the closest seat to the door: A large chair with swirls and squares of brown and felt like an elementary school carpet and engulfed her when she sat down.

"Here we are." Bill joined her by sinking into the couch opposite her and setting a plate of pie in front of her on the coffee table that separated them. "Pecan, if that's okay."

"My favorite," she said, and picked up the plate. The fork that was wedged under the pie made a clinking noise as she pulled it out and dug in. And sweet baby Jesus, Charlie could never have another pie that tasted any better.

"Bill, I don't think I'll ever understand why you never became a baker," she said after her third mouthful.

Bill chuckled again, but it wasn't as happy as usual. "I wanted to, actually. My mother though," he sighed another chuckle. "She didn't think it appropriate for a boy to be in the kitchen instead of playing football or the likes. I tried my hand at baking to spite her anyway, but after some... complications, I moved to business." He ended the sentence with his eyes glossed over and a million miles away. Charlie knew that face because it was one she had made many times before.

"I'm sorry that you had to quit, really. I'm sure giving up your passion was a rough decision."

Bill shrugged. "It wasn't a decision, really. More of—I did what I had to do."

Charlie nodded along. She made to respond, but when the light twisted sickly in the far corner behind the couch, she stopped.

When Callen appeared, Charlie expected him to stare at her like Misfortune did. Instead, Charlie found he had no interest in her at all. His eyes were directed at Bill, gaze encompassing the most hatred and fury she had ever seen a child produce. The air shot down in temperature immediately after his appearance, and Charlie swore she could see her breath materialize in front of her.

"Darn AC. I've had problems with that thing ever since moving here." Bill huffed as he stood, weathered knees cracking. "I'll fix it, just give me a second." He grumbled as he waddled over to a little white box on the wall the stairs shared with the main room.

Charlie peeked back at Callen to see if he would relent anytime soon, but his scorn had only grown. His mouth opened and closed as if he couldn't breathe from his building disdain.

"Darn letters are so small," he huffed and leaned closer. "Hmm, that's odd. The air's not on."

Charlie dared another look at Callen, expecting a fire poker to be leveraged at Bill or something else horrific, but instead he directed his attention at her. His anger was predominant, so much that Charlie could barely breathe. His eyes gaped into hers and his arm was raised, arm ramrod straight as it directed itself towards Bill and a single raised finger solidifying. He was pointing at the old man's back.

When Charlie did nothing, Callen did the first thing that looked very human: His widened his eyes and jut his finger harder at Bill, mouth open in a way Charlie just didn't understand.

When Charlie shrugged guiltily, extremely unsure of what was going on, Callen actually flinched back. He watched her for a second longer before his arm dropped back to his side. Something that should've made a thump should he had been alive.

"What about him?" she mouthed at Callen, who continued to watch her with what she assumed was disbelief and disappointment. Charlie was missing something, and this something was apparently huge.

Callen didn't answer. He closed his eyes and his fists balled themselves with enough pressure that they began to shape. His face became almost pained as Bill's lightbulbs started to flicker and Misfortune, clad in all his black, appeared in Callen's place.

Charlie stared, appalled, while Bill wasn't bothered in the slightest by the light problems. "Don't worry about that. They do that occasionally."

"All good," she somehow managed, still transfixed on Misfortune. What made her attention catch this time was that, staring at the gate of Misfortune, she didn't think he and Callen were truly the same. Yes, she believed they were the same *person*, but not the same *ghost*. Like if someone used a time machine and met their past-self. Sure, they had the same mind and name, but their bodies were different, and so were their minds.

If that meant Misfortune was Callen in another form, why *was* he in another form?

Like a blink, Callen was back, and so was his loathing. This time, it was directed at Charlie. No metal or mesh in the world could've prevented the searing of his stare. Callen reared up, and like a cat going to pounce, he pushed out off the ground and lunged at her.

"Alright, I think that should do it." Bill knocked on the box on the wall, which got Charlie's attention. She sucked in a breath when she looked back and nothing was in the corner. "*Think*, because I have no clue how to use that thing," he sighed out as he sat back down. "Now, where were we?"

Charlie panicked. She stood from the chair, which gave a slight fight to let her go, wanting to forever keep her in the depth of its fluffiness. She pushed her half-eaten pie onto the coffee table. "I'm so sorry, Bill. I really have to go. I'm really sorry for the abruptness." Callen had been trying to tell her something, and whether it had to do with the word, she couldn't understand in the bathroom, it was detrimental enough to him that it had to be important to the case.

Bill waved her on. "No, my bad. I pretty much forced you over here. You get going. How about I give you the recipe for the pie next time we see each other?"

She nodded and inched towards the door. "Yes. Of course. I look forward to it. Thank you for having me over. Sorry, again."

Bill smiled at her. "Everything's good. You know where to find me." His teeth and hand waving her away were the last thing she saw when she slammed his front door.

As Charlie scrambled over to her own house, she felt eyes on the back of her neck. Craning upwards, she saw the movement in one of Bill's upstairs windows. Peering down on her like Rapunzel in her castle, Misfortune stood there. His horns shined in the light and his gloved hand raised in a parting wave. And somehow, Charlie knew she was closer than further from the truth than ever.

Chapter 33

"That is the weirdest game I have *ever* heard of," Sam said in exasperation after Martin had given her the rundown of 'If You Had.'

Martin only shrugged. "Hey, people thought drag was weird when it first started."

"Marty, please don't compare an art form to an old game Dad taught us as kids," Charlie said from behind her menu. They sat at a booth of the diner Scott worked at, Charlie on the outside with Sam next to her and Martin across. She wished Scott had work off today like she and Sam did, but he was required at his other store job today. She supposed it didn't really matter; she wasn't here mentally. Ever since Callen's outburst as Bill's a few days ago, Charlie hadn't been able to keep her mind off it. That was what led to her rereading the menu four times and still had yet to soak up any of the words.

"How's the book going? Did the hero win?" Martin poked at the back of the menu, jumbling the words further, which caused Charlie to throw it down with a huff, the metal ringed back clinking on the table.

"Marty, please," she warned. Another byproduct of noting being able to wander off the topic of Callen in her head was a lack of sleep.

"Don't get mad at me for being an attentive brother," Martin tutted, but backed off.

"How's work been, Sam?" Charlie instead said. She felt bad that they met at her job more often than not. That, and to be in the present and not back at Bill's house and watch his back as he fiddled with the AC.

Sam scoffed. "You know how it is. Boring to the tenth power."

"Who the hell still says that?" Martin mumbled from his side of the table. He was met with a very unfriendly kick from Charlie.

"One thing I am grateful for though," she jutted a finger in the air, "is no more Grant. These past weeks have been very peaceful without him harassing customers."

"He's still in jail?" Sure, Grant was a little on the odd side, but ever since that night she'd run her car off the road, she'd become a tad more empathetic with the old man. She didn't think he deserved a punishment *that* harsh.

"Nah," Sam continued, unconcerned. "They didn't do much to him, but he is banned from the shop." Sam chuckled. "It took my boss realizing that he never brought anything to finally kick him out."

"Well, what happened to him, then?"

Sam peered over at her, looking confused as to why Charlie cared about a stranger. "I don't know, probably at a homeless shelter or something. Hopefully a psych ward, or somewhere that will make him realize that dumb Misfortune ghost isn't real. Either way, best thing that ever happened to me."

Charlie tried to hide her flinch as Sam talked about the psych ward. It was hard not to feel like Sam was calling her crazy when she spoke. Technically, she and Grant were in the same boat. When she picked up her menu again to bury herself with it, she caught Martin's eye over the page. She looked away first.

"One thing I don't like," Sam continued, obvious to Charlie. "Is that now my boss makes me check the security footage every morning to make sure Grant didn't come back during the night."

"*Every* morning?" Martin prompted. "Wouldn't that take a while? Hours of footage and all that?"

Sam snickered and leaned in close. "It *should*. Until I found the fast-forward button. Sure, I don't really know if he comes back during the night, but at least I don't waste my time and my boss thinks I watched it."

Like villains conversing over a map of the city, they tittered together. Charlie would've joined in if Sam hadn't given her an idea. One that seemed took over her mind so viciously that when Martin and Sam began to play 'If You Had,' she couldn't appreciate his answer to his question of having many drag queens to his disposal (to spite Charlie, he said they'd all have to play this game with him. When probed further, he confirmed that this game can be normalized in society just like the many ways or art).

The idea Charlie stumbled upon just might, if they used it right, give them the answer of who Callen's murderer was.

"Do you think the library will let us look at their security footage?" Charlie rushed out before she had even made it into the office.

Scott jumped from his chair where he'd been mindlessly searching another Misfortune book. He turned back to her. "What?"

Charlie dropped her bag on the desk with a thump and sank into her own chair fast enough air rushed out the bottom. "The library," she repeated. "Do you think they'll let us look at their old security tapes?"

"Um, first of all, no? Second, why would we what to?"

Charlie, ever prepared since yesterday when she got the idea, pulled out her computer, popped the lid, and turned it towards Scott, screen already lit up with a map of the town. She leaned around it so she could see too. "Look." She separated her fingers on the trackpad to zoom in on the street Callen was killed on. The screen showed four roads surrounding a block, with her mouse on the southernmost one: Callen's place of death. "This is where Callen died, yeah?"

Scott swapped his eyes between the screen and her, obviously oblivious to what she was so excited about. "Okay?"

"But that's not what it looked like when he died!" She jumped to a different tab. Another map, same area, but the road layout was different. The southern road Callen died on no longer connected to the east and west roads that went north. Instead, it was a dead end that ended to the far west with a roundabout to turn around. The road drove off to the far east and off the screen. "It was under construction to what it looks like today when it happened."

She pointed frantically at one of the little squares that sat off the circular dead end, nail clacking on the screen. "The library would be too far away to catch the hit and run, but it probably caught the car turning around either before or after it happened."

Scott didn't look as hopeful as her. "I guess so. But, Charlie, if the library had the chance of catching the car that killed Callen, wouldn't the police, you know, have already checked with them?"

That rained on Charlie's parade a tad. "Maybe, but I was thinking that because that part of town had remnants of construction, they didn't check with every place because of that."

Scott nodded but sat back, dismissing her need for the computer. "It's a good idea, Charlie, really. But we don't even know if they *had* a camera system then. And even if they did, there is a very high chance they're not going to just *let* us look at it without proper identification or reason."

She'd thought of that, yes, but she also didn't dwell on it for a while. "Doesn't hurt to check though, does it?" She smiled hopefully, praying this would sway Scott.

He softened, but the smile didn't do its job. "I don't want to be condescending but think about it realistically. Remember Lidia? Kyle? Those unannounced visits for personal information didn't work out so well."

Charlie felt her defenses rise. "No offense, but those were terrible examples. We were able to get information from both of them with only minimal problems."

"Minimal?" Scott prompted with a quirked eyebrow.

"More or less," she amended with a shrug. It may have been childish to get defensive, but she'd put work into this idea, and it wasn't like Scott was lining up anything better. She told him as much so (albeit with kinder word choice).

"*I know*, Charlie. Trust me, I know." He sighed, and Charlie was beginning to think Scott was taking the news about Callen worse than she thought, if he was still in a mood even after all these days later. He ran a hand down his face. "I just, I wish we could have a *plan* for these things, you know? Being civil about things, not just barging in and asking for information."

Where Scott pulled back, Charlie pushed forward. "Then we make a plan. We—and if you don't want to—I can go to the library, ask for the footage if they have it. Take it if they give it, leave if they deny." She sat up and made her palms face the ceiling. "Simple as that. If it doesn't work out, it doesn't work out." Her smile grew as she ducked her head towards him. "But if it *does* work out..."

Scott sighed, seeing what she was doing, but he didn't stop her. Charlie's smile matured to full size as she watched the gears behind his eyes turn. "We find out who killed my uncle," he finished.

"That's the plan," she affirmed.

Finally, her smile tipped the ball. "This is some Sherlock crap, you know that, right? Not to mention the craziness of everything." Scott may have still been sitting on the fence, but he couldn't help but peek out a smile, too.

"Whatever gets us closer to the end."

Scott swallowed and looked away, both reminded of what, under all the questions and ghosts and skulls, their objective was. They waited for the lights to blink in confirmation from the ghosts and were not disappointed.

Chapter 34

"You're joking, right?"

"Martin, for the last time, I'm *just* going to the library," Charlie huffed into the phone.

"First of all, you would rather move back in with Aunt Mary than read *new* books for *fun*. Second, I *know* your pretty boy has to be in the passenger seat, because otherwise you wouldn't even think of getting a different book than those weird ones you obsessed over when you were my age."

Charlie changed hands that held her phone so it was further away from Scott. She didn't feel the need to clarify to Martin that Scott was the one driving.

"In case you've forgotten, I go to school, just like you. Which means that I *also* need educational books." She paused, thinking over his words. "Also, I was *obsessed*."

"Tell that to thirteen-year-old me, who had to come with to those weird gatherings of yours that had a bunch of other greasy teenagers with the same addictions to those series."

Charlie turned her head away to Scott to ensure he didn't discover the large scowl that sat on her lips. It wasn't even like Martin needed anything either, because he had called to ask where she was. He'd gotten off school early, and on days like today when she didn't work, she'd usually be home by now.

Ever since answering him, he'd sat on the line and insulted her.

And Charlie desperately, *desperately,* wanted to insult him back, but it was a little hard to tell her brother that she was going to sell him back to their aunt without Scott hearing, and enviably being very confused.

That couldn't stop her from phrasing the insult differently though.

"Aw, Marty. That's so sweet. I'm so happy you want to go and visit Aunt Mary. I'm sure she could use the help in cleaning her house, now that she's getting old."

"That is not what I said," he responded spitefully, then gasped. "You *are* in the car with your pretty boy! I knew it! Aw, Charlette doesn't want him to know she's terrible to her brother."

"Of *course,* you can stay for the summer after school gets out, too. I'm so happy you asked."

Martin hummed. "You know, so am I. That way, I can tell her that you've snagged a pretty boy. Definitely will lighten up holiday gatherings. Hearing about Cousin Jessica's fourth marriage can only go so far in gossip."

"Aren't you a *dear*, Martin. *Yes*, you can come shopping with me tomorrow. I'm in need of someone to carry around the dresses."

The line crackled in silence. "Now you've gone too far."

Charlie shook her head to herself as she saw the library in the distance. "Alright, buddy. I've gotta go. I'll be home in an hour or two. Don't light the house on fire while I'm gone. Love you."

"No promises."

She ended the call with a suppressed huff and a faint smile. As they inched down the road, Charlie danced her eyes on the curbs when they passed the point that Callen died at, but surprisingly, there were no flashes of masks or oppressive feelings.

"Lemme guess, your brother was a lot meaner than your responses let on."

Charlie sighed lightly. "It's almost as if you were talking to Martin instead of me."

"Hey," he said and jut up a finger off the steering wheel to accentuate his point. "Remember? Three sisters, all younger. We're cut from the same cloth."

Charlie chuckled as Scott looked for a parking spot near the library. "No offense, but every day I'm thankful my parents didn't have any more kids." Martin was a handful enough.

"And every day," Scott said as he slotted the car a few paces away from the library's glossy glass doors. "I wish my parents *didn't* have any more kids."

Charlie smiled, but her light feeling could only carry her for so long. Martin's call had been useful in one singular way—it distracted her from the impending library visit. She had been lying when she told Scott about her plan. Yes, she did want to look at the footage if they had it, and would leave if they didn't. But her fib was that she implied she'd be fine I they were denied. Charlie was placing so much hope on this plan, the plan that could possibly tell them who killed Callen and put everything to rest, that it would most definitely crush her if it failed.

So, whatever, no pressure.

"You ready?" Scott asked when she had yet to unbuckle herself from the car like he had.

Charlie tore her gaze, which had been on the building for way longer than what was socially acceptable, away and tossed her belt off, and shoving her door open as an answer.

They walked towards the door and Charlie pretended not to think of it like the hero of a novel greeting the villain for a battle (no, she didn't get that idea from the books she read as a teenager, no matter what Martin thought—not that he wasn't right about her mild obsession).

The inside of the library was spacious and cushy. Windows lined the high ceiling, which shone down with their bright smiles and eliminated the need for artificial lighting during the day. Cushioned chairs and couches spotted the bookshelf-stuffed room. With a shift of her head, Charlie could see through the shelves and into the back, where there were even more literature and chairs. Despite the library being well furnished and well off from taxes, it was relatively bare, save a few elderlies wandering the aisles. At least there were less people to see her embarrassment if her lie—which she had not yet thought of—bombed.

Off to the left was the book checkout counter, which was manned by a woman with skin a shade darker than Charlie's, and deeply unimpressed by whatever was on the computer screen in front of her. As the two moved towards her, Scott hung back. When Charlie looked at him questioningly, he only gestured her on. Apparently, he'd come along for the ride, but wasn't too inclined to help out afterwards. Martin's conversation still fresh out the oven in her mind, she glared at him halfheartedly and turned back to the counter.

The lady that sat behind the desk clacked loudly, not too unsimilar to Helen, but she thankfully did look up when Charlie approached, towing Scott behind her.

"How can I help you?"

Charlie smiled and hoped she didn't sound weird while she said, "Hi, I was just wondering how long this library has had a security system."

The woman's eyes widened as they blinked at her. She frowned in thought. "I'm... not sure? I only work the front counter, not security. If you're with the police department, you'll need to talk to Ted. You'll have to wait, like, two weeks though, he just went on his honeymoon."

Charlie shook her head. "We're not with the police." She regretted telling her that so early, because it was only a matter of time that the worker became suspicious of two strangers coming in and wanting to talk about their security system.

And surprise, surprise, the lady eyed her through slit pupils. "You're... not with the police? Why do you want to know about how long we've had our security system then?"

Bless the cursed day, because she couldn't think of a lie on the spot. She cracked out the truth through her teeth and did her best not to feel stupid. "My friend and I do minor investigation work at home, and the crime we're researching happened near the library. We were just wondering if you had security cameras that might have caught the crime. We hoped to look at them."

The lady gave her an up and down. "That's good to know, but I'm sorry to inform you that I don't know if the library had cameras installed when the library was first built. We have camera's now, but I don't know when they were installed, or even if we still had footage from years in the past. And even if we did, I can't let you see it unless you were the authorities."

"Not even for educational purposes?"

Charlie stepped back as Scott rolled up to the counter, not having heard him approach.

"What do you mean 'educational purposes'?" asked the worker.

Scott eyed her with an eyebrow cocked too high to be normal, almost shocked looking. "Are you serious?" he said, which only confused the poor worker more. "Don't students come down here all the time to study the footage?"

Charlie inched away from Scott, pretending it was just a crazy coincidence they both wanted to look at the old cameras.

The woman watched him incredulously. "I've worked here for over two years. You two are the first to ever ask about the cameras."

Scott scoffed like this was obvious. "Of course, you wouldn't. Research of Digitally Recorded History class took a four-year break. Before that, professors used to take students down here all the time for lectures. They'd always go over the footage, teaching how to study people through the pixels, document the progress of the footage, enhance images, fast forward, you get the idea. My friend took the class, he came here every week to do that."

The woman examined at Scott like he was her computer screen when they first showed up. "Did they now? Hmm, then I have to talk to my manager about this. She's worked here for ten years. She definitely will know about your friend and their classes then."

Scott swallowed to make time for hesitation. "What if I brought the dean of the college down here? Would you believe me then?"

She raised an eyebrow, then too gave Scott an up and down, and sighed. "Sure. If you can get the college dean down here, you can go ahead and do whatever you want. I bet you'll have no problem doing this, since it's a class he *sponsors*."

Scott nodded, but Charlie could see he'd lost some the vigor he'd started with. "I completely agree with you. He's not going to like it though, being dragged away from work and all."

The worker watched him incredulously for a moment, before going back to her work, nails echoing on the keyboard. "Uh-huh. I'll be sure to extend my deepest apologies when he comes around," she said as dismissal.

Charlie waited until both she and Scott and had pulled away from the counter and moved towards the door before she opened her mouth to whisper hiss, "What the heck was that?" She wanted to slump down to the ground and pout to Scott that this was *not* a movie, and telling the worker something so *weird* wasn't a good idea.

Scott shrugged. "She was going to turn you down. You saw that right?"

"Yeah! But that would've been easier than what you just said."

"What I *said* to her was something that's going to potentially get us Callen's killer."

"What you *said* was that we're going to bring the dean down here. Implying, that to have him take our side, *implying* he has to know what we're *doing*."

Scott's conviction wilted at the edges. He looked away first as they neared the car. "Yeah," he rasped. "I thought of that."

Charlie was struck stupid by Scott's idea, and what they now had to do to get those tapes (that hopefully existed) but was more baffled by how resigned he looked.

She sighed and gave up. One more thing to do on their impossible list: Get the dean to back their story and get the tapes by telling him they were investigating his brother's death. Simple plan.

Chapter 35

Charlie and Scott returned to the college in hopes of unearthing the dean, but only caught Helen as she was on her way to the car in the parking lot.

"Helen!" Scott jumped out of the car to call to her.

Helen turned to him with an open face, but he sullied once Charlie stepped out as well. She pivoted back around and continued to march to her car and away from them. "I don't want to hear about your date."

"Helen, we need your help!" Charlie tried.

"I'm not picking out your wedding ring either."

"Have you seen my uncle?"

"Judging by that man's lack of fashion, I wouldn't recommend he pick out the dress either." Then she peered back at Charlie. She made a face as if to say *yeesh*. "Neither should you."

Scott huffed and stepped in front of her. "Helen, please, it's really important we find him quick. Did he go home?"

"I'm his secretary for work, not personal reasons."

"*Helen.*"

"Yes," she harrumphed. "He went home around the time you two left. Now leave me alone. I'm tired of that girl asking me questions."

"I literally asked one," Charlie muttered, but Helen had already rushed off. Scott sighed as he watched Helen retreat to her car but was not subdued for long.

"Come on," he said as he came back to Charlie, already opening his car door. "If we're to explain this to my uncle and get this done today," he checked his watch. "We can catch him at his house. We'll have to be fast."

Charlie joined him in the vehicle, and he sped off. "Wait, so we're just stopping by his house and dropping this all on him? He may be your uncle, but he's the dean to my college."

"Do you have a better idea?" Scott's tone wasn't unkind, but Charlie still thinned her lips. No, no, she did not. But, looking at all the other ideas Scott has had, maybe he shouldn't be the one making them either.

"Besides, it's not like he'll be busy. That's an upside of my uncle never marrying."

When they reached the dean's house, Charlie gave up on her integrity and joined Scott in his franticness to get inside as he pounded on the front door of a modest house on the opposite side of town.

"Hold on!" called the dean from inside, feet landing on the floorboard to accentuate his arrival. Only when the doorknob turned did Scott pull his hand away. The dean took one look at Scott and the odd situation, and his face dropped. "Scottie? What's going on? Did something happen?"

Scott blinked at him. "What? No. no, no, nothing like that. Although, I do have something to tell you that you're probably not going to take well."

Wow. Charlie was amazed, Scott was just going for it.

The dean, no longer worried that his nephew was here to drop off the news that something had gone wrong, realized Charlie was here. "Ms. Kezben? I didn't know you and Scottie knew each other."

Scott cut in. "Can we come in?"

The dean threw his eyes back Scott, switching back into high alert mode. "Are you sure everything's okay? You look like someone died."

"Technically…" Charlie started before Scott answer.

"Really?" Scott frowned at her, while the dean's eyes jumped back to her. He said at the same time, "What's that supposed to mean?"

"We're all okay, Uncle. Let's just go in. I'll be easier that way."

The dean tongued over the sight in front of him but hesitated no longer at hogging the door frame. He wasn't as bothered at Charlie's presence as much as she expected, and didn't give a second look when she followed Scott in.

Trudging down the entry way, Scott sat down at the nearest chair in the living room, providing an example to Charlie and the dean to do the same. Charlie took the chair next to Scott's, while the older man sat in an opposing chair to look at them both.

"This is going to be really hard to explain, Uncle. But the most I can ask of you is to keep an open mind and to stay calm."

The dean's eyebrows did their best to reach the top of his forehead. "Scottie, you know I'll love you no matter who you date."

Weren't they off to a great start?

"Uncle—no, that's not why we're here," Scott rushed out.

The dean blinked and nodded. "Then—are you dating?"

"Why does everyone think that?" Charlie sighed to herself.

"*No*, Uncle. We're not dating."

"Just because we're a boy and girl, that doesn't mean we have to date," she muttered, even though they'd moved on.

The dean watched them for a moment, eyes favoring Charlie. "No offense, but then why are you here, Ms. Kezben?"

Scott had apparently reached his limit of being misinterpreted because he cut to the chase. "We're investigating the death of your and mom's brother."

The dean flinched at the speak of death but said nothing else.

"Uh, should we bring up the ghosts?" Charlie whispered when the dean continued to stare at his nephew.

"Maybe not quite yet. We've already broke him," Scott said through the side of his mouth.

The dean snapped out of his stupor. "I'm sorry, Scottie. I think I heard you wrong. Did you say you're… investigating a death?"

"Of my uncle, your brother, that you told me about," Scott finished.

Again, the dean was struck back into being dumbfounded. At least this time he didn't have plausible deniability over hearing what Scott said. His jaw had slackened when Scott finished, but he worked it back into feeling after a moment, face much more frigid. "Scottie, I don't know if this is a prank, but—"

"It's not," Charlie cut it. "Believe us, we wish it *was* a prank."

The dean flicked his eyes to her, then something over her shoulder, like he couldn't look at her. "Forgive me for my rudeness, Ms. Kezben, but I believe I want to hear about this nonsense from only my nephew."

"It's not nonsense," Scott pleaded while Charlie snapped her mouth shut.

"Scottie," the dean looked resigned, disappointed, almost. "I understand that people make dumb decisions when they're your age. I did the same, but speaking about Callen like this with such disrespect is not something I will tolerate. Just tell me why you are doing this horrible prank and then we can speak about the effects of our words."

"Uncle, listen to me, *please*. Just *listen*. I know what we're saying sounds crazy and insensitive, but just wait until I tell you the whole story of why we're here."

The dean examined his nephew for seconds that employed themselves as hours. "Fine," he said quietly. "But do not think I am happy about what you've said to me so far."

Scott took a deep breath. "You know how you have all those books in the office about Misfortune?"

The dean's face was unreadable beyond his disappointment. "Yes."

"Well, long story short, Charlie and I decided to look into where Misfortune came from. We found that not only did he first appeared around forty years ago, but he also wanted someone to… understand how he died."

The dean said nothing.

"Charlie and I worked towards this, and we found out that Misfortune... is Callen. They're the same ghost, anyway," He ended his words rather anticlimactically.

The dean sighed.

"Callen told us he wanted us to find out who killed him, and—"

"That's enough, Scott." The dean held up a hand and used the other to run it through his budding gray beard. "This may be a joke to you, but you have no idea how much pain you two are causing me. This is my *brother* you're talking about, for God's sake. Your own mother's brother. Just because you are young, it doesn't excuse these horrible words you've said to me. I have those books, but I stopped believing Misfortune was more than a tale years ago, and I will not have you telling me my brother's a ghost, too. I would appreciate if you left my house, now."

Scott shut his mouth like someone stuck a lemon in there without his knowledge. "Uncle," he begged.

"Dean Manfree, please—" Charlie tried.

"Ms. Kezben, I suggest you stop before I feel the need to suspend you from your classes."

She continued anyway. "I've met him."

The dean sighed and stood from his chair. Charlie and Scott weren't inclined to follow. "Please stand from the chairs." The dean's voice bordered a plea.

"I've met him," she said again, quiet voice a shout in the room. "I've met Callen."

Anguish spread itself over the dean's face like an infectious disease. "Please, Ms. Kezben, I of all people don't need a reminder that he's dead. There's no possible you could've talked to my brother. No matter how much I don't want to, I will involve the police if you don't leave."

"Uncle!"

Charlie paused, refusing to remove herself. She desperately sought to think of a way to get the dean to believe their crazy story. Did Callen have a birthmark she could reference? Eyes? Hair? No, that wouldn't work, anyone could look up a photo of the dean's brother. Those articles told everyone the basics of Callen.

No, they told of everything, expect for one huge detail.

"Scottie, please, don't make this hard on me." The dean reached down to help his nephew to his feet, but Charlie spoke before he could touch him.

"Callen doesn't speak."

The dean flinched when Charlie looked at him for confirmation. The dean's face blotched slightly when he tried to compose himself, however possible that was in their situation. "I do not know what pleasure you get out of torturing me, but I don't appreciate looking up my family to get secrets—"

"He doesn't talk," she continued, words articulated carefully. "He only mouths words." She furrowed her brows. "Why didn't he learn signs language?"

She'd taken a shot at guessing Callen didn't learn sigh language, and by the stricken face of the dean, she'd guessed correct. The dean hardened and backed up, but he no longer tried to pry them out of his living room. "I don't know how you know that—"

"I told you I met him!"

"No, you didn't!" The dean finally let his anger snap. "My brother is dead! You will not come in here and tell me that you've met him!" He swung around for the kitchen, which connected off the side wall. "That's it. I'm sorry, Scottie, but I'm calling the police."

Scott flew from his seat and barred the way. "*Please*! Just hold on! We're telling the truth, I swear!"

"No, Scott. You're not. Neither of you are."

"Why was he so angry?" Charlie whispered. "Was it because he was killed, or something before that?"

When the dean turned around to spit his grief filled venom at her, Scott intercepted him. He put his hands on his shoulders to soothe him. "Just listen to her, Uncle. I beg of you. She's telling the truth. Just listen, and then we'll leave."

The dean glanced at Scott, a pass of eyes that conveyed pain and grief that rivaled Lidia's, and then pulled them back to the point just over Charlie's head. When he said nothing after Scott pulled away, she took it as her invitation to pursue her point.

She told him of how she met Misfortune, that terrible catastrophe on the road, and then the following days. How she couldn't get rid of him, how every waking hour turned to something out of a ghost movie. She recalled her thankfulness when Scott said he'd help her fix the problem, and how they realized something deeper may be going on.

She talked about Lidia and Kyle, and that they started to understand Misfortune wasn't as sinister as she thought, but merely wanted attention. That brought her to the theory of finding out why he would want attention, and then, by proxy, looking into who he was.

It was unavoidable to tell the dean that yes, the bear he had seen in the office was indeed his brother's. When she said this, she had expected a reaction of some sort. She got nothing.

The recounting of seeing Callen for the first time was vague, but she did her best to mention his clothes and face, along with the *anger* he radiated because she couldn't understand him, and the bear he gave her.

Finally, she ended with her epiphany of finding Callen and Misfortune were two sides of the same coin, and when she did, she embellished the story with how she could tell Callen only wanted someone to finish his story. And when she took a moment to let her words sink in, she saw that even though the dean had yet to look at her, his body was filled with sorrow.

The dean sighed and walked towards Charlie with a slouched back. Both she and Scott tensed, but it was only to return to his chair. "You're missing a detail about him," the dean whispered.

Charlie opened her mouth, looked to Scott, who was also bewildered and hopeful, and then snapped her mouth shut to ensure she didn't ask *Wait, you actually believe me?*

"Callen wasn't angry at one thing. He was angry at *everything*."

Scott slowly inched forward to return to his seat, so cautious like he imagined one puff of air will flip the dean back into unbelieving-mode. It didn't matter, because the trauma the dean had endured was bubbling back up his gut and spilling forth onto them, all because of Charlie's little recap.

The dean slung his head into his hands, which leaned on his knees. "The dog, school, me, our parents. All of it was too much for him. Callen had no way to cope; he'd smash things and hit people. Going purposefully mute was another one of his rebellions. And when he'd get mad when people didn't know how to communicate with him, I tried to teach him sign language." The dean shook his head and his hands along with it. "He had none of it."

The dean sighed. "I know you've read those articles. Everyone knows about how we came home to our parents arguing, and he ran away because of it. But did you know that they didn't even notice? Ma and Pa didn't know Callen ran until after the bear was identified by someone and the police came knocking on the door of our bakery.

"But *I* noticed. *I* noticed that he ran, and I chased after him. *I* chased after my baby brother to keep him away from those fucking roads, but our parents were raging alcohols, and Callen knew how to hide when he didn't want to be found." The dean sucked in a breath. "God, he knew how to hide. Why did he have to hide from me?" he worried to no one.

"Uncle," Scott repeated for the umpteenth time, but the dean only dropped his hands and waved away Scott's concern. His eyes were empty with pain.

"Somebody killed my baby brother and drove off and got to live their life without the consequences of killing a child. And the police didn't do a goddamn thing." He sighed and sat back in his chair. "I don't believe in Misfortune, and I don't believe in ghosts. Which means I have no idea how you two know what you do, but I do know that, for whatever reason, you're trying to solve Callen's murder, and for that, I'm not going to call the police."

"You're not?" Charlie asked without thought.

He stuck up a finger, body clinging to the hair's length worth of authority he still had.

"Don't mistake it for trust. I don't know what your motives are either, but I make it clear that I too want to convict my brother's murderer. Ma and Pa only ever cared about that fucking bakery, not Callen. Not the hit-and-run."

Scott blanched. "So, you'll help us?"

The dean sighed. "I think that after all these years of doing my own research for Callen's murderer, you two are the ones helping me." He swallowed. "But yes, I'll add onto whatever else you need. Although, might I remind you, I don't fully trust nor understand you."

"Of course." Scott nodded. He tried to hide his eagerness as he sat forward. "So, you want to assist, yeah? Well, are you free for the rest of the day?"

Chapter 36

"What kind of plan is that?" the dean groaned out from the passenger seat of Scott's car.

"I panicked!" Scott huffed.

Charlie leaned on the middle console from the backseat. "You panicked? You looked pretty confident when you told the lady that they had classes at the library all the time."

Scott sighed and pointed a finger at her. "I *had* to jump in, Charlie! Because, really, she was definitely going to kick us out."

The dean hummed from his place in the car. "I have confidence that, from what you've said, just walking in there with me isn't going to work, but at least you two didn't try and impersonate the authorities."

Scott looked over. "Thanks, I guess? Please have a little more of that confidence put towards knowing we're not going to break the law." He shook his head. "Anyway, all you really have to do is act, like, self-righteous about the class when we talk to them."

The dean chuckled. "I've dealt with overprotective parents and the board for years. I think I have an idea of what to do."

His smile faded a tad and he cleared his throat. "I suppose I should thank you two. Even if this amounts to nothing, this is the most attention my brother's murder has gotten in decades." He paused for their appropriate responses, then continued. "Oh, Ms. Kezben, that reminds me. You spoke of my brother's bear when we were at the house. Do you, by chance, still have it?"

Charlie sobered. "Sorry, sir. After we found out who Misfortune was, he took it away. I don't have it anymore."

The dean tried to hide his deflation. "It's alright," is all he said. "And please, call me Mitch. Perhaps a little less formality is needed while finding justice for my brother."

Charlie smiled at for a response. It didn't meet her eyes. She could've said something about how her aunt would've never let such informality slide and refuse to refer to him as anything as 'the dean', but she had broken life changing news to him just that day. He was right. Using formality at this time seemed sickeningly inappropriate.

They drove the last few minutes and silence, and when the car was slotted back outside the library, Mitch straightened his lapels, dragged a finger through his salt and pepper hair, and opened his car door to strut towards the library. Charlie and Scott hitched themselves along for the ride, jogging to keep up with Mitch's long strides. Charlie could tell Mitch definitely hadn't been lying when he said he had a work persona.

By the time the two leaked through the glass doors, Mitch was already a few feet away from the counter and booming, "What is the meaning of this?"

"Wow, he's really going for it," Charlie chuckled.

The worker, who was the same one from earlier, startled from the loud noise that echoed along the book's spines. She wasn't the only one. The few stranglers that haunted the aisles peeked around the corner to see what was going on.

"I'm sorry, sir," she sputtered. "Who are you? What seems to be the problem?"

Mitch raised a righteous arm and thrust it towards Charlie and Scott, who hung back with awkward waves. "I'm Dean Manfree and I was told the students at my college were denied their education for their class Research of Digitally Recorded History. Why is that?"

The woman blanched. "Oh, wow, okay," she nearly chuckled out. They must have done an unbelievably bad job of selling their story if this is how she reacts to it now.

"What's so funny?" Mitch snapped. Charlie too almost laughed. She'd never seen Mitch so worked up (the previous thirty minutes didn't count).

The woman shook her head. "Nothing, Mr., uh, Dean Manfree. My apologies for the misunderstanding. What can I help you with?"

Scott jumped in. "We want to look at the security tapes for research."

"They want to look at the security tapes for research!" Mitch boomed.

The worker finally seemed to accept the situation and sighed. "Alright, then. Just give me a second to get the keys to the backroom." As she rolled away from the desk to stand, Charlie heard her mumble, "I don't get paid enough for this."

"Thank you!" Scott called.

"I'll thank you after my students get their education!" Mitch followed.

Charlie took Mitch's other side and patted his arm. "I think Scott can take it from here," she whispered.

"Oh, okay," he grumbled, and settled on crossing his arms and looking menacing. His fatherly air could only go so far at looking mean.

The worker came back, dangling a key ring off her middle finger. She gestured to a hallway behind her with her head. "Are you coming? Don't want to waste time to learn now, do we?"

Charlie gave her most thankful smile as she ushered the rest of them behind the desk and past the worker.

"It's the farthest door on the left," she said when Charlie paused to take the keys from her. "You've got about an hour before I ask my manager about your class." She closed her mouth and gave Charlie the sweetest passive-aggressive smile. Charlie should've taken mental notes of the smile so she could use it on Martin.

"Thank you so much," she whispered, and the worker waved her on. She was thankful that in the jumble of lies, the worker didn't remember the truth. "Just be quiet while you're in there."

Charlie departed with a nod and skipped down the hall to unlock the door Scott and Mitch were waiting in front of with a hard click. Inside was a room that told Charlie nobody else ever needed the library's security footage. Virtually every item in the room had a gray sheet of dust over it. Spider webs added for extra padding in the corners. Charlie, being the first person to break this dust time-capsule, hacked when a pop of dust rushed through her nose and placed itself in her eyes like she had new eyelids. Mitch and Scott weren't far behind on the coughing train.

She coughed as she spoke. "We've got—about—an hour."

Scott sniffled and waved at his face. "That's fine, that's all we need." He finished his sentence just to sneeze a second later.

"Here," Mitch said, and began to open and close the door, trying to waft out the dust, but the most it did was displace the dust in the air more.

"Uncle, stop!" Scott and Charlie both raised their shirts over their noses, muffling voices. "Just let the dust calm itself." Like heroes in a movie afraid to startled a sleeping monster, they didn't twitch a muscle until they could drop their shirt without falling back into a fit.

"Off to a great start," Charlie sighed out. After they all hesitated to move, she took initiative and began to brush dust off the chairs and shelves of the room. Like shoveling away snow, she soon uncovered that, yes, the library had a security system, and they thankfully kept recordings (Charlie thanked every Holy Being she could think of in her head). The only issue they she had now was that she still didn't know how far back the tapes went.

She walked up to another shelf and crouched down to pull back a cardboard box that had lost the top half years ago. She peered inside. Stacks of VHS tapes sat inside, unorganized. Glancing around, this was how all the tapes were stored, and there were many, many boxes. Picking one up, she could see that the dates were on the side, but the dates on the tapes and the boxes they were didn't match each other. "See if you can find out how old these tapes go back. These boxes aren't in order, so the boxes they go in don't really matter."

With the help of Scott and Mitch, they all picked a place in the room and began to sift through the past.

"What day of the year did Callen die?" Scott asked.

"May 26th, four forty-six p.m.," he responded without pause. Charlie got the idea that Mitch mourned his brother every day of the year at that time.

As they drifted off into silence and their heads respectively, Charlie knew she had a confession: She had expected the hour that the woman had given her to be more than enough time, but when the clock in her head mentally ticked down more and more, it became apparent they needed to hurry.

It was good news when Scott found a tape labeled a few years before Callen died, which meant that it was likely they had a tape of that day, but it was like it wanted to play an extreme game of hide-and-seek. They hunted the tape vigorously, but as the pile for discarded tapes began to build, it became obvious it didn't want to be found.

"Why couldn't they have just put the tapes in chronological order?" Scott whined.

"Because that would've made too much sense," Charlie groaned. Her patience was ticking down as fast as the amount of time they had left in the room. And with each degree the temperature rose, so did the people's.

"Would they have had any reason to move some tapes to a different place?" mused Mitch.

"Oh, yeah, I bet it's in a different room and we're only going to find it at the last second, like some movie." Scott sighed and checked his watch. "If we don't find this thing soon, we won't be able to watch it at all."

So Mitch asked, "Do you think the worker will give us a little more time?"

"No," said Charlie. "She told me she's telling her boss about our 'class' at the end of the hour."

"Ah," sighed Scott. "That makes our lives easier."

Charlie took a break to lean her elbows on her knees. "I know you don't believe in the ghosts, Dean Manfree, but usually, if we get stuck, they help us. Give us a hint or something." She shrugged. "But after we found out who Callen wa—"

She stopped when the sound of plastic rubbing against metal came above her, and something sharp bashed her right in the head. Charlie shucked in a breath and flinched back, covering the crown of her head with her palm.

"Woah, are you okay?" Scott stood from his crouch to walk over to her.

Charlie waved him away with her free hand. Using the one on her head, she felt for blood, but only found a rising bump. "I'm alright." She looked down. "A tape just fell off the shelf, that's all."

"Wait." Mitch joined Scott at standing come over to Charlie, instead of it being because of worry, his eyes were only for the VHS tape. When he picked it, his face paled. "This is it."

"What?" Charlie and Scott said in unison. She pulled herself off the floor and joined Scott at craning their heads to the said to check the date on the tape. Sure enough, it was for May forty years ago.

Charlie gave a sneak peek to the top shelf that had been above her. She caught a glimpse of white skin pulling away and frowned. Scott caught her face. "What's wrong?"

She sighed. "Nothing." Of all things, she wished Callen would be less passive-aggressive.

"At least we have it," Scott said, giddiness in his rising. "Come on, Uncle, put it in the player."

Dean Manfree hesitated to move. He blew out a breath like he was steadying himself. Charlie knew she would feel the same if she was about to possibly see the murderer of Martin.

She nodded at him. "It's alright. This is the end."

Mitch nodded with her like she was the oldest adult in the room. "I know." He pivoted towards the back of the room, which held one measly chair and a box T.V. that was probably older than Martin, and possibly Charlie herself.

Mitch handed the tape to Scott, who shoved it into the player connected to the T.V. Mitch took priority and, as such, sat in the only chair. Scott and Charlie kneeled next to him while Scott fussed with the T.V.'s controls. He turned it on with the click of a button and danced through settings when the T.V. snapped on and bathed the room in blue. It sputtered with every button Scott pressed, when finally, more colors of the rainbow spectrum speckled the room.

Charlie recognized the layout of the road from the old map she showed Scott. Sure enough, the road no longer connected to other roads, and minor construction work dotted the dead-end filled with stores and the rest of the road, which drove offscreen.

When Mitch said, "This is the road." She knew that was the only confirmation they needed.

"Four forty-six, you said?" Scott wondered as he began to forward through the tape.

"Yeah," rasped Mitch. They all watched as casual traffic invaded the screen every so often. The camera mainly tracked construction workers building off the road and patrons for the nearby stores. Charlie could tell why the police never took these tapes: Road construction cut off all solicitation for the library. A mini clock in the corner, as well as the sun in the sky, told them that the time was getting closer to the latter half of four. And by each skipped second, Mitch grew tenser. And Charlie knew she was following his example.

"Here. Stop here." Mitch sat forward even more, like he could duck his head through the screen and see higher up the street.

Scoot removed his hand from the controls and the screen quit sputtering and went back to normal. The camera had no audio, causing Charlie's ears to ring terribly. It would've bothered her if her blood hadn't already beat the ringing to it.

Charlie knew what was going to happen when the little clock turned to four forty-six, but she still flinched.

It was after the workers and patrons had cleared out. Just in the far corner, almost off the screen, a blurry little boy burst out of an alley and bolted across the road. The camera could see the car just as poor as the boy, because there was a flash of metal, and the boy was launched through the air at an unnatural angle.

And even though it had no sound, Charlie could hear the crack of Callen's skull against the concrete. She could guess this was where the cuts on Callen's face and his bear came from.

Something tugged at Charlie as the car drove further into view. It maneuvered around Callen and parked in front of him. A man with white skin and broad shoulders jumped out of the car and rounded on Callen. Examining the man's back, a funny feeling built in her chest.

The man bent down to Callen, but whatever he saw, he flinched back like he was the one to be hit. The man straightened and glanced around. When he found no one witnessed him kill a child, he peered down at Callen's dead body for what felt like hours. Again, looking at the man that killed Callen, the odd feeling multiplied, tenfold like.

It was when Charlie really focused on the broad shoulders and lean stature of the rest of the body, how the man's clothing was deep in color, military grade, did she realize why he looked familiar. This epiphany answered one question, and when she focused on the low placement of the wheels and the navy coloring of the car, and its unfamiliar lack of adornments, did the answer for who killed Callen Manfree come crashing down on her. She recognized Charlette the car.

When Bill Forester turned around, the blurriness of the VHS tape did its best to hide his features, but the way his face contorted into anger, even the old technology couldn't stop them from finding it. Bill stomped away from Callen with a face Charlie imagined was bared teeth, got in his car, sped around the dead-end, and drove away, leaving the pile of skin and bones in the road to create a bigger puddle of blood.

Chapter 37

From the stiffness beside her, Charlie could tell all movement in the room ceased to exist. The shock of their realization persevered for as long as their minds refused to believe it. But no matter how many times Charlie repeated to herself, it had yet to sink into her flesh.

Bill Forester killed Callen Manfree.

Bill, Charlie's sweet, caring neighbor, who was one of the nicest people she'd ever met, who sent her home with cookies, who invited her over for pie, who collected cars because his father gifted his own collection to his son. Who was humble to admit he was a good neighbor, who was the father to play pool with them when their own dad couldn't. How could someone who was so amazing and thoughtful be the same person who killed Callen Manfree?

He was a sweet, loving old man who quietly lived next door and gleaned smiles everywhere he went.

But no, Bill's loving nature didn't discredit the video. Didn't discredit that he'd done the same thing that Brandon Fredricks had done to her own father. Taken to behind the wheel and unrightfully stolen a wanted life. And no matter how painful to think it, Bill being the murderer *made sense*.

That day that Misfortune appeared in her bedroom looking out the window, he hadn't been looking out there for nothing. Charlette the car had been parked in their driveway that day. And, God, when Callen showed up for the first time in that bathroom, he *had* been telling her who killed him.

He had been saying "Bill" over and over again. No wonder he'd gotten angry that Charlie didn't understand.

Charlie had to suppress a self-loathing sigh. Then there was the day she had been having pie with Bill. Callen with *right there*, shooting daggers at Bill and *pointing at him*. She was too caught up with thinking Bill part of her personal life and Misfortune part of her work life to realize the two were already merged.

And then not to mention the similar build of Misfortune and Bill.

"Bill Forester," whispered Mitch.

Charlie glanced over at him worriedly. She was still battling with her own feelings, but Mitch had known Bill for decades, and Callen was his *brother*. She had no clue how he was going to react. Will he explode? Cry? Shut down?

So far, option three was closest to ringing the bell.

"Uncle, I'm so sorry. Mitch, please, are you alright?" Scott tended to his uncle kindly, but Mitch was in no shape to respond. He kept repeating Bill's name to himself, like his tongue was unfamiliar with the shape and no matter how many times he practiced, it would not take.

Charlie watched on warily until the hair on the back of her neck began to stand. Slowly, she turned around, still leaning on her knee like she was proposing to the T.V.

Standing behind her was Misfortune, facing the wall opposite them, back to the group. Misfortune's black hair was visible at this angle, but the swimming of the dark made it hard to focus on him. That didn't matter, the way he stood was the same as Bill had when he stood over Callen's mangled body—stiff, tense.

"Scott," she hissed.

"What?" he shot back, busy trying to get Mitch to respond.

"He's here."

Scott paused, hands still on his uncle's shoulders, and tilted his head towards the opposite wall. "Oh."

Mitch, in his grief and trauma induced stupor, snapped his head towards Scott. "What? What's wrong?"

"Misfortune's here," grimaced Scott.

Mitch shot up from the chair fast enough Scott's hands where wrenched with him and the chair wobbled. He joined them in staring at the ghost's back. Finding her feet with Scott, Charlie peered at Mitch. His face was pale, and the only thing she could hear was his ragged breaths.

"Is that him?" he rasped.

Scott's eyes wondered to Misfortune for a second, but his attention didn't wander from Mitch for long. "That's Misfortune, yes."

"No, you said…" Mitch swallowed. "But he's… He's so… Cally?"

The snap of a neck turning 180 degrees made Charlie gasp and throw a hand over her mouth. Misfortune was staring at them, or more likely Mitch, his head sitting on his body backwards.

Scott copied Charlie. "That's disgusting."

Mitch was unfazed. "Is that really Cally? How… Why is he so…?"

"He took on the shape of Bill of when he killed him," Charlie answered. "Look, same shoulders and height. That's why there's two of them. One for show. One for truth." She recalled how Misfortune copied Bill's wave when she left his house after pie.

"Why?" cried Mitch. "Why the skull? Why do all of this?" Charlie cringed. Mitch had apparently moved on from denial and onto anger.

"To get people's attention," Scott finished. Charlie didn't voice it, but from what she learned from Callen, she guessed Misfortune looked so demonic because Callen thought of Bill that way.

Misfortune patiently watched them unravel his identity. She could almost see him blinking at them lazily.

Scott gasped. "God, that's why the kids are disappearing, too."

"What?"

He gestured to Misfortune with inappropriate enthusiasm. "If Misfortune is the Callen version of Bill, he's probably *acting* like him, too. Bill took a kid's life, and so—so is Misfortune."

"I've seen him copy mannerisms of Bill's!" Charlie followed.

Scott slowed. "But why? Is he doing it for revenge? Attention?"

Charlie had no answer. She saw movement out of the bottom of her sight and looked down to see Mitch's hands shaking. She wasn't the only one.

"Uncle?"

"Bill killed my brother," he spat with newfound malice. "Bill killed my brother and went to his fucking funeral. He came to every fucking one of our birthday parties." He shucked a vibrating hand up and onto his face. "He was at your parents' wedding, Scottie."

"I know, Uncle. I get it," he soothed.

"I went to the bar with him last night!"

Charlie spied Misfortune again, and when he gave no intention of moving or fixing his neck, she scampered back to the desk with the T.V. as Mitch continued.

"He's lived free for all these years! And the police didn't do anything else than call it a tragedy!" He breathed hard. "And my parents didn't care! All they cared about was their *fucking bakery*!"

She pulled out the tape and stepped back to them brandishing it like a sword of a hero. "Then we give this to the police. They can't ignore Callen's death anymore if they have it on tape." She handed the tape when Scott asked for it with an open palm. "And I know Bill still has that car, I've seen it."

Scott sighed and inspected the tape. "He knew what he did and didn't have a problem with it. Did you see the way his face looked after he hit Callen?"

Their silence answered for them.

Scott turned to Mitch. "Uncle? What do you think?"

Mitch only had eyes for Misfortune, and Misfortune apparently the same. Mitch took a deep breath and put fingers over his eyelids like he had to physically close them. When he opened them, his eyes were flat with the

Misfortune

acceptance. "Let's just get this over with. I can't stand thinking about Bill being free for another second."

When no one made the first move to leave the room, and Misfortune continued to stare at them with a broken neck, Charlie cleared her throat. "It's probably late, we'll need to get there—"

She was cut off by a voice outside. "Yes, they're in here."

Charlie groaned at the familiarity of the voice. She may have assisted in solving a decades old murder, but that didn't mean the shock of it all could stop her from being annoyed.

The worker from before opened the door first, and an older white woman with a lanyard full of keys that clacked together and an irritating habit of smacking her gum. She snapped her fingers at the three of them like they were children getting into something. "Okay, yeah, y'all can't be in here. There's never been a class that researched history with our tapes. You need to get out right now, leave all our stuff here."

"God, they've made a mess," complained the original worker.

Charlie snuck a look at Misfortune, but from the way the door opened, he was hidden. She then flicked her gaze to Scott, but he'd done something with the tape, as his hands were now free.

The older library worker snapped at them again and pointed out the door and down the hall. "C'mon, let's go. But before I call the police, and *trust me*, I *really* want to."

If the situation wasn't so dire, Charlie would've agreed with her that she too *really* wanted to call the police.

Charlie was the first one to move. She heard Scott and then Mitch shuffled out after her. She did her best at looking like a punished child rather than a traumatized one. Like prisoners connected by the ankle, they waddled past the older librarian and the self-righteous worker that bathed in satisfaction that she'd caught them in the lie.

After being kicked out into the late air (and told they couldn't come back), Scott rushed past them to his car. "Come on. We have to get their before it gets too late."

Mitch continued to shuffle forward without seeing while Charlie paused. "Wait, where's the tape?"

Scott angled away from the library's cameras, as well as Charlie, and pulled something out of the front of his pants. Charlie turned away when he brought out the tape. "Great job," she muttered. It was awfully great to know the tape that would convict Bill of murder and finally put Callen to rest was stored by being shoved down Scott's pants.

Scott chuckled self-consciously, bubbly and near a cough.

When Charlie settled into the backseat and they drove by the spot Callen died, her phone rang as she looked for Misfortune in the shadows. "Hello?" she asked quietly to Martin on the other line.

"No way have you been at the library for this long."

In the craziness of everything, she appreciated that Martin was still untouched by Misfortune and Callen. "Sorry, Marty, got caught up in some things. I'll be home soon, I promise."

"Yeah, I'm sure you got caught up in *things*, if *things* is that boy toy a' yours."

And there goes the light feeling he gave her. "Martin, I am not in the mood for this right now. Is there something you need?"

"Oh, yeah, I was just calling to say I won't be home when you get there."

Charlie glanced out the front window, checking their progress to the police station. "Why? Are you going to a friend's?"

"Nah, I'm actually going to play pool at the bar with Bill. He came over and asked, and, honestly, I wasn't going to, but the old dudes got some *killer* pie. I'll have you know I was bribed, that's the only reason I'm going with him."

Charlie's brain stopped computing once it put together that Martin was going out alone with *Bill*. She sucked air into her chest, but it wasn't enough anymore. "No. *No!* Martin, you are *not* going out with him!"

"Everything okay?" Scott asked from the front seat. Charlie ignored him.

"Charlette, sweetheart, I think I'm a little old to ask my twenty-some-year-old sister for permission. Especially when I'm a grown adult."

Her mind was sputtering like a waterlogged machine as he continued. "Besides, it'll be *fine*. It's not like we'll be alone, if that's what you're worried about. Well, I suppose we will be alone because we'll be in his car. He names them, did you know that? Stereotypical, I tell you. Anyway, the one we're taking is... Charlette, I think? I only remembered that because it's your name, too."

Charlie's body was sitting in the backseat of Scott's car, and her hand held a phone to her ear, but her mind was in a future where Martin was the one found dead. It was him who haunted her day and night. It was him, whose anger was so putrid and saturated, it caused her physical pain. "Scott, you need to go back to the college. I need to get my car."

"What?" Martin and Scott asked at the same time.

Scott continued first. "Wait, what do you mean? We're almost to the station."

"I need to go home. Drop me off at my car. Scott, *please.*"

He looked at her in the mirror. "What's wrong?"

"Charlie?" She heard her brother sigh over the line. "Look, I don't know who you're talking to, but Bill's sitting in the car waiting for me, I've gotta go. Meet us at the bar if you're going home. Tootles, darling."

The line clicked off before she could warn him. Her mind was twisting too fast, and it didn't help Scott had yet to relent with his questions. "It's a little off course, Charlie. We'll want to get to the station before everyone goes home."

"Martin's with Bill."

Scott swallowed and looked away. "Charlie, I know that we all know Bill is a terrible human being, but I don't think he's going to kill your brother just because we sudden know what he did. Besides, the college is a couple minutes away, the station is a block away. We're almost there."

And with force in her voice she'd never used on anyone, Charlie bore her eyes at Scott's in the mirror, where he refused to meet her, and stated, "Scott, let me out of this fucking car right now."

Scott glanced at her, then at his uncle, who seemed to have yet to remember he had a working human body, and sighed. "Alright, I get it. Are you sure?"

"Scott," she warned.

"Alright, alright, here." He flicked on his blinker and pulled over. "Be safe, okay?" he told her when he turned around.

Charlie didn't bother with an answer. She kicked open the door and shot onto the cement and then down the sidewalk.

It wasn't that Charlie suddenly believed that Bill would randomly kill Martin now that she knew he was a murderer; she'd spent time with him alone. She didn't want Martin with him because she now knew that Bill, having shown that terrible face on the VHS tape, and had lied for all these years, and knew his way around manipulation.

Chapter 38

The run to her car and the following drive to the bar was more excruciating than the officer knocking on their door the night her father died. And, by God, fuck Brandon because she ran more than three lights. When she reached the bar they'd played pool at with Bill when Charlie had been oblivious to what her neighbor did, she frantically ran through the place with filling horror. Martin nor Bill were there. Bathrooms, bar, back tables, bathrooms, pool area, everywhere in the damned place she hunted for her little brother and came up with nothing. She was trying to call Martin again when the owner came over to kick her out. She didn't care because her phone rang and rang and rang.

Charlie tried to quit her hyperventilating when she was forced to retreat back to her car. Maybe she shouldn't jump to conclusions. Maybe they went to a different bar, or they did go there but left for home already. Home, she had to check home.

Her phone buzzed a couple of time from what she assumed was Scott's number, but it wasn't Martin, so she didn't bother to pick up. At that moment, she didn't care if they got the tape to the police or if Callen got his closure. She didn't care about anything that had to do with Misfortune.

She just wanted to make sure her brother was okay.

Breaking another multiple road laws (and mildly wondering where the town police were that should've caught her were) Charlie was back at her house. She didn't bother to close her door when she jumped out and bolted into the house. It fell back to the car with a dull click.

And her house was empty. The walls mimicked her panicked shouts for Martin like a sick mocking.

No. No, Bill couldn't have done something to him. Bill was their friend; he wouldn't want to hurt them. He hadn't hurt anyone in a long time. Or, as far as she knew.

But she's seen his face the day he killed Callen. He was *angry*, and made no move to help him, or even call the authorities.

Bill knew what he did and didn't want anyone else to.

She really needed to find Martin.

Back outside, she crossed the grass barrier of their houses and stalked up to Bill's door. Conjuring bravery and her own anger, she righteously wrenched open the door.

To find Martin sitting on a chair in the living room sipping tea and munching on pie, crumbs sprinkled all over him.

Charlie, in all her panic and haste, froze at the sight of her brother safe and content. Hand still gripping the handle, she examined the room for Bill, and her survey came back negative.

Martin watched her lazily and stuck another forkful of pie in his mouth and raised the utensil to point at the ceiling with it. "You're letting out all the heat, Charlie."

She snapped back to him, and without permission from her head, her body stepped inside and closed the door behind her. She fought terribly to come back to her senses as she sputtered, "I thought you we at the bar."

Martin shrugged, unbothered. "Meh, we did, but the place was too busy." He shrugged again. "Doesn't matter to me, he still held up his side of the deal." He lifted his floppy plate to wave it jovially in the air. "Have you had this pie yet?" He took her lack of answer as a no and tsked. "Charlie, darling, your life will be *changed*."

"We gotta go, Marty." She moved forward to pull him off the chair.

He pouted. "You just got here! Besides, I'm not done with my pie, and to leave this precious half eaten would be a *sin*." He waved her off when she tried to pry him from his seat.

"Charlie! Wonderful for you to join us!"

Charlie felt the anxiety and fear burrow itself into her spine, causing her to fight a flinch when she heard that sickly sweet voice come from the kitchen doorway. She forced herself to turn towards the sound. There stood Bill with his padded hands holding a piping hot circular pan. "Perfect timing, I just finished another pie."

The knowledge that Bill killed Callen and her mental construction of him killing Martin too had already stuck itself too far in her head. Fear curled around her muscles and prevented her from making the next move.

Martin must have caught on to her sudden stiffness. He looked her up and down with an odd face and said, "You good, dude? You're looking a little... mannequin like." When Charlie looked back to him, he furrowed his brows. "Is something wrong?" His face dropped. "Mom?"

"Yes," she said immediately. Charlie didn't feel guilty for lying. She'd do anything to keep Bill away from Martin.

"God," he rushed out and shucked his food away and found his feet, face etched out of stone that only knew worry. "What happened?" He sucked in a breath. "Did she drink and drive?"

"What's wrong?" Bill asked and wandered forward with concern.

Charlie flinched back, not being able to look at Bill, not being able to see his soft face feel something so human and fatherly. She propped herself between him and Martin, finding him. "Let's go home. We'll talk there."

Martin swore under his breath and wasted no second listening to her. He whipped towards the front door and pulled it open shakily, looking around and seeing nothing as he waited for her. Already he expected her to tell him they were orphans.

"Is everything okay?" Bill came close enough to set the pie down on the coffee and table and pull the oven mitt off each respective hand.

Charlie forced herself to look the murderer in the eye. "Don't worry about us. It's a family issue. Thank you for the pie," she said and backed away.

Bill nodded, but his eyes were still sharp on her, following her every move up until she took the front door's knob from Martin and made to close it. The past thing she saw were the lines that strung themselves around his mouth and eyes.

"What happened to her, Charlie?"

"Get inside the house," she hissed at him, quiet so Bill couldn't hear, and forceful enough to make Martin listen. They trudged the rest of the way, with Martin giving her troubled looks and Charlie watching Bill's house and fighting her perturbation.

It was only when her own front was closed did Martin spill his toppling bucket of fear. "What happened? Is she alive? Are the cops involved? Who told you, Aunt Mary?"

"Mom's fine," Charlie said stiffly as she peeked out the living room blinds. Slowly, the realization of what was happening, and what was *going* to happen bit into her. Well, it had been weeks. Anytime was a good time to tell Martin what she had been doing.

"Woah, wait, what?" Martin stumbled. "What do you mean *she fine*. Then why the hell did you pull me from my one true love?"

Charlie tamped down the irritation that rose at Martin's questions. He didn't know what was going on, that wasn't his fault, but she had had a *hell* of a night, and was not in the mood for this. "I mean that there's *nothing wrong with Mom*." She sighed and turned to her brother. "Martin, I need you to listen to me right now, because I'm going to tell you something that's going to be really hard to comprehend."

Martin frowned at her and crossed his arms. "Well, I don't know how much of a *comprehending* mood I feel I'm in if you start out this conversation by *lying* to me."

"*Martin*," she hissed. "You need to *listen* to me." It was like she was speaking with Mitch again.

He continued to frown at her, but didn't say anything.

"Do you know about the town ghost story with Misfortune?"

He made the same odd face at her that he did at Bill's, like thinking over her oddness. "Yeah? Who doesn't?" he said at the same time she remember he had asked her about the story in the past.

"And do you remember how you said that Misfortune might have something to do with that skull I found in the middle of the road the night I crashed my car?"

"...Sure?"

"Well, you were right. Misfortune, yes, the town ghost, has been haunting me ever since. He was who I heard the night I thought someone broke into the house. Saw him in the kitchen." She began to pace as all the experiences burst out of her for the second time that day.

"That's why I've been hanging out with Scott. He's been helping solve the problem of *why* Misfortune was haunting me. So, then we found he's been kidnapping kids, but that's like his way of—what revenge? I don't know. Anyway, turns out he's actually a kid that was murdered forty years ago and he wanted us to solve his murder," she ducked down her voice. "I met him bathroom, and all. Anyway, and so we *did* and then—it turns out Bill killed him." She sucked in a breath. "So now Scott and his uncle, who is actually Callen's—that's Misfortune's real name—brother, are now at the police and giving them the evidence to convict Bill for Callen's murder."

She stopped and pivoted back at Martin; her hand frozen in the air where they had been flying around as she explained. Sure, it had been choppy and *definitely* should've been rehearsed, but no going back now. Martin's eyes were stuck in an unblinking widened state as she stuck a finger up. "Oh! I forgot to say that's there's two of Callen. One's like a manifestation of Bill, and the other is Callen as he was when he died."

She stopped and dropped her hands, waiting for Martin to respond. Her unwilling mind laid out every possible response he could have, good and bad.

She didn't know where saying nothing fell on that scale. "Marty?" she prompted.

She watched his Adam's apple bob. "One question," his voice grated. "Of course."

Martin took a hard sigh and let his shoulders drop. "How many beers have you had tonight, Charlie?"

She tried not to flinch, but it hurt worse that Martin, of all people, didn't believe her. "I'm not drunk!"

He lifted his disappointed arms to soothe her. "I promise I won't tell Aunt Mary or Mom, but you have to tell *someone*. Drinking yourself into oblivion as a coping mechanism isn't a good thing. You need help."

She shook her head at him, scrunching her eyes to compose herself. She opened them with newfound vigor and approach Martin with a finger in his face. "I am not drunk, I am not high, and I am not crazy. What you need to understand is that Bill is not who he says he is. He was involved with a hit-and-run years ago and hid it from everyone. The police and the family of the child he hurt. He is not a safe person to be around."

Martin's eyes flicked between each of hers. His body softened, and finally, *finally,* she thought she got through to him before he backed up and wouldn't look at her. "Until you get help for your addiction, Charlette, I'd appreciate if you didn't speak to me." He sighed with disappointment written all over him. "I'm not mad at you for drinking, I just—you gotta understand. I couldn't bear mom when she was drunk, you know how she was. Now—just…not you too. I can't take it from you, too."

Charlie pulled back like Martin had hit her, and he used the opening to slide by her and reach the stairs, purposefully not touching her. She watched her brother's shadow disappear up the stairs with a poisonous arrow through her heart, feeling like she'd lost her last family member.

Chapter 39

Martin wasn't talking to her. And now, neither was Scott. She hoped the latter was because he was busy with work or other things, and not because it had something to do with Misfortune.

Since that night some days ago when they found the tape of Bill killing Callen, she hadn't heard much from him, only that the police would 'take it into consideration' when they turned in the tape. She desperately wished to know if that meant they believed the tape was real or not (she could only go so long knowing Bill was living next to her without consequence, which was *still* going on).

Martin, on the other hand, she knew was purposefully avoiding her. He wasn't aggressive with his newfound distance, but the opposite. If he had to be near her, he was more passive anything. He took the bus home when she was still out, then suddenly had something to do when she got back from work. If Charlie didn't have work and was home before him, he was up the stairs and slamming his door before she could say hello.

And all because he didn't believe her when she told him about Misfortune. That she'd taken up drinking.

Charlie's heart tore itself over her brother if this is how he reacted to even the mention of alcohol. She hadn't realized their mother's crippling alcohol addiction had affected him so badly. But at the same time, she was childishly resentful that he didn't believe her. She had researched this for months and worked with Scott and *communicated with goddamn ghosts* to find out what happened to Callen, and pin Bill as the killer, just for Martin to call her drunk and then sulk.

And not to mention that since Misfortune's case was solved and evidence was given to the police, that was no longer a need to meet with Scott after school. No need to visit people or taunt Helen. No need to help with weekly coffee runs. No need for her.

And Misfortune, in his lovely black clad and goat skull mask, had yet to relent in his hauntings.

It was dramatic to think so, but ever since that night they solved the murder, it felt like her life was just falling into a downward spiral (if Martin wasn't going to be the melodramatic one, *someone* had to).

Today, after checking in with the office, and finding no Scott, she returned home on another work-free day. As expected, when Martin got home, the only acknowledgement the house gave that someone was home was the front door opening, a drop of shoes, and then a bolt upstairs.

Charlie stayed where she was in the kitchen. She had stopped trying to get Martin to talk to her and figured that he'll come to her when he was ready. Nevertheless, she still called out, "Welcome home, Marty," from her place at the kitchen table with a hot cup of tea in her hands.

She was met with the click of his door shutting and sighed. She'd raised Martin ever since their mother couldn't function without their father, but sometimes she wished that she didn't have to, or that he had someone better to raise him. Martin didn't deserve a caregiver that hunted ghosts and lied in her spare time.

Charlie hadn't realized that she'd zoned out until her phone buzzed rapidly, jostling the hand that lofted the quickly cooling tea in the air and spilling it onto the ground. She sighed and set down the cup, replacing it with her phone and pulling it up to her ear, allowing her shoulder to hold it.

"Hello?" she asked as she stood to grab a towel to clean up the tea.

"Hi, hon, it's me."

Charlie unconsciously felt her mind harden. It wasn't her mother's fault that Martin was unhappy with her, but she *was* the reason that Martin had developed trauma over alcohol. But she wasn't going to share this with her mother.

"Oh, hi, Mom. How have you been doing?"

"You know me, baby. I'm always doing the same." Charlie ignored the small curves around her mother's vowels, which she always talked like after she'd had something to drink. "Are you alright? Anything happen?"

She also didn't feel the need to share to her mother, who couldn't parent right, that she too couldn't parent right. "Not much. Martin and I are pretty caught up in schoolwork, so there's that."

"Are you *sure* there's nothing going on?"

Charlie paused mid crouch with a towel in her hand. Had Martin called her and told her what happened? It didn't seem like something he'd do, considering the situation, but she wouldn't put it past him. She sat back on her hunches, cloth still stuck between her fingers. "Why do you ask?"

She could almost see the hesitation of her mother. "Oh, sorry, I just assumed you'd seen the news."

She frowned. "The news?"

"Oh, um, well, like I said, I'm sorry about throwing it on you like that, it's just that since, you know, you live so close to him and you've talking about him in the past, you'd know. But I'm sure it's a shock, once you do—"

"*Mama*," she cut her off. "What are you talking about?"

"Right, yes, I suppose I should tell you."

Charlie waited for her to continue. Her mother did not. "Suppose you should tell me what? Mom—" She pinched the bridge of her nose. "How much have you had to drink today?"

The pause her mother took to answer made Charlie double check the like to make sure it hadn't been hung up.

"I don't know," she murmured, so low the line barely picked it up.

"You don't know?" Charlie started out; voice harsher than she intended. She needed to take a breath and figure out what was going on. "Are you alright, Mom? What do you mean you don't know?

"Today's been a hard day, Char. I miss your father." Her voice broke on the last word, and despite all of her pent-up anger at how she was raised, Charlie felt herself split down the middle. Once side was still resentful, the other side pitied her poor mother, having lost the man she loved so soon.

"I know it's tough, Mama, but you can't turn to drinks to ease the pain." She heard a sniff on the other end. "I know. I know, baby, I know." That was the first time her mother had ever agreed with her. "I just miss him so much, and I don't know how to make the pain go away."

"Try therapy, Mom. It'd be good for you. You need to talk to someone about losing Dad that's not me or Aunt Mary."

Another sniff. "You're right. I know I do. Of course, you're right."

She listened to her mother sob softly and began to wipe up the tea. "Are you better now?" she asked when the hiccups on the line calmed. "Will you be alright if I hung up?"

"Yeah, baby. Thank you, I feel better. I'm sorry of what I've put you through, I am. You and Martin both." Charlie froze at the apology, but her mother continued. "Anyway, I never did tell you about why I called."

Charlie was still stuck on the fact that her mother *finally* apologized for her terrible actions. And with calming her down, she'd forgotten all about the original question. "Don't worry about it, Mom."

"No, I called to ask if you were okay, because I saw on the news that a man in your town named Bill Forester had a warrant for arrest, and I remembered that you talked about a neighbor named Bill before. I was just worried that that Bill was your neighbor because it'd said he was evading police and all. Can't equal anything good, neighbor or not."

This phone call was really trying it's best to stop Charlie's heart. "Wait, what? Did you say *Bill Forester*?"

"Oh, no, it must be your neighbor then. Char, I'm so sorry. You've gotta stay safe, okay?"

Charlie opened her mouth and then quickly closed it. Then opened it again and sputtered, "Hold on, Mom. When did you hear this? Did they say anything else?"

"Charlie? Is everything alright?"

"Don't worry about it, Mom. Just—was there anything else?"

"Well... I just saw it on the news just a few minutes before I called you. I think it said something or other about a past crime. I wasn't really paying attention after I noticed he was in your town."

Charlie scrambled from the ground, soppy towel in hand, and tossed it with a wet *thunk* onto the counter. She exited the kitchen and reached the living room in four steps, stopping right in front of the T.V. with the remote in her hand.

She flashed through channels while her mother continued to toss irrelevant and concerned questions at her. Charlie didn't notice, didn't care, as she finally landed on the news channel. Sure enough, they were running a mini segment about Bill, with his face plastered on a rectangle and the reporter detailing cops knocking on his door to no help. The report said that they assumed that Bill knew the police were looking for him and skipped town. She was confused when it told her his neighbors were asked about his whereabouts, and they told him they hadn't seen him. *She* hadn't been asked, but she supposed with work and school, she was almost never home before sundown.

But above all that, their evidence had been taken seriously, and it was finally going to happen. Callen was going to get his retribution.

"Charlette, you're scaring me. Why aren't you answering?"

She tried to speak, but with her mind glued to the T.V. and her body trying to answer her mother, Charlie had to take a moment to work out her sentence. "Sorry, Mom. Something came up. I'll have to call you back. Love you."

She cut off her mother midway through her name. Charlie dropped her phone back into her pocket and raised the volume on the T.V., like that would make it easier to comprehend. No matter how long she listened, they didn't give the reason police wanted Bill beyond mentioning he had evaded police for a previous crime, and when the segment came to an end, she tossed down the remote and brought her phone back out to call Scott but stopped when the bottom stair creaked.

Charlie slowly turned around, expecting Misfortune to be standing level with her door, and instead found Martin, eyes adhered to the T.V. with his hand gripping the banister hard enough to white out his fingers.

Chapter 40

"I'm sorry, Charlie."

"Marty, it's okay, I'm not mad."

"Well, you should be. I acted like a butt and didn't believe you."

Charlie sighed lightly and leaned back on her side of the couch so she could pull her legs up and get a better look at Martin on the other end of the cushion. "Honestly, buddy, I really need to teach you how to swear better."

"God, be serious!" Martin huffed. "I called you drunk when you told me that you *solved a murder*."

Charlie shoved down the urge to tell Martin that he was a little behind on everything. She knew she had to be patient with him. It wasn't every day people solved murders outside of a T.V. screen.

"Really, it's all good. What matters now is that the police find Bill and we can all put this to rest." *Put Callen to rest*.

Martin thinned his lips and looked down in thought. "Fine. But how—what did—what did you do to *solve a murder?*"

When Martin brought his eyes back to her, Charlie had to remember that while he was a senior in high school, her brother was still a child. "Everything I told you that night was true," she said soothingly. "It may have sounded crazy."

"That's for sure."

"But it's what really happened. Misfortune, ghosts, bathroom meetings and all. I solved it with Callen's help. And Scott's, of course."

As the clock ticked and pulled them along into a newer present, Martin seemed to be coming back to himself. "Hm, so I *was* right about all those times I said you were with him."

She sighed, suddenly wishing the shellshocked Martin was back. "Yes, Marty."

"A true genius is never wrong." Martin paused for a second, but was never quiet for long. "So... you *really did* solve a murder during all this time? With, what, *ghosts*?"

"I know this can be hard to understand. Just take your time."

Martin shrugged. "Honestly, the part I'm having a tough time with is believing that you've been willingly doing extra work for weeks."

She threw a decorative pillow at him. She didn't feel bad when the beads hit him in the face.

He grinned at her, but it didn't take long for his body to dull again. "What was it that Bill did? I mean, if it was so bad, how did he end up getting away with it for so long?"

"Bill killed Callen in a hit-and-run, and the area where this happened was under construction, so a lot of buildings were closed, and police had a hard time getting through the place. Why Bill did what he did, I don't think I'll ever know."

Martin shook his head and leaned back against the couch arm rest, forearms knotted together. "And to think he was so nice to us. Someone that terrible shouldn't be allowed to bake comforting pies and be so welcoming. I wish I still didn't like him after that day we moved in."

Charlie smiled to placate him, but it was more brittle than her own mental state over Bill. "Yeah, me too."

In the time that followed, the police had yet to find Bill, and any the room for second thoughts on his innocence evaporated once he didn't surface from his hiding. Police searched his house like spiders exploring a ghost town, but nothing else was found except more antique car memorabilia.

The only thing out of place was that one of the many cars under his name was missing: Charlette. Charlie didn't need the police to tell her that Bill had skipped town with the car he killed Callen with. The knowledge of what he did, and how long he'd gone unpunished, and then how he took Charlette have her a stomach ache built out of unease and foreboding.

Scott, on the other hand, didn't care in the slightest which car Bill used to leave. He was too caught up with dealing with his uncle to indulge Charlie in her worries when she visited the office from time to time. And Mitch was too rung out from learning about his brother's death to deal with running the school.

And so, with no ghost/murder mystery to solve or friends that weren't either dealing with dead family members or a sudden vacation with a sister (Sam), Charlie designated her time to schoolwork and pretending the life she'd had in town so far was completely normal. She went to work, and both she and Martin went to school. The temperature cooled as the days moved towards the end of the year and Charlie focused extra hard on her driving skills.

She was a few weeks into this plan before it came to a sputtering halt.

"Don't you have a spare one?" Martin whined.

"No. I don't." She sighed hard and dragged her hands down her face as they stood outside of her car on the road Scott had seen Misfortune on for the first time.

Martin flapped his hands in the air. "Who the heck doesn't have a spare tire?! Isn't there always one in the back or something?"

Charlie groaned and fought the need to kick the deflated tire that had failed its singular job. While they had been driving to the store, she had felt the dreaded *pop* under her feet. The culprit: A blasted nail the size of her nail.

"Yes, there usually is," she gritted out. "But the mechanic used it when I drove into the ditch."

Martin huffed loudly and spun around, hands raised even higher in the air. "Why can't you just go one drive without something going wrong!" he pleaded into the cool air like the gods were listening.

Charlie frowned at his back. "Stuff always happened when you're included. Maybe *you're* the problem."

Still facing away from her, Martin gasped and slapped a hand on his chest. He pivoted at the waist to stare back at her heartbroken. "I am *not*, you evil, evil woman."

She shrugged. "Just sayin'."

Martin's eyes slit themselves as he hummed. "Suddenly, I don't feel like helping you fix the car." And he stomped off and around it, slamming the passenger door after himself and staring forward with his arms neatly folded. He pretended not to see Charlie when she peered at him through the driver's window. She nearly indulged the feeling to tell him that he wasn't helping her at the start.

Bending down to examine the tire again, it was clear there was nothing she could do. The air had already emptied out soon after the initial burst, and the most she could do now was call a truck to come get her. Charlie was pulling out her phone with another angst-filled sigh when she heard the engine down the road.

It was the first sign of relief she'd felt since stopping. It would be easier to have someone help her now, over waiting for a truck to come. That, and it would be cheaper. Her wallet was still smarting from the first time her car was in the shop.

She pushed off her knees, which gave a gentle *pop*. Charlie stepped away from her car and waved. She wanted the attention of the driver but kept her distance from the middle of the road. If they didn't want to help, she wouldn't make them. The shoulder of the road was wide, so if the car wanted to go around them, it would have no problem, but Charlie's chest began to unbind itself when the car started to ease over to their side of the road. She watched and waited patiently. The car was still moving a little fast, but maybe the driver had a place to be, and only had so much time to be a considerate human being.

She worried about its speed as it got closer. The car was much too fast to slow down, but it was also much too close to their side of the road to not indicate they would stop.

Charlie was a few feet away from her own car, having backed up a few steps, when she realized too late that the car's deep navy color looked too familiar. Too late to notice that the model was old. Antique-like.

Too late to notice the car was not slowing down while it charged right for her own.

Charlie tossed herself behind the front of her car and out of the way not a second too soon. The navy car barreled right over where she had been standing without remorse. It was only when she was out of the way did the brake lights began to shine.

"Oh my God, are you okay?" Martin burst open his door and had one foot on the ground before she scrambled to her feet. She didn't feel the minor scuffs on her palms and knees.

"Martin, get in the car and get down," she stiffly ordered, eyes only targeting the quickly slowing car now in front of them.

"What?" he started.

Charlie didn't turn around to him. She didn't want to give the indication there would be another person added to the situation that was about to happen. "Get down in the foot space, Martin. *Now*."

She could tell he hesitated by the lack of sound, but eventually she heard his foot displace gravel as he picked it up. Still, she faced forward, but prayed that he had listened to her. His door closed at the right time because the navy car that almost hit her came to a stop.

Charlette the car's door kicked open hard enough to make it find the entirety of the radius of its hinges. When Bill exited the car, Charlie expected him to be red-faced. Angry at what she did. While his body still moved with a purpose when he walked towards her, his face instead housed a dull resignation on it. Like he was disappointed, almost.

"I'd say I didn't see you there, but that'd be a lie," Bill said once when he was ten feet away.

"If only you'd given that mercy to Callen," she spat back. If Charlie was terrified that day she'd come home to Misfortune in her kitchen, what she was doing now had no equivalent. But what sparked her anger and was bigger than her fear was the resentfulness of all the *lying* Bill did. How nice he had been. How welcoming and helpful and empathetic he'd been.

And how he'd killed a child.

And she wasn't going to hide her anger, even if she should've had no idea what he did.

"Even if I did see him, it wouldn't have changed things," he sneered. Never in her life had Charlie imagined that look on her next-door neighbor's face.

When she didn't answer, Bill held his sneer for another few seconds, before dropping with a hard sigh, like a father who yelled at their child and then regretted it.

"I was thinking you knew." He took a step forward. "It became pretty clear after that night you took your brother home. A problem with your mother, the excuse, wasn't it?"

Charlie still didn't answer, ensuring her footing was ready in the case that Bill decided to attack. The idea itself was foreign to her, but after all she'd learned about her neighbor, she wouldn't put it past him.

Bill took another step forward. "I don't know exactly how you figured it out. And you knew before the police were at my door, so don't try and feign ignorance. But I do have an idea of who told you." He paused midway through another step.

"I felt him that night, you know." Bill breathed in the quickly cooling air through his nose and glanced around the forest. "I knew Callen was around the house somewhere. Always so angry, that one, ever since he died." He shook his head. "I've lived with that fucking ghost ever since that night outside those shops. That oppressive, fucking anger. I'm sure you know what I'm talking about."

Charlie made a promise to herself that if Bill came any closer, she would dash to the woods. She racked her brain at how fast she could find a stick to pummel Bill with before he noticed Martin was in the car.

"He's chosen others in the past to... help him, you could say. Always trying to get revenge on me, but..." Bill trailed off, pained almost. "I just didn't think," a deep breath. "Just didn't *wish* he chose you. I liked you and your brother. Wonderful neighbors, you were. It'll definitely hurt the worse to see you go."

Charlie's brain was too slow on the implication of what Bill said, her head too busy processing his words when he lunged.

Bill was no small man, with a grandfatherly belly and skinny arms and shins, but he moved faster than any retired person should've been able to. Charlie managed to back away from him, Bill's nails just barely skimmed her arm, but could go no further when the back of her knees found her car's bumper.

Bill reared up again to reach for her—

And was thrown back when Martin punched him in the face.

Charlie flinched at the sudden moves, and her heart dropped when Martin bared the way to her. Bill held a hand over his face. Blood seeped through his fingers in the region of his nose.

"Get back in the car," she hissed at him. Charlie still wasn't over the fact that Bill said he was going to *dispose* of her and Martin.

Martin didn't move. "The police should be here soon," he whispered before Bill regained his bearings. Charlie could tell he was trying to be brave, but his voice warbled terribly and his fists shook. His fingers hung slightly—he'd used the wrong form and hurt himself. She'd never seen him punch someone before.

"You don't know what they did," roared Bill. Both Charlie and Martin flinched at his tone, but the old man came no closer.

"Who?" Martin prompted.

Bill laughed wetly, causing anxiety to slip under every fold of Charlie's muscles. "Those entitled fucking Manfree's. They had a bakery some years ago. I'm sure you've heard about it by now. I've seen you hang yourself over that younger Manfree."

Charlie tried to grapple with Bill's words. Yes, she remembered Scott talking about how his grandparents had owned a bakery around the time Callen died. How they had been obsessed with it. She wasn't entirely sure where he was going with this. "So?"

He chuckled again; this time the hiccups of the laugh were filled with unadulterated hatred. "Those rich fucks. *I* was supposed to buy the bakery at the auction. *I* was supposed to be the one who owned it, but *no*. The only thing those rich assholes saw was another way to make income. They barely had to work for the money they bid, while I had bet my *life savings* for *nothing*. And they could barely run that bakery either! Couldn't bake for shit, yet Daddy's money kept them afloat." He growled low. "My own father disowned me because I tried to buy that bakery. I hate him and those fucking cars."

Charlie blinked at him. She recalled asking him if he had ever wanted to open a bakery, and how pulled-back he'd become afterwards.

Bill took a moment to cool the fire on his tongue. He pinched his eyes. "I didn't mean to hit Callen that day. I hadn't been watching the road. The murder was a complete accident."

"You walked away from his body!" cried Charlie.

"Because those Manfrees deserved payback for what they did to me! I moved here just to buy that bakery! I shackled myself to that house with the rest of my money, and now I can't leave, and all for nothing!"

Charlie balked at his words. All this, over a *bakery*? Bill had *murdered* people just because Scott's grandparents had outbid him.

"Like I said, it was an accident. One that I'm happy happened every single day," spat Bill.

The sirens reached Charlie's ears first, and the other two followed, everyone's body language singing stiffness.

"Got anything else to add before you get arrested?"

Bill glared at Martin, still seething from the assault. Blood dripped down into his teeth as he bared them. "And what are they going to do? Just because I wasn't home when they came knocking doesn't mean I did anything. You have no evidence." His words were sure, but Bill started to inch away from them and back towards Charlette.

Martin ducked down and whispered, "Like hell we don't." Glancing down, Charlie could see the hand Martin hadn't used to bust open Bill's face. Clever as ever, he had recorded the entire thing.

"This won't amount to anything, and you know that," Bill said during his steady retreat. "Callen was an ungrateful child. Do you really think anyone ever cared about him? That he would ever mean anything to anyone? He was a *burden*."

Charlie watched as Bill got closer to the shoulder and the forest beyond. She grabbed onto Martin's forearm in instinctual protectiveness when the shadows behind the old man began to shift wickedly.

"Charlie," Martin gasped. He saw it, too.

Bill had yet to notice, yet to feel the heaviness of the anger and anguish in the air. He foolishly continued to back away, closer to the manifesting blackness.

Charlie thought of Bill's parting words. "Yes, Bill," she told him when he was two feet away from the dark. "I do."

The slab of shade found its form when Bill's left heel snapped its barrier. Misfortune rose from the grave, blocking the rest of Bill's path. Those same shoulders and build slammed into Misfortune's, and Bill halted with wide eyes. But it wasn't Charlie and Martin he was looking at.

Callen walked past Charlie from the opposite side of the road like she didn't exist. Charlie startled and Martin fully jumped out of his skin, but Callen was already closer to Bill than them by the time they accepted there was another ghost in the vicinity.

"What are you gonna do?" sneered Bill at Callen. "We've been here before, and you've done nothing for the past forty years. You'll do nothing now."

Charlie was still trying to process seeing Callen and Misfortune in one place at the same time while Bill talked. From the way they stood, she couldn't see Callen's face, but from the terribly oppressive feeling that kicked at her, she knew it probably didn't look good.

"You were a pathetic child then. You're *nothing* now."

Callen was unfazed by Bill's words, having most likely heard them for years. He paused his journey to Bill when he was just out of reach. The sirens were getting closer, and yet they were so far away. Ringing stuck in time. Charlie could tell they wouldn't get here soon enough.

Callen lifted a bloodied arm and pointed a skinned finger right between Bill's eyes.

Bill smirked at Callen again. "Like I said, you can't do—"

He stopped when Misfortune placed a hand on his shoulder. From the looks of it, the touch was not kind.

Callen began to retrace his hand and jut it out at Bill, over and over, as if to say *get him get him get him.*

Misfortune diligently listened. With his other hand, he grasped Bill's upper arm and yanked him hard backwards, towards woods that were shaded too darkly to be natural.

Bill had yet to panic, but Charlie knew it would happen soon. The most she could do was hold onto Martin and continue to breathe, watching on pathetically as Callen pointed more and more violently for Misfortune to drag his murderer into the woods.

"You are *nothing!*" Bill roared. Over and over, he roared at Callen. It did not stop Callen from directing Misfortune, and it did not stop Misfortune from listening.

Finally, Bill seemed to understand what was happening. "Demons," he hissed. "You can't do anything to me."

It could've been the wind—it must have—but Charlie would never know, because at that moment, she could've sworn she heard someone whisper, "Yes I can." She looked over to Martin in bewilderment, but he was too enraptured by the sight in front of them.

"Nothing! *Nothing, nothing, nothing,*" Bill chanted. And yet, nil he said nor any of his kicks and bucks removed him from Misfortune's hold. They were getting dangerously close to the woods, sirens now howling down the road.

Charlie watched numbly and dumbly as Callen neared his one goal—revenge. It was odd, but Charlie finally, *finally,* realized why Misfortune chose her.

It was because she had easy access to Bill.

That was it. All of this pain and fear and mysteriousness to be used as a conduit. She didn't even have the mercy of being randomly picked as she had previously thought. This all happened to her just because of the house she moved into.

The shadows of the woods skimmed by Misfortune's lifeless flesh and wrapped around Bill, who paused mid "Nothing" and looked down at his arm. It didn't take long for the dark rope's brothers to follow. Misfortune tugged him back harder, and fear finally found Bill, digging claws into his cheeks, and pulling them down. He looked to Charlie one last time as if to beg for help, but with another yank, Misfortune disappeared first, and Bill not long after.

That's when the screams started. Deep, guttural, and built out of pure *agony*.

Callen, being the last one to join Bill in his damnation, paused before the gate to the darkened woods. He didn't turn around, but tilted his head just far enough to the left for Charlie to chance one last glimpse of the tattered skin on his cheek.

And with that, Callen moved beyond the shadows and disappeared the woods.

Screeching of tires made Charlie flinch, and right as sirens tried to cover her hearing, she felt the loss of Bill's own screams not long after Callen disappeared.

And as officers began to pile out of their cars, Charlie had the feeling that she would never see Bill nor Callen in any spiritual form again.

Chapter 41

The police deemed Bill a criminal on the run, but Charlie knew that no matter how much they searched for him, Bill would never be found, but that was something that only she and Martin would ever know. Scott, she believed, had an idea of what happened, but would never hear the story from her own mouth.

It took a while, but the police finally deemed them just witnesses, that they didn't do anything to help Bill escape. The video that Martin took (which had recorded the entire Bill fiasco, but gotten corrupted around the time Callen showed up) did wonders for ensuring their own innocence.

And just like that, she was back to her normal life. As if the horrors with Bill and Callen never happened. Of course, it still had its ups and downs with the added stress of what had happened. The police had looked into Bill's mention of supposedly taking care of others that had figured out what he did, which had then led them to a number of disappearances in the city. It was too early to tell if Bill had been telling the truth, but Charlie had a feeling that they would find something that had to do with her old neighbor.

But after that, she still went to work (with her boss none the wiser to what she did) and went to school. It took multiple weeks for Mitch to come back to doing his deanly things, but he did eventually, returning with a bruised soul and Scott by his side.

Charlie may not have had a reason, but she still visited the office and made coffee runs with Scott. She was unsurprised to find Helen training him at the front desks one day, finally having been satiated with the need for more hands in the main office. It was sweet, and Charlie had to hide the smiles that Helen caused her (Helen couldn't know Charlie could tell she had a soft spot somewhere under all her wrinkles).

Mitch himself had a hard time looking at Charlie whenever they passed in the halls but smiled at her at the times he managed to work up the ability to. She didn't blame him for associating her with the death of his brother.

Sam continued to make minor snide comments about people who believed in Misfortune, as Charlie had denied any affiliation with Misfortune and Bill's case, but her amount of comments withered as sightings of the ghost dwindled substantially after Bill disappeared. Almost as if he no longer existed.

And one of the oddest things happened a few days after Misfortune disappeared for good—the children came back. All the kids that had been taken over the decade suddenly appeared back on the doorsteps of the houses they were taken from, unharmed, and aged as if they had grown up. From the articles Charlie had read about the crazy phenomenon, none of the kids (or adults, as some of them now were) remembered anything, like they all shared a care of terrible amnesia. It was terrible to hear about people learn they'd been gone for years, and hadn't even known it, like they were in a coma, but the foremost thing Charlie cared about was Lidia. She never did hear from the woman, and her own attempts to reach out weren't received, but she hoped that Gen was returned to her.

Charlie herself liked to pretend that her life wasn't changed; only her memories of the past few weeks. But that was incorrect. At first, she had felt an overwhelming hollowness that *this* was all that everything had amounted to. Sure, Callen had his revenge and Mitch had his closure. Lidia hopefully had her daughter and Scott had his uncle back to normal. Everyone else each had their reasons to solve Callen's murder, except for her. Not beyond the selfish reason of safety.

But she'd been a fool to not think she was doing it for those stolen kids and Callen. Deep down she'd held agony inducing fear for the kids' whereabouts and Callen's terrible end. They'd all reminded her of Martin and brought out the viciously protective side in her. It had been so subtle, the worry for them, that she hadn't noticed until the knot in her chest unwound its petal thin fingers and unveiled only the inherently sisterly worry and care she held for Martin.

In her dreams, it had been Martin hit by Charlette on the road outside of the library. It had been him she'd imaged as the next victim of Bill or Misfortune.

But here they were. Bound into one piece and bound to being safe from Bill and Misfortune until the end of time.

And something Charlie couldn't begin to be thankful for was Martin's mental health. She had worried about how he would cope since he hadn't handled her car crash or the news about her conversing with Misfortune well. Instead, he took it like a pro, and was unbothered by what happened. Like that day outside the woods was a dream, he went back to acting like he did before. An example of this was when he *still* refused to have the paint in his room match.

"I'm *not* buying two different shades of green just because you can't decide which one you want," she huffed, arms crossed as Martin faced away from her, examining the large hole in the wall he had created after trying his hand at 'Unorthodox Karate Personal Defense.' No, Charlie did not know what that was.

Martin held up a finger to his sister. "You aren't following, dear sister," he tutted. "I would appreciate the means to both greens as so I can replicate the previous look of my room. In order to do this, I *must* have both shades. I would be in absolute and utter despair if I was to be denied my final wish."

Charlie peered at his back boredly. "You are not dying," she said slowly.

"I'd die of a broken heart." His hand disappeared as he placed it on his chest.

"Drama."

"Grandma."

273

"You're kind of an idiot, Marty."

"Meh." He shrugged and dropped the dramatic act. "Part of my charm."

Charlie shook her head to herself as she took her eyes off him to retrieve her phone from her pocket, which had begun to buzz. "You're seventeen. Like you could have any," she muttered.

Martin gasped and spun around, wounded. Charlie was already turning away with the phone to her ear. "Hello?"

"Just your mom, honey." It was nice to hear her voice clear of sullied vowels and alcohol. Her mother had *finally* started to talk to others about her alcoholism and the loss of their father. It was a blessing she'd finally gotten help.

Charlie smiled, even if her mother couldn't see her. "You don't always have to announce yourself, you know that, right?" Charlie had finally saved her mother's caller ID a few weeks after Bill disappeared.

"Ew, you're smiling. Is it your pretty boy?"

When Charlie turned back to her brother to glare at him, he had the audacity to look disgusted. "Quit calling him that, Martin. It's Mom."

"Oh, is Martin there? Will you put me on speaker? I wanna hear his voice."

Charlie did as she asked, also mouthing threats to Martin to be appropriate while on the call while she was at it.

"Hey, Ma," he greeted in his sweetest voice. And then he stuck his tongue out at Charlie, who didn't hold back on her kick at his shin.

"Hi, baby, how are you doing?"

Martin scowled at Charlie and rubbed his shin with his other foot. "I'm fine, Ma. Just in some *minor pain*. Otherwise, we're all good."

"Minor pain? Why, are you hurt?"

"Yeah, Charlie, why *am* I in pain?"

"Char—"

"We're painting Marty's room right now, so we're a little busy. Did you need something?" she cut off. She gave Martin one last warning, which, for his sake, he better heed.

"I don't like you talking over me, Charlette," said her mother.

Misfortune

In the background, Martin mouthed, "Busted."

"But yes, I actually called because I got good news that I want you two to hear."

Martin dropped his dramatic acts and raised a brow at Charlie as if to question if she knew what their mother wanted. She shook her head. "What is it, Mom?"

She gave a pause for effect. "I'm moving out of Aunt Mary's house."

Charlie opened her mouth in a mix of surprise and happiness. Even Martin took a whammy from the news. "Mom! That's great! How do you feel? Are you excited?"

Their mother sighed in relief, like she had expected her children to be disappointed. As if. "Yes, honey, I'm so excited. I'm proud of myself. You know I've been working hard for this."

Charlie did, exceptionally. Ever since getting help for her addictions and mental health, their mother had racked up jobs and spent more time at work than in Aunt Mary's home. Then at the bar.

"Mom, you should be! This is amazing news!"

"Congrats, Ma," Martin added quietly. He still had reservations over welcoming their mother back in their life truly, but his walls had crumbled substantially since her call about forever sobriety.

"Oh, thank you, babies." A sniff. "Great, now you've got me all worked up."

Charlie had to do her best to wrangle her own tears. "Where are you moving to?"

Her mother paused a second too long before answering. "I hope you don't think I'm trying to impede on your lives, but the apartment is actually in your town. I know there are still… difficulties between us, but it's a really nice place, and it's on the opposite side of town." She hesitated. "Please don't be mad."

Charlie looked to Martin for an answer. She knew she was alright with the plan but give the entire go ahead if Martin as against it. She felt her chest unwind as he gave a subtle shrug and nodded. "We're not mad, Mom. That's wonderful. We're so proud of you. You deserve it."

Another sniff. "Oh, darling, I'll never know what I did to deserve you two."

"I'll never know what I did to deserve Charlie either," Martin muttered. He snickered and danced away before Charlie could kick him.

"When do you move?" Charlie asked and pivoted away from her annoying brother.

"Oh, a few weeks from now. I still have a few things to wrap up at work. I think Aunt Mary is having a hard time with me leaving, too."

"As if," Martin mouthed. Charlie shrugged in response. Aunt Mary was a caring woman. There was a chance she'd miss their mother when she left.

"Anyway, that's great, Mom. It'll be nice to see you more often."

"Really?" she said quietly in disbelief, and Charlie knew that one word softened both Martin's heart and her own. "Thank you, baby. I can't wait. I've gotta get going, but I'll call you later tonight, okay?"

Charlie agreed with a hum and hung up. Martin, resting his hands on his hips, brought her attention to him.

"You know, I think it'll be good that she moves here. Nice to see her and everything. I've missed Mom. After all, I know you've missed her, too. It'll be healing for both of us."

Charlie melted into a smile but slit her eyes midway and dropped the happy feeling. "Agreeing with me won't make me buy two shades of green paint."

Martin groaned, tossed a hand over his eyes. "I am not just *agreeing* with you to get you to buy the paint. We have a great mom who's trying to better herself for her kids and you're a smart woman who one can't help but side with." Martin shifted his arm to peer at her through his fingers. "Is it working?"

"*No.*"

Martin harumphed and dropped his hands in their entirety. Charlie grinned at him with the finesse of a con man selling a striped car. If she were to be honest with herself, she really wasn't lying when she said she was proud to see her mother again. She herself had grown up without a mother for so long, and, staying with this honestly, fixated on making sure Martin never felt the same loneliness and isolation to older family members she felt. The façade of maturity she told herself. But the fixation had turned obsession then anxious—worrying for their relationship, worrying for his safety, worrying for his happiness. She'd done it because they were things that she'd never felt like her mother had worried for when she was Martin's age. She'd worried she would never be enough to raise him, even after he was a legal adult and didn't need anyone to raise him.

But here they were. One murder case and murderer confrontation later, their bond was stronger than ever.

Charlie wasn't Martin's mother. She knew she needed to understand that, and no matter how tough he wanted to act, he needed more than just his sister. He needed his mother too.

And so did Charlie.

A slam of a car door outside drew her attention away from the sin of Martin's room. She smiled wide and turned towards the sound like there weren't any walls dividing them.

"Ew. Whatever's going on, your face is way too happy to be appropriate."

Charlie rolled her eyes for the umpteenth time. "Shut up, Marty. The new neighbors must be here."

Martin continued to stare at her blankly. "And what does that have to do with us?"

Charlie didn't wait. She sailed out of the room. "It *means* that we need to go greet them!"

"Sick, I call baking the cookies."

Charlie sighed as she found the stairs. "Not funny!" she called back. The downside of Martin being pretty much unaffected by what happened to Bill is he had a bad habit of cracking jokes about him. She herself was still coming to terms over what Bill did. She didn't think she'd ever get over it. Memories of Callen and the pain she sees in Mitch not allowing her to.

Flying down the stairs and making a detour to snatch her shoes, Charlie was out the door and onto her little deck in a matter of seconds. Unloading a car not unlike she had all those months ago was a middle-aged woman with ivory skin that had freckles meticulously pressed into every spot. Two little boys swarmed her legs as they peered at the boxes on the ground that she had unloaded.

"Afternoon!" she called. "Need any help?" The air had warmed from the changing of the seasons, welcoming her sweetly. Already fall and winter had gone by, and spring was here. Another thing that washed Charlie clean of Bill.

The woman startled and looked up at Charlie. She grinned back politely and set down the box in her arms. "If it wouldn't be too much trouble…"

"None at all!" Charlie practically floated over the grass and onto the driveway that used to house all of Bill's many cars. She held out a hand to shake, which the woman took. "Charlie Kezben. It's so nice to meet you!"

The woman smiled as her boys jumped behind her legs, suddenly timid at the sight of a new person. "I'm Monica Jones." She stepped to the side, which forced her sons, who were little copies of her, to become the center of attention. "These are my boys. Mark and Mickey."

Charlie smiled warmly at them, but the two boys weren't too receptive to her nonhostile nature. They jumped back behind Monica's knees.

She sighed but didn't try to move again. "I'm sorry about them. They're very shy."

Charlie flicked a wrist. "Don't worry about it. My brother is shy too, and he's a teenager."

"Don't talk bad about me!" Turning around, Charlie found Martin had followed her out and was standing on the porch.

"Apparently not shy enough," she murmured.

Monica was unfazed. She chuckled lightly. "I suppose I'll learn what it's like to have teenagers in a few years anyway." She raised a hand to Martin and waved. "Hello!"

Evidently, Martin wasn't as outgoing as he tried to convey, because he ducked his head down and returned the favor by not responding at all.

"I'm sorry, Monica. That's just how Martin is. I'm sure he likes you."

It was Monica's turn to throw a wrist and toss the slightly awkwardness aside. "All good. It's so nice to meet the neighbors. Honestly, I'd heard some bad things about the house and had hoped that didn't mean anything about the house's new door."

Charlie shook her head and did her best to smile wide enough to placate her new neighbor and ensure she would be nice.

By each second, Monica looked more and more soothed by Charlie's personality. Relieved that she was welcoming and kind.

"Well then, if you're still up for it, will you help me with these boxes?" Monica backed up to unload more from her car.

"We'd be thrilled to," Charlie said loudly, as to cut off Martin's remark off. "I hope you didn't add me to this equation."

Charlie bent down and picked up the first box nearest to her, and with a threatening glare to Martin when she turned around, he sighed and trudged off the deck and towards them.

Charlie smiled to herself as she carried the box towards the front door. Monica called for her to deposit the cardboard cube in the furthest upstairs bedroom. And when Charlie immediately remembered that was the room she'd seen Misfortune standing at the window of last time she'd been in the house, she looked to it instinctively.

Charlie breathed easy when she found the window to be empty and pulled herself up the steps of the deck that now belonged to her new neighbor and new friend.

Chapter 42

Lidia had opened the book ten minutes ago and had yet to turn a single page. Like a pathetic repeat of time, she reread the passage over and over, eyes skimming over the ink and absorbing nothing. Almost like she'd lost the ability to understand the language.

Lidia couldn't afford a therapist, her terrible paying job made sure of that, but a quick search online told her picking up a hobby was a good way to keep her mind off of her grief. So, she tried her hand at reading. Even went to the bargain section at the store to pick up a few novels.

It didn't work, that much was obvious. Nothing would ever take her mind off the agonizing and never-ending sorrow of losing her daughter. Her Gen. Her sweet, beautiful baby Gen.

It would be a lie to say Lidia didn't put more faith than she should have into those people that came to her door talking about that ghost all those weeks ago. She'd thought, no, she *expected* for something, *anything*, to happen and tell her about her baby girl.

Lidia had long lost hope her darling child was still alive. Didn't that mean she deserved the mercy to know how Gen died? It ate at Lidia at every moment. Did she suffer? Was it fast? When did it happen? Did she cry for her mommy after that damn ghost took her? Lidia didn't think her life would be easier with the answers to those questions, but they still swirled in her, nonetheless.

Lidia sighed to herself when she finally realized she had gone back to staring at the floor again. She got up off the couch and paced, hoping a little movement might get her brain on track. It did nothing more than make her think about how she'd run herself into exhausted debilitation that night Gen was taken.

So much for keeping her mind off Gen.

But how could she? Gen was her *daughter*, not just a traumatic time in her life to forget and move on with. And it wasn't like Kyle was any help. He'd sent a card some weeks back, but she didn't know what it was about; Lidia's hadn't bothered to open it before her trash can claimed it as its new tenant.

Lidia tossed down the book, throwing away her attempt at reading past the first paragraph, and leaned on the kitchen counter with her head in her hands. It had been months since her baby was taken, and it was like the pain never stopped. Every waking second her heart was in a twist and begging to be filled with something over than hurt.

And as long as Lidia lived on this Earth without killing herself, the thing she filled it with was alcohol.

As Lidia weakly pulled herself off the table, she felt the familiar guilt as she pried open the liquor cabinet. She always had the feeling that Gen would be disappointed in her for being a drunk mother. Would her baby still think her mother was strong even if she passed out from overdrinking?

It wasn't like she would ever get an answer to that question.

Lidia didn't bother to grab a glass this time. She pulled the cap off without wasting a second and sucked down a third of the bottle in just a few gulps. A year ago, this amount of alcohol would've made her dizzy. Now, after stretching her alcohol tolerance to the max, it barely made her thoughts buzz.

She slammed down the bottle on the counter. A little harder and it would've broken. She breathed in, out, in, out, in, out, and tried to keep herself under control.

Her efforts meant nothing. The tears had already been flowing since she started walking over to the cabinet.

What did she do to deserve this pain? Was it because she cut off her family? Was it because she had a baby as a minor? Was it because she hadn't been thankful enough for the most wonderful present life could give her? Lidia would fix every problem she had, every mistake she ever made in her life, just to have her daughter back for one day, to make sure her baby knew her mother loved her before she died.

The pain was so bad, Lidia could almost hear her daughter calling for her. That whistle in her teeth from the large gap in the front.

"No," Lidia pleaded to the hallucinations.

They did not care. The calls continued, more hurried than the last. "Mommy, mommy, mommy," they called, muffled.

"It's not real." The tears were falling harder. Lidia was unsure if it was more pain to wish away the hallucinations or wish they really were real.

"Mommy!" shouted one that rose above the others.

"Leave me alone!" Lidia shouted.

The voice stopped, and all Lidia could hear were her own sobs. She let go of the bottle and covered her mouth.

It was almost inaudible, and Lidia could've been making it up, but it was nearly like the voice was mimicking her. It sobbed too, still pretending to be Gen. Lidia knew her mental state was getting worse.

But then, even after Lidia calmed herself, the childish cries went on.

And that's when Lidia noticed that the voice wasn't originating from her head, but from behind walls. Gen's room. They were coming from Gen's room.

Without thinking or caring about what was happening, Lidia tore away from the counter and to the hall, closer to the voice she needed it to breathe. She followed it into Gen's room, somewhere she usually sat and cried in for hours on the bad days, but that's not why she was here now. The voice continued to bawl, and Lidia could draw it back further to where it was coming from: Outside Gen's shaded window.

The room was dark, as Lidia never bothered to turn the lights on and remind herself that the pink and girly covered room would never be in use again, but she didn't need light. She was across the room in three steps and threw aside the princess themed curtains.

And sitting there on the ground, just on the gateway to the forest she was taken to, was Gen, on her bottom and sobbing.

Lidia's body worked faster than her mind. She didn't bother to go back to the front of the house to get outside. She instead broke the seal on the window at break-neck speed and jumped over the ledge and onto the grass. In her speed, she landed wrong on her ankle and dropped to her knees. Lidia didn't care about the pain, didn't feel it, and crawled the rest of the way to her daughter. The first place she grabbed her daughter by was her face, holding it gently in her hands and looking, looking, looking at it, and ensuring that, yes, this was her baby girl, sitting here alive and breathing.

Gen's sobs turned into sniffs as she saw her mother was with her. "Mommy!" she cried and threw her arms around Lidia's neck.

Lidia engulfed her daughter in her arms and pulled her onto her lap. "Gen, baby, you're here. You're alive," she said over and over. In the back of her mind, she was bewildered on *how* her daughter had reappeared right there.

She placed a hand on her back of Gen's head and pulled back from her, frantically searching for wounds or blood. There was none.

"Mommy, I wanna go home," sniffled Gen.

"You're home, baby. You're home. Are you okay? What happened?" Lidia tried to keep her voice as stable as possible, so Gen wouldn't be scared.

Gen looked up at her mother with clear eyes. "We were going to have supper, Mommy. And I was playing with Goaty."

Lidia peered down at her daughter. Did she have no memory of where she was for the past months?

She hiccupped from the tears. "And then—you were gone, and—I was out—here." A sniff. "I was scared because I couldn't—find you."

"I'm right here, baby. I'll always be right here."

Gen, suddenly soothed from finding Lidia, smiled up at her with a tear-stained face and pink cheeks. "Can I go inside and—play with my doll now, Mommy?"

Lidia stared at her daughter for a moment longer. So many questions filled her head, but now, with Gen back in her arms, she didn't care. Her daughter was *alive*, and it didn't matter what happened for this to happen.

When Lidia smiled down at her daughter, it was as if her cheeks had forgotten how to feel happy until this moment. "Of course, baby. Whatever you want. I love you so much."

Gen giggled bubbily and hugged her mother again, no longer bothered about why she was outside.

Lidia clung to Gen like she was life support. She closed her eyes and breathed in the smell of her hair, which still was the same scent of the strawberry soap she used to bathe her with the night before she was taken. Opening her eyes again, Lidia's attention was pulled to movement in the woods. She looked passed Gen's head and all the spinally trees into the forest and, for the last time she ever would, swore she saw the horns of a skull as it retreated into the woods. Lidia couldn't help but feel like whatever debt she owed to the ghost was paid.

Printed in the USA
CPSIA information can be obtained
at www.ICGtesting.com
LVHW012153261024
794913LV00008B/154